LOCKED OUT
OF HEAVEN

Jamie Lyn,
Mermaids, Dragons + the Fae
Oh my! all of these
are waiting for you in
the Veil!

DANIELLE M. ORSINO

Danielle M. Orsino

LOCKED OUT OF HEAVEN

Birth of the Fae Book 1

SECOND EDITION

— ♡

4 Horsemen
Publications, Inc.

4 Horsemen
Publications, Inc.

4 Horsemen Publications, Inc.
1497 Main St. Suite 169
Dunedin, FL 34698
4horsemenpublications.com
info@4horsemenpublications.com

Cover by Horsemen Publications, Inc.
Typesetting by Michelle Cline
Editor Vanessa Valiente

"Los" Dragon concept by: Danielle M. Orsino
Los Flying over the Forehelina Forest by: PandiiVan
Map is illustrated by Daniel Hasenbos—he goes by Daniels Maps

Library of Congress Control Number: 2021948159

Paperback ISBN: 978-1-64450-368-3
Hardback ISBN: 978-1-64450-367-6
Ebook ISBN: 978-1-64450-366-9

TABLE OF CONTENTS

DEDICATION VII
ACKNOWLEDGEMENTS XI
FOREWORD XV
PROLOGUE XIX
CHAPTER 1   LISTEN TO THE WIND 1
CHAPTER 2   A WARRIOR WITH NO NAME 10
CHAPTER 3   THE JOURNEY HOME 25
CHAPTER 4   "STAR LIGHT...STAR BRIGHT" 30
CHAPTER 5   THE HIGHER YOU CLIMB THE
             FARTHER YOU FALL................ 35
CHAPTER 6   WHAT'S IN A NAME?.............. 48
CHAPTER 7   WINGS 57
CHAPTER 8   LEARNING CURVE................. 63
CHAPTER 9   MEMORIES IN THE WIND.......... 70
CHAPTER 10   REUNION 76
CHAPTER 11   GIRL TALK 81
CHAPTER 12   HOLD MY HAND 84
CHAPTER 13   THE COURT OF LIGHT............. 92
CHAPTER 14   THE CROWN MAKES IT REAL 100
CHAPTER 15   JUST BREATHE 104
CHAPTER 16   BEST OF INTENTIONS............ 111
CHAPTER 17   THE ROAD TO HELL IS PAVED..... 113

CHAPTER 18 WHERE THERE IS LIGHT THERE
            IS DARK..........................124
CHAPTER 19 A WING AND A PRAYER...........126
CHAPTER 20 EVERYONE NEEDS A MERMAID ...135
CHAPTER 21 YOU'VE GOT SOME
            EXPLAINING TO DO..............149
CHAPTER 22 YOU HAD ME AT-WE
            SHOULDN'T BE DOING THIS... 155
CHAPTER 23 WHO SAID CREATING A NEW
            DIMENSION WAS EASY? 160
CHAPTER 24 DIMENSIONAL ANALYSIS 167
CHAPTER 25 IT'S ALL IN HOW YOU SAY IT......180
CHAPTER 26 WORSHIP EQUALS POWER 200
CHAPTER 27 EVEN A GOD BLEEDS 207
CHAPTER 28 WHEN THE RIVER TURNS RED 216
CHAPTER 29 DON'T KILL THE MESSENGER.....222
CHAPTER 30 OLD FRIENDS 227
CHAPTER 31 FIRST THERE WAS DARKNESS.....239
CHAPTER 32 EMPATHY FOR THE DEVIL 246
CHAPTER 33 I AM THE STORM.................251
CHAPTER 34 KEVAH 257
CHAPTER 35 LET THERE BE... WATER?
            OR LET MY WEEPERS GO.........263
EPILOGUE   WE HAVE ONE GIGANTIC
            PROBLEM.......................272

DEDICATION

To all of the freethinkers and anyone who was told they had a vivid imagination, were too dramatic or flamboyant, never be ashamed of who you are. You never know where it will take you or the worlds you will create. Believe in yourself. I never said it was easy, but it is so much more fun.

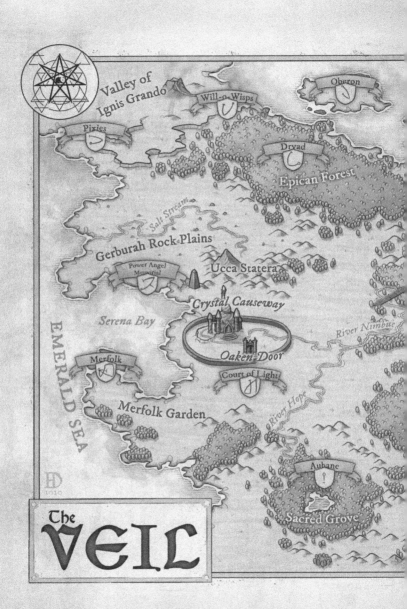

Valley of
Ignis Grando

Will-o-Wisps

Oberon

Pixies

Dryad

Epican Forest

Salt Stream

Gerburah Rock Plains

Ucca Statera

Power Angel
Memorial

Crystal Causeway

Serena Bay

River Nimbue

EMERALD SEA

Merfolk

Oaken-Door

Court of Light

Merfolk Garden

River Hope

Aubane

Sacred Grove

HD
1919

The VEIL

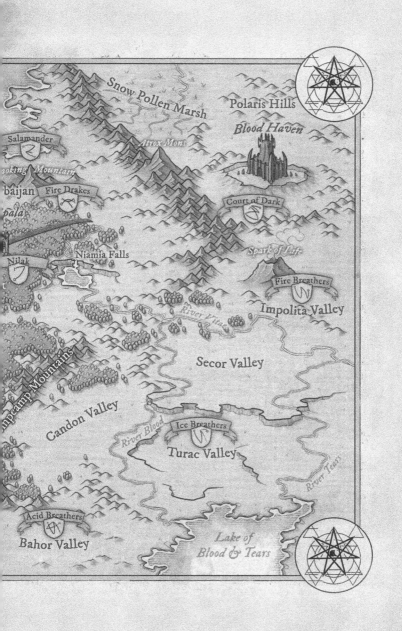

ACKNOWLEDGEMENTS

To my father, who never said, "you can't" or "you shouldn't." Instead, he said, "Why not go for it?"

PMD.

To Carlos and Penelope for showing me the meaning of unconditional love.

Carlos, for a nine-pound Yorkie, you have the heart of a dragon and the loyalty of Dragor. My special little guy.

Penelope, for a twenty-pound Cheweenie, you certainly have the stomach of a dragon and the spirit of Yanka. My heart melts only for you, my little one.

Jenn G.: Remember all those times they called me weird? Hahaha! Okay, I'm still weird, but heck, I have a book now! Thank you for dealing with me and my weirdness all through middle school, high school, and beyond. Best friends until the end. All my love and light.

Dr. Gil Stanzione, DVM: Thank you for indulging my questions regarding dragons. I know I had more than a few doozies. Most of all, thank you for keeping my pups happy and healthy. Carlos and Penelope are not your average pups. Thank you.

Professor Ioannou of Westchester Community College and his students: Thank you for helping me give my dragons their wings.

PandiiVan: Such a talented artist! I am so grateful to have found you. Thank you for helping give my dragons their colors.

4Horsemen Publications: Thank you for letting me ride with you: Val, Erika, Jen, and Vanessa—welcome to the Veil.

J.R.: My sister from another mister. Lip gloss, Yorkies, and now the Fae bond us.

To Clete Barrett Smith: Thank you for smoothing out the bumps as we journeyed into the Veil. I learned so much from you. I look forward to more excursions into the Fae world with you.

To the Muppets: Yeah, I said the Muppets! Kermit, Piggy, Fozzie, Gonzo, Uncle Deadly, Animal, and the entire gang. Thank you for showing me you never outgrow imagination.

Just remember, in the blink of an eye, it's all over. Enjoy the ride. Ignore the trolls. Instead befriend the mama Rus, comic book geeks, the guy who you would never guess has a good old-fashioned left jab, and rays of sunshine who walk into your life. Hopefully, you'll experience it all on the back of an oversized white deer with gilded antlers or an acid-breathing dragon. That is, if you have the balls to take the risk.

For the readers taking this ride with me: Chaos be with us! You will learn what that means soon enough. ;)

FOREWORD

I have never actually been to most of my favorite places. But I had some amazing tour guides, anyway.

Tolkien, Clarke, LeGuin, Lewis, Butler, L'Engle, Martin. So many others. They all took me by the hand and pulled me into the wonderful worlds that they created.

Through their words, these creators not only made me feel as if I were physically there, but they also tied me emotionally to these places. They made me care deeply about the residents. They showed me things in these lands that were beautiful and terrible and mysterious and infuriating and miraculous. No wonder I keep going back to visit again and again.

If you are holding this book, it means that you are lucky enough to have met your new tour guide. Danielle Orsino has built a world that will capture both your heart and your imagination.

You will become connected to the world of the Fae in ways that you don't even realize at the moment, and it will be a place that lingers in your memory long after you put the book down.

I was fortunate enough to work on this story with Danielle as an editor and to have the opportunity to play a very small part in getting this book into your hands. I had a front row seat to watching her create this world. And I can assure you that I have never seen a writer more invested in fully creating a vivid and authentic place—the outlines and diagrams and pictures and maps and notes and character sketches. After summoning this world into existence through an imaginative force of will, Danielle has scoured every inch of the landscape several times over. Critics often praise a story's worldbuilding by saying that it feels "lived in." Well, the world of the Fae certainly seems like that because Danielle herself has happily lived there for years as she worked to put all of this together.

My favorite part of this story is that while it is gloriously depicted in vibrant images... it is not going to be easily explained to you. You will have to visit the Courts of Light and Dark for yourself, spend some quality time with the intriguing beings who dwell there, then make up your own heart and mind concerning which place is better—on which side you belong. But beware: there are no easy answers here. You may find your personal alliances shifting from chapter to chapter. Sometimes even page to page.

After seeing firsthand the enormous creative effort that Danielle poured into this endeavor, and also getting a chance to visit myself, I am so excited that this story is finally out in the world and ready to be enjoyed by readers.

So get ready. Pack up your bags and allow your new tour guide to take you by the hand and lead you into an intriguing new world.

And the best part? When Orsino has you riding on the back of one of her dragons, the view of your new favorite place is going be spectacular.

~Clete Barrett Smith
Author and mentor extraordinaire

PROLOGUE

T he innermost levels of the Shining Kingdom were quiet. But sometimes, silence was louder than sound. Very few ever saw the innermost chamber; only he and his brothers were ever allowed to gaze upon the doors.

As the angel stood, his back gave a quick jerk, and his large gold and silver wings unfurled. His dark hair swayed, the long length a symbol of his mounting rebellious streak. The protocol was to keep their hair short, but with what his Father had done, long hair was another small way he could show his defiance. His blue eyes with their silver irises complemented the shadow of stubble growing along his strong jawline. With his helmet tucked under his right arm, he scanned the cavernous room.

The one-hundred-foot-tall arched double doors stood before him, hewn from Black Tourmaline Crystal to repel negative energy and create a protective aura for those behind them, with handles of Labradorite which shielded from psychic attacks and angelic runes inscribed down the length inlayed with Black Obsidian to reverse hexes, the doors were a line of defense—not the final line but formidable.

He placed his helmet over his head. It would only be a matter of time before the others came. Stalking up to the door, he clenched his jaw. His right fist opened, and the scent of ozone filled the air as a plasma ball formed. He lifted his arm and threw it. The energy orb dissipated as it slammed against a door, the branches of power crackling and popping—his version of a knock.

"You cannot do this to me, Father! I am the Light Bringer! I want answers!" he screamed, his breathing growing frenetic. "Answer me!"

The rustling of wings coming from behind did not surprise him. Another angel with oversized wings of white, silver and indigo with hair of metallic gold stood beside him. "Lucifer. Brother, the Creator doesn't want to speak with you. Leave."

Lucifer gave a derisive snort, but he did not turn to face his brother. He was on a mission to speak with their Father, not engage in petty squabbles. "Gabriel, I am not here to speak with you. You must leave. This is of none of your concern."

Lucifer inhaled, picking up the ozone's scent, accompanying the forming of the plasma orbs which meant... Gabriel's attack was imminent. "You dare draw against me for wanting answers?" He slowly turned.

Gabriel looked Lucifer up and down. "What have you done to your armor? It's Blue?"

Lucifer smirked, stretching his arms away from his body to show off the armor. "I wear Blue Kyanite for the truth, and He is our Father! We are not his toys. We are his beloved Archangels." He pivoted back toward the door and pulled on the handles. "And I want answers!"

Gabriel watched as an angel flew into the watchtower. He briefly dropped his eyes before returning his attention to Lucifer's futile attempts to open the door.

"Brother, I will not ask again. You are not allowed in the inner chamber. Step back. I do not want to fight you."

Lucifer dropped his hands from the handles and growled, "I am not leaving until I speak with Father, and I am not as passive as you are, Gabriel." Lucifer drew his Elestial blade. His auric weapon was blinding red as he charged.

Gabriel unsheathed his own sword from his right inner forearm; it blazed to life in his color of indigo. The two Archangels clashed with their weapons, both putting everything into each strike, blows sparking off their blue and Black Kyanite armor.

Lucifer slashed Gabriel across the face. The blue blood leaked from his wound as he launched into the air, Lucifer chasing close behind. The two continued fighting mid-flight, barrel rolling and colliding. Power Brigade Angels gathered as their commanding Archangels battled. They dared not interfere but couldn't look away. Gabriel made a sudden cut and landed, preparing to make a stand against his brother.

The two Archangels circled on the ground, stuttering and stopping, trying to fake each other out. They were now by the gates of the Shining Kingdom. Many Power Brigade Angels gathered, watching and waiting. With the crowd, Lucifer grandstanded, addressing them: "You deserve names! That is what I want to for you—identities. Free will. I want an answer. That is all I am asking for. Why can you not have your names?" A few Powers seemed to harken to the rebellious Archangel.

Seeing his brother distracted, Gabriel glanced at the watchtower. Touching the Angelite disc on his forehead, he made his decision. "Now, Uriel. Do it."

A long horn pushed through the window of the tower, the surface gold with runes and sigils. Gabriel softly whispered, "Father, Your will be done. Forgive me, Lucifer."

Lucifer looked up, horror gripping his face as Gabriel and the Powers launched skyward a second before the horn blasted, the sound hitting Lucifer three times. Gabriel watched, unable to tear his eyes from the body tumbling like a meteorite from the gates of the Shining Kingdom.

"My dear Brother, what have I done? What did you make me do?" His voice was just above a whisper, laden with sorrow and judgment.

Lucifer's body tumbled head over feet, his wings unable to help him. With so much velocity, his wings caught fire upon re-entry to the planet below. This immature planet was to be home for his Father's latest toil. Now, it was his crash site. His glorious wings no more than skeletons, he landed in a broken heap.

Gabriel called his Power Brigade to his side. "Follow him and bring me the body." Five Power Brigade members left to retrieve Lucifer's body.

In a deep chasm, a body lay broken—but not defeated—his face scarred and burned. His glorious wings were gone, their skeleton a reminder of what he lost. His skin red from the blast, no longer translucent or pristine and flawless,

Lucifer sat up and grimaced. "They used the Wormwood trumpet on me. Me, the Light Bringer." He released a primal scream.

The Power Brigade landed, surrounding him. A Power stepped forward, raising his chin. "Lucifer, by the glory of the Shining Kingdom and Archangel Gabriel, we are here to send you into Oblivion."

The angels flicked their wrists in unison as their Elestial Blades unsheathed.

Lucifer scanned the group and cracked his neck. He was injured but not defenseless. "What is your name?"

The angels exchanged glances between them, and the same Power who delivered the Archangel Gabriel's orders spoke for the group. "Excuse me?"

Lucifer inhaled and coughed. "Well, I want to know my executioner's name. It only seems fair."

The Power shook his head, pointing his Elestial blade at the Former Archangel. "You know Powers do not have names. We give up our identities to protect the Shining Kingdom. Stop delaying the inevitable."

Lucifer put his hands up in surrender. "I am not delaying anything. I am injured. What can I do? But aren't you tired of being a body? They used the Wormwood trumpet on me for asking a question. Me! The Creator's favorite. An Archangel. The Light Bringer. What do you think they will do to an angel without a name?"

The group of angels murmured with one another.

"Join me, and I will give you back your names. You will be more than bodies. You will have identities. I will never abandon you."

The Power narrowed his gaze and leaned forward. "Betray the Creator?" His voice was low. The other Powers backed away.

Lucifer braced himself, grunting as he stood. His skeletal wings were slick with blue blood, their previous glory now horrific and gory. "No! Free yourselves!"

A second Power pushed forward through the group. "What do you want in return?"

Lucifer growled, low and primal. "Loyalty. Join me, and we will take what is rightfully yours. Freedom!"

The Power ripped his gold angel wing symbol from his shoulder and threw the metal pieces to Lucifer.

The first Power who had delivered the order of execution shook his head. "No!" He turned to face off against the betraying angel, but before he could do anything, Lucifer grabbed him, plunging his Elestial blade into his back in a killing blow. He let the body drop to the ground.

Lucifer showed his blood soaked Elestial blade to the rest of the Powers. The shadow of his blade cast a light, making his eyes look like deep bottomless caverns. "You have my word. I will protect you."

The other angels threw their gold wing symbols down at the feet of Lucifer.

Thunder boomed from the sky.

"LUCIFER!" the Creator's voice echoed from above. "You take my Angels! How dare you! You believe you can defeat me? I am the Creator! You were my Light Bringer, and now you bring me disappointment."

Lucifer looked above, his sword pointed skyward. "You are wrong, Father. It is time for a regime change, a new king to sit on the throne of the Shining Kingdom. I will take more of your angels, and we will conquer. I am coming for you, Father. You took from me, and I will now take from you."

Lightning crackles. "Come, Lucifer, you will be defeated. I will not treat you as my son but my enemy. My Archangels will defend the Shining Kingdom, and when they do, if you grovel long enough, maybe I will let you sit like a dog at my feet. As for the angels you have taken..."

The angels began crying out in pain, dropping to their knees. They twisted and contorted their wings, losing their feathers "You are not worthy of my Glory or being an angel of the Shining Kingdom."

The angels stood, their wings no longer covered in feathers, but different, scaly, with red skin like leather. They had lost their armor, their eyes now reptilian.

Lucifer smiled, looking at them. "Is that the best you can do? Red skin and scary eyes? Armor can be made, my angels. Fear not. Frankly, you look better." He looked toward the storm clouds. "I am coming for you, Father. We are coming for you."

Then there was nothing but demonic screaming.

ONE:
LISTEN TO THE WIND

B efore human history, when the Earth was still a cooling spark from the Creator's hands, Xi stood atop the highest mountain she could reach without the help of her wings, which had proven a monumental task. She wanted to be as close as possible to the sky. Whether *He* answered her or not was no longer the point. She wanted Him to hear her. She had much to say to her absentee Father. Creator or not, *He will hear me.*

"Do you know what the wind sounds like? I mean, really sounds like. Stop, take a deep breath, close your eyes for a second, and try to listen. Do not imagine it. Do not think about how it should sound when it howls across the plains or whistles through the tree branches on a cold winter's morning. Just be for a moment. See if you can pay attention to it." She tipped her chin skyward, crimson hair billowing behind her, emphasizing her defiant stance.

"Of course, You won't. Why would You? After all, You invented it," Xi taunted, true disdain coating each word. "You never listened to anyone or anything. You may

have heard me a few times, but You didn't listen. That's Your problem."

"Let me explain, dear Father. The wind has its own language—a unique dialect that is audible when your wings carry you above the clouds. In the moment, you can listen and comprehend the wind because you are one with it. I speak its language. I know every delicious facet of air. As you pick up speed, the airstream echoes like the ocean crashing onto the shore. However, before you land, the blustery gusts sound like the crackling of a roaring fire. When you climb into the atmosphere...if you close your eyes, the wind hums and quakes like the earth. The elements meld together in a symphony. Earth, Air, Fire, and Water become raw power—I was power. Just as you ascend as high as you think you can on a current of raw power and bathe yourself in the morning sunlight, ribbons of sunshine enveloping your body, the wind can whisper into your ear with a soft caress, a stroke like the softest kiss from the cherubs themselves."

She glanced away. Her eyes softened and her mouth turned up ever so slightly as tranquility set in fond remembrance. Deep down, she hoped in this moment of recollection He might answer her. The air was now eerily silent. Her hair fell to her back. She closed her eyes and released a sigh. He would never give her the satisfaction of a response, so she gradually opened her eyes. Her expectations disintegrated in the cool mountain air. Gone was the angel who had been hurt and sad, looking for her Father's attention. Here stood a creature poised, demanding answers. The ground shook under her feet as she stepped forward, the icy crust of snow crunching with each placement of her foot. She watched the clouds pass overhead with a fiery, determined gaze.

"You never understood your creations, your angels or the elements. Listening to the wind, being one with its power, allowing myself to fly, I felt free and loved by it. I paid attention to the wind, and I felt those intoxicating emotions because I was power. An angel. Your Virtue! Xi Guardian of the Wind. A Shining One You made to protect nature. You gave me power over the elements. Earth was my domain. I watched over and nurtured her. Just as You asked. I served you well, my Father." She choked up as she spoke skyward.

The tears came. Xi had promised she would not break, but as she made her case, the wall of emotions strained under the stress of her confession. The tears burned as they ran down her face. She only allowed a few to fall. The cold air mixed with the warm, salty water, forming small webs of crystals as the breeze caressed her face. It was as if her old companion was trying to soothe her.

"In the blink of the cosmos, I was no longer a Virtue. I fell from grace, and I don't know why!" Xi searched the heavens. "You changed the rules in the middle of the game. I didn't join Lucifer, nor did I commit a sin. It appears...I did something far, far worse. But I have no idea what that is." Her voice trailed into a whisper.

A sharp inhalation helped gather her resolve. Xi sneered as she spoke, her intonation louder than it had just been. "Did I spend too much time as the wind?" Her voice ricocheted through the mountains, rumbling enough to cause an avalanche. It was strangled and hoarse from the feelings she had suppressed for weeks.

"When the Archangels and their Power Brigade launched their attack against Lucifer, the other Virtues and I were too busy doing our jobs, getting the earth ready for Your new pets to acknowledge what was happening. So, You punished us? You never trained us to fight! That was the Power Brigade's job! You closed the gates, cutting us off from the Shining Kingdom's Glory. All to teach us a lesson? I guess the adage 'if you aren't with us, you're against us' seemed apropos in Your eyes. This is how You treat Your children? One mistake and we are cast aside?"

Xi paused, waited, hoped. Nothing happened. The anger boiled up again, rage spilling out.

"Answer me!" she screamed into the mountain air, falling to her knees in the snow and ice. All her body felt was fury. The heat kept the ice at bay. The battle against her tears was lost. Even if it was a one-sided conversation, she couldn't stop now, and once the floodgates opened, there was no way to cease the deluge.

"No amount of pleading, crying, or praying made You notice us. We no longer existed in the kingdom's eyes. The almighty Glory, disintegrated like a castle made of sand, washed away by a small wave." A dry, bitter laugh fell from her lips. "The silence was the worst part. The sweet blissful melody raining down from above was hushed, and the world...it became so still." She wrapped her arms around herself. Just remembering those first few days brought a chill to her bones all over again. As her rage waned, the hurt settled in. Points of the granite and limestone beneath the snow cut into her knees. Their chilly edges digging in brought her out of her head and grounded her to the present.

"We were so forlorn for Your love, for the first time in—I can't even remember how long—the Virtues agreed on a plan. Your insistence on ranks and seniority kept us divided, but desperate times call for desperate measures." She shrugged and slapped her hands to her sides, rubbing her legs as she strengthened her resolve to finish.

"We gathered on a beach—a place where the earth and sky met—to feel closer to You. We gazed upon the bright water, sparkling as if thousands of gemstones hid under the currents. The white sand of the shoreline glistened when the sun shone upon it like stars had dusted the earth. The sky, a sapphire blue hue streaked in yellow, orange, vermillion, and lavender, caressed the water at the horizon, creating the perfect backdrop. Standing in Your moment of flawlessness, we were optimistic, gazing upon magnificence. How could we not be?"

Xi picked up a handful of cold snow and watched it fall like the white sand she had played with on the beach that day. The breeze took the white powder into the air, reminding her she was far from those warm shores. Focusing back on that moment on the beach, her mouth tightened and her eyes squinted as she struggled to keep the sadness at bay. "A warm breeze carried a faint salty musk, pure in its own right. There was a balance to all of it, earth, water, air, and the fiery sun as it made its way above the horizon." Lifting her eyes to the sun, she let the warmth caress her face as a fleeting smile crossed her lips at the memory of how beautiful that morning was.

"We thought perhaps this was just a misunderstanding, and we only needed You to listen to us." A hearty chuckle rolled from her as she placed her right hand over her mouth to stifle it. "Looking back, it seems so trite to think You had perhaps made a mistake, and much less that You would admit to it. But we were despondent. I remember watching the sunrise as we held hands. We prayed and hoped all our voices together would somehow open the gates. We sang, our voices carried on the wind, and we listened for a response. We watched and waited. We remained on the beach for what felt like an eternity, but signs about the truth of our predicament took hold." Her shoulders relaxed, her face held no malice. Her eyes were soft and unfocused. Unshed tears glittered in the sunshine.

"Our wings felt the effects first. They began to wilt. A few feathers fell, and we noticed the discolorations in our veins, crawling insidiously in our plumage like black snakes delivering their venom. The thick lines marred our symbols of angelic status, displaying the signs of true decay. When the corrosion set in, the panic took root along with the pain." Her bottom lip quivered as she relayed her account into the ether.

"We all dealt with this in our own way. As Virtues, we knew Your rules for taking one's own life. You gave us life; therefore, You had authority over it. We have no souls. If we kill ourselves, we don't return to the Shining Kingdom. We cease to exist. A cruel joke if you ask me, but You never asked. However, many still felt death would stop the searing pain encompassing our bodies and minds. I did not begrudge those who chose Oblivion. We went from having a purpose as high-ranking Virtue Angels to being nothing, from bathing in Glory to being plunged into darkness. I understood why Oblivion appeared to be the sweet tincture to the sickness. I did not judge—unlike *You*." Irritation made her body rigid as she chewed on her bottom lip. She had come close to making the choice more than once.

"Some of the Virtues retreated to parts unknown. Others used the last of their Glory to shed their wings before the decay finished taking them. A few chose a different path, using the last bit of Glory to bind themselves with the flora and fauna they had vowed to protect. The remaining Virtues shrank to the size of insects in hopes of escaping Your eyes should You ever return." She shook her head.

"But You will never return for us. You have new pets. Perhaps that is why You tossed us aside without a second glance or thought. We all heard the rumors, Father. We knew why You sent us here, but we did not know we were being replaced."

Her smoldering fury morphed into a raging inferno as she clenched fists, her fingernails digging into her palms until drops of blue blood speckled the stark white snow around her.

"I did not allow the hopelessness to take me. I let my wings fall off, one feather at a time. I wanted to feel every bit of the decay and pain. I needed to remember it: the feel of the black ink seeping and pulsing through my veins. Each agonizing minute gave me strength. I was not going to let this beat me. I would not let You beat me."

"As my last sick, blackened feather fell, it was but a brief second I took to mourn. Holding the oily feather in my hand, I stroked her, and Xi the Virtue Angel, protector of the element of Air, died. I saved it for You."

She dug into her white, silk gown pocket, blue blood smudging the fabric from her hand as she pulled out a slick, blackened, ebony feather in her hand. It was limp and devoid of hope. A thick crust of sludge had dried the edges, crinkling and bending the feather into an unusual, contorted position. It looked pathetic, as if begging to be put out of its misery, like so many of her kin. There was no evidence it was once a symbol of angelic pride.

Staring at it for a brief moment, she raised her arms skyward as an offering. "Take it! Go on. Take it! I want You to see Your work. Aren't You proud, Father?" Her tears were warm against her skin as the mountain air kicked up around her, stinging her eyes. Nothing happened. She dropped the feather off the edge of the mountain, and it plummeted, twisting as it fell, slowly making its way down the mountainside and out of sight. The tears dried up. She did not bother to wipe them away. A slow deliberate sneer grew from her grief.

"You are such a coward." The lopsided sneer shifted into a maniacal grin as she spoke in a low growl. She scanned the sky one last time. "You can't even look at what You have done to me. It is fine, for in this moment, I have been reborn." Xi's voice rang out in notes of vindication. She tilted her chin upward, facing the sunlight. She pulled her shoulders back as if her wings would reform in the moment. Her will unshakeable, she was as obstinate as the mountain she stood upon. She extended her arms over her head in mock worship.

"I will rise again, and it will not be by Your blessings but by my own mastery! I will fly with my own wings. One way or another, I will hear the wind again. The next time I grasp power, I will never allow anyone to take it from me. Ever. Goodbye. You are no longer my Father. Just the Creator... of pain."

Xi dropped her arms, turned, and began her descent. The wind strengthened, billowing her flaming red hair like a banner.

As Xi walked away, her old friend—the wind, had other ideas for the feather as a breeze caught the feather, slowing its descent before sweeping it up, cradling it like a precious jewel toward the western shores. Some say the universe works in mysterious ways, others say...it was just timing.

ᚈWO:
A WARRIOR WITH NO NAME

A lone, contorted feather fell; it had a crust of black ooze, the feather appeared, *pathetic*. That was the only word he could think of, *just pathetic*.

He picked it off the rock and looked around. *Where did this come from?* There were no other angels in sight. He held it up to the light, examining the twisted edges. He shook his head and placed the feather in his hip pouch; it was an enigma for later.

Where's the rest of my platoon? Did I miss the flare to reconvene for the injured? It was protocol after all.

Shifting focus, his eyes and mind attempted to grasp what he saw. He reconciled the landscape, his injuries, and confusion as nothing more than a distant memory lost in a fog. The morning mist had lifted from the darkened stretch of sand before him. The salty air was motionless, the silence striking him as the waves hushed. Not even a gull could be heard.

The mutilated bodies of his fallen brothers littered the ground, slain, not by Lucifer's army, but by the Powers'

own Elestial blades. Their bodies bore the auric signature in every punctured eye, slashed throat, and defaced wing. The sand was not wet from a high tide but covered in blue liquid—

He fell to his knees, sinking into the blue-stained ground, overcome by emotional pain. The air crackled with his grief, his cries disrupting the stillness as he dug his hands into the wet sand. Every grain under his fingertips was warm from his brethren's blood. Even now, it still held the energy of those Powers who had passed on.

He did not know nor cared how long it would take, but he would gather each Power's body along with their Angelite disc. They would be given a proper sendoff, regardless of the nature of their departure. This he vowed.

He pushed his body aches aside and locked away his grief.

As he gathered himself, flashes from the past few hours played out in his mind: the memory of the demonic howls, walking onto the empty beach, how every part of his body ached. *But at least I am alive.*

He rubbed his wrist as he recalled the pain when his Elestial blade had unsheathed from his inner right forearm. His back contorted as his auric blade's energy jolted through him, the searing bright light distorting the blade's white glow in shadows. With a flick of his wrist, the blade sheathed into his arm as his aura reabsorbed the weapon.

His shoulders and chest heaved; he had struggled to catch his breath from the surprising onslaught of pain. Even now as he tried to gather himself to clean the corpses, his body was reacting to the memories. His breathing was uneven, and he was sweating.

His left hand trembled as he brought his fingertips to his forehead, attempting to activate his Angelite communicator and homing beacon. The commanding Archangel inscribed his sigil on it with his Elestial blade, making it possible for the Power to communicate with him and for him to sense their location. When an Archangel deemed it necessary, he could link the Brigade through their Angelite discs, allowing them to function together equally in the role of one mind, like a beehive for a short time. It could store a small reserve of Glory for emergencies, just as important as their Elestial blade during dire situations. When a Power expired, the disc was taken to the Power's Archangel Commander as tribute, ensuring no one else could use the disc to gain access to the Shining Kingdom.

He felt the shallow fissure running down the center of the pale blue crystal. The rough edges snagged his skin as tiny shards of crystal stuck to him. "Damn it to Lucifer!" he huffed. A cracked crystal communicator meant he was cut off from his Brigade and the Shining Kingdom.

After Lucifer's betrayal, their Creator's divine tears dried, forming a light blue crystal called Angelite, a gift given to the Archangels and the Powers in the Brigade they had each commanded.

Angelite could only break under very specific circumstances, one of which was the fall of the Shining Kingdom. He turned and retched at the thought. Wiping his mouth with the back of his hand, he swallowed the rest of the vitriol. If the kingdom had fallen, he would know. Demons would be everywhere, the sky crimson red, and the Power Brigade would be under Lucifer's command. There was no indication any of these events had come to pass.

He had to get moving. Staying still would only lead to his demise, and he had bodies to burn. Attempting to rise, he braced his weight on a nearby boulder, grimacing as he rubbed his burning shoulders. He circled them a few times, attempting to lubricate his joints.

"Oh, damn it to—" He gritted his teeth, fighting the symphony of curses from the ache in his knees. When he tried to stand, his knees buckled. Resting his hands on his legs, he took in a few breaths and stood. *My injuries must be more severe than I realized.* To complicate matters, being cut off from the Shining Kingdom slowed his healing process.

As he began formulating a plan to gather the bodies, his legs moved as though stuck in quicksand. He attempted to fly to survey the area, but feathers fell from his wings. He picked a feather up, examining the slick black ooze similar to the contorted feather but different.

He shook his head. The memory of a plasma sphere hitting him vaulted through his mind's eye. Perhaps this was a side effect. It would not surprise him if Lucifer had a new spell. But there were more immediate issues to worry about. It would be best to conserve his energy.

His armor creaked as he moved. He inspected the armor for battle damage. It was made of Black Kyanite because of its unique protective and healing abilities. Black Kyanite pushed the aura's excess negative energy into the earth while simultaneously drawing positive energy, aligning the Seven Chakras, and creating a shield of positivity around the wearer. For Powers, too much negative energy meant their Elestial blades wouldn't unsheathe, unable to generate defensive plasma orbs, leaving them susceptible to Lucifer's temptations.

At least the Black Kyanite crystal didn't need cleansing after destroying negative energy, an invaluable quality when fighting Lucifer and his demons.

He had never comprehended how heavy his Black Kyanite armor felt. His magnificent wings had always carried the load. Now, he had to shoulder the weight. He had no choice; he was a member of the Power Brigade and a soldier. Powers might be one of the lower factions of angels, but it was an honor to protect the Shining Kingdom.

Lucifer's demonic army contained former Powers who had chosen pride over oath. Many times, he had fought ex-Powers with whom he'd trained side by side.

He briefly closed his eyes. Those friends' faces, now contorted into demonic fiends, passed before his eyes. They had chosen their path—the *wrong* one—by breaking their oaths when they sided with Lucifer. He had stayed and fought, an angel of honor, but shaking his head could not clear the memories.

Angels were nearly impossible to kill, especially skilled warriors like the Powers. Few weapons could mortally wound an angel. Elestial Quartz blessed by God and fashioned into a blade could become such an instrument of death—making the Elestial blade a Power's most trusted weapon. Once the angels made rank, the blade was implanted into the Power's right inner forearm, aligning with the projection side of the body, the side which the Power Angel can use to manifest energy and express it to use power their blade.

The Power's commanding Archangel gave a second blessing to the blade to identify it. If a Power fell in battle, only another member of the Archangel's Brigade could acquire the fallen angel's Elestial blade, ensuring it didn't fall into enemy hands. The Shining Kingdom's main enemy for now was Lucifer and his demons, but Commander Gabriel had told him many times, "One never knows what else is out there. When you are king of the mountain, everyone wants to come for you."

Cut off from help, he knew if he ran into any reanimated Powers or demons, one Elestial blade wouldn't be enough. He flicked his wrist, and in one fluid motion, the energy engorged the veins in his forearms. And like a ghost, his Elestial blade extended. Over twenty-four inches of raw auric power illuminated from his right forearm, allowing the body to project their energy.

He scanned the field of at least two hundred bodies. Each of them were mutilated, some beyond recognition. Wordlessly, he asked to find the compatriots of his Commander, Archangel Gabriel. He needed to find Gabriel's Power Angels to collect their blades, sooner rather than later. Beads of sweat formed on his brow, but he did not falter.

"Commander Gabriel, I draw my strength from you. My will is bound to you. Guide my blade to find what is yours."

Maintaining focus, his breathing quickened, and his fist shook from tension, but his perseverance paid off— one body emitting a white glow.

He moved in long, quick strides, shoulder-rolling over the other bodies to get his target. The fallen Power's Elestial blade appeared when he ran his own blade over it. Small currents of energy flowed between the two blades in branches of force, zapping and crackling as they played tag back and forth. He closed the gap between his blade and the one contained inside the forearm of the deceased

Power. The space narrowed, and the two swords magnetically charged as the dead Power's blade liquefied, coalescing into his in a streak of bright-white light.

His blade grew two times its normal size, and without having to concentrate, another body illuminated, ready for him to take the next sword. By the time he had reached the fourth body and merged his blade, his Elestial blade had grown spikes at the tip. He gazed wide-eyed at the shape change of his weapon. He swiped it in the air, trying the extended reach his bladed offered.

Glancing at the body, he removed his helmet and dropped it on the wet sand, shutting his eyes at the thud. He rolled his tongue around his mouth, holding back the scream building in his throat before falling to his knees to pray over the bodies of his fallen brethren, thanking them for their sacrifices.

He moved to the next important piece of a Power's arsenal, the Angelite disc. The disc was embedded into every Power's forehead. The sky-blue crystal with its cloudy, white streaks allowed the Glory of the Shining Kingdom to flow through each Power; the procedure was an unavoidable rite of passage for every Power. The procedure was pure, blessed agony to endure but a necessity as a key step in the angel's initiation into the Brigade while they swore the oath to defend the Shining Kingdom. It either took to them, or it did not. If it did, they were a Power. If not... Oblivion was their only refuge. Once the disc bonded with the Power, he had the ugly task of carving out each disc from the fallen Powers.

He slowed his breathing and focused his energies on his Elestial blade, controlling the length until it was the size of a dagger. He carefully cut around the pale blue crystals, slicing into their skin, the blade cauterizing most of the gore. With a sickening pop, he flipped the disc onto its front side so he could sever the cranial nerves anchoring the disc. He could only imagine what it would be like to perform this on a living Power. He was aloof and efficient, not overthinking as he inspected a disc, holding it up to the light between his thumb and index finger. They all had the same fissure running through the center, but this mystery would have to wait. His priority was to gather them and burn each Power to prevent demons from reanimating their bodies. Once this task was completed, then he could collect their bodies for the funeral pyre.

As the bodies burned, he did his best to ignore the bitter smell of flesh. He had gotten better at disregarding its rancid stench since burning Powers had become standard protocol due to the threat of reanimation. Even at ten paces away, the heat burned at his back as the fire crackled and popped behind him. He turned to face the blaze, moving back another few paces. He had respect for fire. It was one of the few elemental powers he envied. Fire was purifying. It was all-encompassing, and it did not discriminate. He understood why Lucifer chose to live among fire. Good or evil, everything burned.

The glowing embers bounced and snaked in a fiery dance, glittering like stars in the hot, swirling air dissipating into the sky above him. His face softened. He tried to wipe the sweat from his right cheek with the back of his left hand and ended up creating a thick smudge of soot across his face. He stood in solitude. He liked to think the cinders were the essence of the fallen Powers finding their final repose in Oblivion. His mouth quirked, then his lips stretched into a smile, but it didn't reach his honey-colored eyes. The glow from the flames highlighted the sadness. His morose mood was not for their loss. He had seen too much death to be affected by it. He was desensitized, and that was what troubled him. However, as the moment came, it went. He exhaled and looked around at the pieces of armor, realizing he needed a method to organize them all by.

He was a member of Commander Archangel Gabriel's Power Brigade, and it was more than enough for him. The best way he could demonstrate that pride was honoring those who had come before him and had fallen in battle. He sifted through the driftwood stacked beside him, running his fingers over it. The sea salt had devoured the bark, leaving behind the smoothest wood he had ever felt. He painstakingly traced the ridges and grooves, swirling into a partial curl; it reminded him of ocean waves. It was rare of him to visit the ocean. He did not have many experiences like this.

Reaching for another piece and with twine from one of the leftover belt pouches, he bound the two pale sticks together into a cross. Once he tested the structure, he stuck the shape in the wet sand. He stood back, thumb on his chin, checking for the level of his work. He made a few subtle adjustments, tipping the left side of the cross for better balance.

He scratched the back of his neck and looked down at his hand. "A cleaning is necessary when all is said and done," he huffed, disgusted by the grit and grime.

Carefully grabbing the Black Kyanite armor of the first Power he had laid to rest, one piece at a time, he arranged the armor around the driftwood so it hung from each side of the configuration. Saving the helmet for last, he placed it on top. He stepped back and walked around the structure, adjusting each piece, whether it was a slight angle change or stripping off one side to start again. He did this until he was utterly satisfied. He repeated the procedure for every piece of armor owned on the beach, his attention to detail never wavering.

He finished the final armor memorial marker as the last body burned. He rubbed his weary eyes. It had taken him days to clear the field, but he had given his brethren a proper sendoff. By the end of his task, his skin was stained blue. The sand embedded into every pore of unarmored flesh. His hair matted to his scalp with a thumbnail-thick layer of sea salt. His lips blistered from dehydration, and his hands felt like unfinished, raw crystal. However, all of it would have to wait. His heart was heavy, and for a moment, he wanted nothing more than to close his eyes and lie down, forgetting about the pain. The mystery of why they had chosen Oblivion was not his concern right now. As Powers, theirs was not to judge but to follow their Commander. They were the hands of the Creator.

The sun hung in the sky as he drifted, his eyelids growing heavy, when a splashing sound came from the shoreline.

Is it a demon?

He sprang up as quickly as his tired body would allow. He crouched, finding cover behind rocks and driftwood. There was more splashing. His eyes darted to the left. He flexed his wrist and set free the new, improved Elestial blade. He stalked toward the sound, the damp sand keeping his footsteps' stealth. He coiled his body, every muscle tense and loaded with energy, ready to spring. He froze when his eyes landed on the source.

There on the rock, with the ocean waves crashing around her, the sea foam encircling her womanly figure, sat his salvation. Her skin glistened. Her thick, wavy hair was the color of a morning sunrise, long enough to cascade down her back and onto the rock. *It must be covering her wings because a creature this exquisite could only be a Virtue.* He believed if he stood beside her hair, it would radiate warm, summer rays.

Well above him in rank, he was not supposed to speak to her, but this was not an ordinary situation. She could contact the Shining Kingdom or Commander Gabriel for him. He wanted to break protocol. He could offer her an Angelite disc as tribute, then take his punishment later for speaking out of his rank.

He retracted his blade into his inner forearm. Under normal circumstances, he would have a chaperone. He took a deep breath, placing his head low and palms up, to show he bore no weapons, and approached the Virtue, trying not to make eye contact unless she gave him permission. He could not speak until she spoke first. She remained looking at the horizon, combing her fingers through her luxurious hair, unaware of him.

He cleared his throat as he hopped onto the rock across from her. He peeked up to see the Virtue glance over her left shoulder at his approach, giving him a quick once-over through her long, green eyelashes. She sensuously tucked her hair behind her ear as she twisted her torso to face him. She perched upon the jagged rock like she sat on a throne. Her lower body disappeared over the edge of the rock. She was even more spectacular up close. She said nothing but gave a subtle tilt of her head. Her eyes were large, the blue was like the deepest ocean, sparkling beneath the sun, while the teal hue shined like rare sea glass.

He found himself staring. Realizing he had broken protocol, he assumed the traditional position of humility; he went to his knees, made a triangle with his hands and placed his forehead on the rock between his fingers. Waves broke over the smaller rock, the spray splashing his face, but he did not budge.

The Virtue shifted closer. She moved to her elbows, dipping her head low, trying to make him look at her. He felt the weight of her stare upon him and blinked one eye open to meet her gaze. Her face softened as she rested her cheeks on her fists. "Do you wish to bathe with me? It is safe, I promise you."

He kept one eye opened, winking at her, more out of surprise, as he thought for a second before he answered, not sure of what to say.

She mimicked his wink and smirked.

He tried swallowing the lump lodged in his throat but winced. He glanced at the crust of sand on his armor. He knew she offered him a bath because, by the universe, he needed it. The saltwater spray dried, clinging to his skin. He was relieved the waves had died down. At the very least, the salt water had washed off the first layer of dirt from his hands, but his matted hair combined with the salt made him itchy and uncomfortable. The sun beat down, sucking the last bit of moisture from his body. His thirst grew, his body demanding fresh water to rehydrate.

"I am most humbled by your generous offer, dear Virtue, but I am not worthy of bathing with you, for I am a lowly Power. I should not be in your presence without a chaperone. I require your assistance. I have tribute for you." He took the Angelite disc, held it up into the light, and scurried forward on his knees, placing it on the edge of her rock.

"Wait," she said as she tried backing away.

He knelt, returning to the position of humility, keeping one eye on the Virtue as he remained close to the edge of her rock.

The Virtue glanced at the disc but did not move toward it. Instead, she leaned forward, stretching her arm toward him. The slightest touch of her fingers lifted his chin toward her as she asked, "Tribute? Help? Why?" She held his gaze, her voice enveloping him like warm caramel. She stroked his cheek. "No one can help us, and no one is coming." She pulled back and met his eyes, continuing to stroke his face.

She was divine yet different from the other Virtues he had met before.

He cleared his throat, the dryness almost unbearable. "Are you refusing to help me, my sweet Virtue? Have I offended you? Was my tribute not worthy?" He searched her face for any spark of hope.

Her lips curled, and her eyes held a fleeting ember of pity and empathy. "No, I'm not refusing you," she cooed.

His shoulders released their ribbons of tension. Alas, this was his only moment of sweet relief. The Virtue's next words sent a shudder of confusion through him.

"Why do you still abide by such antiquated protocols? I am not a Virtue, and you are so much more than a Power. Labels do not bind us any longer. These are dark times. Be the light or be one with the shadows but decide for you. Not for Him." She pushed him back as she spoke. "I can't help you. As for your tribute, I am not worthy of such things, nor will I play by His game any longer." Then, she picked up the light blue-and-white-veined disc and threw it into the sea.

"No! Do you know what you have done?" He jumped from the rocks and charged into the waves to recover the crystal disc.

"No, and I don't care. There are no longer conse-quences." Her voice was flat, devoid of emotion.

He heard her yelling at him, but he was waist-deep in the cerulean waters. And the more she yelled, the more the tide pulled at him. His wings caught on the coral reef. Feathers floated on the waves. The foam crests became more frenzied, white lace over the blue, slamming into him and knocking him off his feet, sending him under the waters. He fought to stay upright, spitting out the brine in between each tumble.

He regained his footing and retreated for the shore.

Her voice called him. He searched for her on the shore. Her blue-green eyes reflected like abalone shells atop a high rock, catching his attention. He raised his hand to shield the sun reflecting off the sand. Her eyes changed from their blue-green to glowing red, her shoul-ders squared. She looked majestic.

The waves had calmed, and he could hear her once again. "We are not bound by Him! Now go, my star, and find your own way. Do not let Him dictate your destiny!"

Enthralled by her gaze, he hadn't noticed her hair move, exposing her back. She did not have wings.

"Where are your wings? Are you sick?" he called back, worry lacing his voice.

She smiled over her shoulder and dove off the rock.

His eyes widened, and his mouth fell open. He was still in the surf when he tried to run to her, but his wet wings weighed him down. His muscles flexed, and an explosion of wet, white wings erupted from his back. Twisting and shaking to alleviate the extra weight, more than a few more feathers were lost in the process. He cracked his neck on each side and swiftly retracted his wings, the pain making him scowl.

He bit his lip and turned his head away.

No, she didn't have wings; she had a tail! A beautiful, rainbow tail.

He scrambled to where she had sat. He searched the water but saw no signs of her or her rainbow tail. He waited, twisting his black hair at the nape of his neck, hoping she would resurface. The ocean had calmed with her departure.

"A Virtue with fins instead of wings? How is this possible?" What had she meant by "not bound by Him?"

He stood on the rock, dumbfounded. He lifted his head, listening, but all was quiet once more.

Where's the rest of my platoon? Did I miss the flare to reconvene for the injured? It is protocol.

THREE:
THE JOURNEY HOME

H e waited for hours on the rock, but the Finned
Virtue never returned to the surface. The sea
remained calm. Waves rolled in and out, their rhythm as
steady as his beating heart. The sun dipped low in the sky.
With daylight soon to be scarce, he moved to the sand
dunes for tonight. He would try to rest. There were no
bodies to burn, no Virtues to speak with. Tonight, as the
stars began to reveal themselves, he would quiet his mind.

He found an area of sea grass. The ridges of sand created a steep slant in which he could conceal himself for
the night. First order of business was to make a small fire
for warmth and find some fresh water. His lips had split
from dehydration. His throat felt like he had swallowed
shards of crystal. His skin was dry and itchy from his
unexpected swim. Running his fingers through his hair,
he scratched at his scalp trying to shake the sand free. The
Power unfolded his wings, stiff from the salt crust, and
more of his plumage fell. Picking up a few feathers and running his fingers over the quills, he raised one of the feathers

to his eyes, examining the faint black streaks discoloring the veins. Shaking his head, he gave a long, slow exhale.

Tossing the feather aside, he pinched the bridge of his nose with his fingers and rested his elbow on his knee. There's too much to process. His frustration and confusion mounted. He pulled at the hairs on the nape of his neck again, the salt and sand coating his hair and skin causing a crunch in between his fingers as he pulled. He slapped his hands on the tops of his legs. *I need answers.* In training, he had been taught to start with what he knew, then formulate a plan. *What do I know?*

Taking a stick from the sea grass brush, he drew spiral shapes in the dry dunes to help settle his mind. He sat, compiling a mental list of the information he had at hand.

Powers had chosen Oblivion by self-infliction. The battle was over for now in this area.

He was cut off from the Shining Kingdom and its Glory.

Virtues would not help him. Healing would be slow.

Concentrating on the list, his honey eyes searched the words for a pattern. He rubbed his temples and closed his eyes. Training had taught him to use logic not emotion to examine evidence. The evidence pointed him to an impossible conclusion—the Shining Kingdom had fallen.

He opened his eyes and scrutinized the sky. *It hasn't turned red?*

The scrolls stated:

Should the Shining Kingdom fall, the skies will burn and boil until the rage of those who control the throne corrupt all which we see.

He stood and slowly raised his hands, palms up at heart level. He inhaled, and on an exhale moved his arms away from his body, palms facing outward. He reached and circled his wrists, grabbing the air as he repeated the motion, linking his breath and his movement. He did this one time in each cardinal direction—north, south, east, and west. Colorful, translucent plasma orbs of red, yellow, blue, and green sparked between his palms as he moved. The space between his hands felt thicker as the plasma manifested, the scent of the salt air mixing with the orb's sweet yet heady aroma.

He wrinkled his nose as he drew his hands closer. He hoped aligning his chakras would give him a better perspective.

Going through his moving meditation, he spoke in a low monotone so as not to break his concentration. "Perhaps a small group of Archangels and Powers fought in the kingdom. Maybe they were still holding Lucifer and his horde at bay?"

The sudden revelation made him pause mid-motion. It was even more of a reason to find a way back. It was his solemn duty to defend the Shining Kingdom and help those in the throes of combat. He dropped his arms to his side and his jaw twitched as his teeth clenched. Hands tightening, his blade itched under his skin, begging to be discharged. He would not abandon his fellow Powers or Commander Gabriel, no. He was a Power. He had to get back. The building rage in him demanded release in the form of violence against the demons that dared attack the Shining Kingdom.

Meditation time completed. He lifted his hands over his head, crossing his wrists, and pulled downward sharply, separating them. He brought his right fist to meet his left palm, meeting at his heart, and bowed his head. "With heart, head, and hand aligned, the warrior is complete." He nodded in each direction as the colorful plasma orbs he created from his meditation faded.

He looked at the beach. The stretch of shoreline would be the best place for him to try. He ran, gathering speed to take off. Each step burned and each flap of his decaying wings brought tears to his eyes, but he pressed forward. He stumbled and fell. The Black Kyanite armor cut into his flesh and tore away chunks of skin. Blue liquid oozed from his wounds. He paid it no mind. The waves crashed up around him, saltwater blurring his vision. He coughed as he gulped the water but it did not matter. He got up and started all over.

He had fallen twenty times. It took all of his spirit but again he ran, pumping his arms, chest heaving. He refused to give up. It paid off. He caught an air current. He lifted only a foot off the ground, but it was something. He struggled to maintain it before what was left of his once mighty crystal white wings came alive. He was five feet off the ground.

"Almost!" he growled, the strain in his voice piercing the air around him.

He thought about the Powers fighting alone in the kingdom and how much he was needed, how much he wanted to help them. A primal sound escaped the back of his throat. The guttural moan helped break the spell gravity had over his body, and he gained more than a hundred feet. It took all of his perseverance to keep going. He drew his Elestial blade against the twilight sky, pointed in the direction of the heavens. With a battle cry that would have scared Lucifer himself, he screamed above the rushing air to unleash his fury like a volcano erupting, helping to rocket him upward. He used his last bit of Glory.

A cruel sneer formed on his face, and he leaned forward into his trajectory. The wind at his back, his crystal wings carried him upward toward the gates of the Shining Kingdom. His feathers fell fast as he propelled upward to fulfill his angelic duty.

Or so he thought.

FOUR:
"Star Light…Star Bright"

The scream from the meteorite tore through the early evening like a shard of glass tearing through a heart. Every creature and angel stopped and watched the lavender sky. The bursts of stars acted as a backdrop to the ball of light shooting upward. They knew not who or what it was, but they sensed this was their last hope. They held their collective breath. Not a cricket chirped. The wind stopped blowing, and it was the quietest the earth had been since the morning the Virtues had stood on the shoreline. No one knew the nature of this star streaking the sky, but they felt the anguish. The ache and determination were obvious. The yearning to return home was the same for all of them. It didn't matter who or what it was. The star carried them all on its back. Of course it didn't know the responsibility it carried.

Heavy was the head that wore the crown.

On a mountain ledge, Xi's knuckles were white and her skin cracked from the cold, Xi stood, clutching the granite. She had not traveled as far back down the mountain as she would have liked. Her anger had propelled her journey upward but coming back was not as smooth. The flash of light drew her attention up, a pang striking her. Whomever or whatever the star was, it was power at this moment. It was the wind. She longed for the feeling again. She cried every night, missing the wind. She held her breath as did every Virtue and creature who watched. The higher the bright light climbed, the more hope they all gained.

Several miles away from Xi and the mountain on a throne of jagged rocks, with the waves cresting around her, the Finned Virtue held court among the other sea creatures. She held the Angelite disc he had given her and pressed it to her lips. The coolness of the crystal felt like home for a second. Somehow, deep down inside her heart, she knew the star rocketing upward was her stranger from earlier today. His mix of passion and humility had struck her. Perhaps that was why she scoured the sea bottom until she found the Angelite disc she had thrown away. The Finned Virtue had recognized his agony and loss, but she also saw a fire burning behind his honey-colored eyes. It was unlike anything she had ever witnessed in a Power. No, he wasn't a lowly Power. He was something much more, and she knew it in her very core.

The star's light dimmed into a small glint in the sky before it disappeared. The Finned Virtue rolled her wrist, and with a splash, a group of narwhals raised their gilded tusks from the depths below, crossing them in a moment of salute to the star. The Finned Virtue gave a soft smile at her unicorn porpoises as she gazed skyward.

A moment of relief blanketed the earth, but in a flash the star reemerged screaming into existence once more. Faster and faster the star tumbled. The burning yellow comet streaked downward, no longer a bright beacon of hope but a harbinger of broken dreams. The sky set ablaze, a brilliant streak of white and red as it accelerated. A loud crash echoed for miles, shaking the earth upon impact. A plume of fire exploded into the silence of the earth.

Xi had an unabashed view of the star's path from the mountain ledge. She slammed her eyes shut tight and turned her head away from above, burying her head against the rock. Tears leaked. She knew all too well how hard and cold the earth felt after one had been the wind. Her heart broke. It would be best if the fall eviscerated it. Oblivion would be the kindest fate after a fall like that. She hurried down the mountain.

It had flown one last time and died trying to return home. Xi would have given anything to fly one more time. She wanted to cry and curl up somewhere, but she had done that for too long.

"I refuse to hide anymore," Xi whispered.

Her kin were out there, scared and alone. She squared her shoulders and looked back at the inky blackness symbolizing her past. The hurt and hopelessness had almost swallowed her. She titled her head, staring into it, her mouth tight, and her forehead creased. It did not hold power over her anymore.

Xi turned to the horizon lit up from the crash. It called to her. Her face softened. The time for looking to others for hope was gone. She needed to be someone's hope. Whomever or whatever had crashed to the earth would not die in vain. She would find each Virtue and lend her shoulder to cry on or use her arms to lift them up. Whatever it took, she would rebuild this world with them. Let them know they were not alone. Yes, the Shining

Kingdom had abandoned them, but she would not. Never again would she discard anyone. She would not allow her kind to be treated as if they were disposable.

Xi scanned the sky again. She didn't gaze upon it as a lost home anymore. No, that was her past, one she cared not to recall. No longer a symbol calling to her as it had before, it was now the last bit of an unattended fire burning itself out, much like the desire for a dream that no longer belonged to her. Tonight, she was to make good on the vow she swore on the mountain. She brought her hands to her lips and kissed her fingertips, then raised them in a salute to the fallen star.

"I will begin my journey now. Each Virtue, no matter where they hide or what form they took to stifle their heartache, will know there is still room in this world for faith and hope." Her voice penetrated as power rolled off every word, invoking magick.

The wind picked up behind her, coming out of nowhere from another side of reality. It swirled her scorching, fiery red hair as the navy sky was torn open, revealing all its secrets, bleeding streaks of orange and yellow above her. Smoke particles churning in the air delivered their woodsy aroma as the world around her burned.

At the shore, the Finned Virtue put her hands to her face and cried as she witnessed the star's crash back to the earth. Her porpoises and other sea creatures had dispersed, leaving her to grieve. She sat for hours on the rock after the crash, as the pitch-black curtain of night was sliced open by the star's fiery tail and revealed a gaping wound of red and orange as far as she could see. She had been a fool to hope, a fool to have faith. She had been wrong about the stranger. There was no room for faith in this world anymore. The hole in her heart felt deeper than the cold and unyielding sea. *How can I go on? Do I want to?*

She slipped off the rocks and into the depths below.

FIVE:
THE HIGHER YOU CLIMB
THE FARTHER YOU FALL

T he thick, grey smoke trail streaked the sky, reminding all who looked up of what had transpired. Burned treetops led to the blast radius of scorched earth, everything in its wake decimated in each direction. Ash still rained from above, coating the ground in a layer of dirty snow. The large particles were the remnants of the incinerated vegetation. They fell noiselessly, filling in the newly formed landscape.

The new topography traced the trajectory of his fall. Large, seared marks as long as the tallest evergreen trees lay out as far as the eye could see where he had skipped along the ground like a pebble over water. Each hit to the earth left deep impressions with mounds of dirt. These slowed his velocity enough to allow him to skid over the ground before a final toss plummeted him into a deep crater—his final place of repose.

Molten in texture, the trench glowed red around the edges as it dropped off into a deep, dark chasm. There in the darkness was the heart of the shooting star. It lay silent but still beating, the burnt earth sizzling around it.

Through the thick smoke and choking waves of scorching air, the Power lay. The heat sat on his chest like a boulder, sticking to his skin, sucking what little life force he had left. Without the protection of his Black Kyanite armor, he was at its mercy. His broken body lay twisted in odd angles, but he was too weak to move. His eyes burned more from the acrid smell of sizzling flesh than the smoke. It had been different when it was others' flesh, but now his skin burned, the scent sickening him. What was left of his Black Kyanite armor was now part of him.

Fighting the urge to breathe fast took every fiber of his being. He concentrated on slow breaths. Nothing too deep, it hurt too much. He swiveled his head slightly to the right, and the small motion caused the acid to rush up into his throat. *Is vomiting worth the effort?* He swallowed it down, and it felt as though broken crystal lined his throat.

He released an involuntary grunt.

When the world to came back into focus, he saw the skin above his right gauntlet was blistered and bubbled. The Black Kyanite crystal had melted during his reentry, cooling into the pink tissue of his arm. The thick black lines were eerily similar to the ones marring his wings.

He gave a low, cynical chuckle at the irony, coughing as he did. His gauntlet had settled into his arm, along with chunks of his armor unbroken from his landing.

The moisture from his body had evaporated. Therefore, nothing in the burned areas bled or wept. The tissue pulled as it precariously draped over his muscles. One subtle movement, and other sections opened up, exposing the viscera underneath.

The physical pain was unbearable. His spirit was shattered in a million pieces. There was no tincture to fix that. To breathe was agony. He felt as though his lungs were filled with lava. He couldn't move. He didn't want to. Why am I still alive, and how? The pain...why can't it just take me already? Maybe I am in Hell. It would explain the burning and heat.

He couldn't see anything through the gray smoke and darkness. He closed his eyes.

Please let a demon show themselves and just get it over with it. He didn't want to think anymore because the same thought raced through his brain and his heart. *The gates are closed; they are closed, and they don't want me back. Yes, I must be in Hell.*

The pain in his chest returned. "Oh, my Fathe—"

He couldn't even finish the statement. No one was coming for him; he'd learned that. He choked up. That's what the Finned Virtue meant. He understood now. *So stupid!*

He had been a pawn in all of this. He had given his life to the Brigade. He'd sworn his allegiance to them; he'd given his word, but for what? For what? He was injured, and they'd left him. They'd abandoned him. *How could they? How could Gabriel do this to me?*

He had used the last of his Glory to return to the kingdom, thinking they needed help.

"My wings?" He whimpered as he tried to reach for them but the agonizing pain stopped him. They were gone. He recalled the feathers falling as he flew up. If he hadn't lost them on the way up, they had surely burned during the crash.

"My wings..." he cried, but there were no tears.

He had given everything, only to be rewarded with lies in return. Now he would die alone in a dark hole with no honor and no name. Every thought stung, only fueling the fire that set his heart ablaze. He longed for Oblivion.

"I want to hear my mother call me by my real name." His voice was wheezy and strained. He remembered his name. He had never forgotten it, unlike many others. He wanted it back. He would take it back. He would not go to his Oblivion nameless, forgotten. But there was no one there. He would be forgotten.

"My name, someone call me by my name," he mumbled. But only silence answered him.

The pain in his body was minuscule compared to the throbbing in his heart as the revelation suffocated him. They had pissed on his oath and loyalty. He knew what he must do.

He opened his eyes and focused on his breathing. *There is no need to pray.* He released a soft chuckle at the thought, coughing again.

He unsheathed his Elestial blade and grimaced at the energy expenditure as the blade broke his skin. The glow from his auric weapon blinded him with pure white light. Squinting against the harsh light, he took a deep inhalation, coughing as his lungs burned. With his last focus of will, he shrank the blade to the size of a dagger. He counted to three and slowly pointed the blade toward his face, breathing ragged and sharp as his arm shook.

The skin on his body pulled and moaned as it tore, but he ignored it. This was more important. Using his left arm to grasp and steady his right hand, he aimed the blade at his forehead, his arm trembling from pain, anticipation, and fatigue. His jaw clenched and nostrils flared in preparation for what was to come next. He plunged the blade into the Angelite disc. His tortured scream erupted into the reticent night. It echoed up from the dark chasm, his angst carried on the wind.

Birds flew in every direction to escape the wretched sounds of torture. The group of Powers looked up and felt optimistic he had survived the fall. What had started out as a body retrieval mission might be a rescue after all. They followed the grey smoke trail for hours, but it was beginning to dissipate. His scream gave them a solid lead. They ran toward the outcry and found a path of trees whose tops were smoldering orange embers, not the blazing fireballs they had been hours ago.

Refusing to give up even after his howls had died down, they persisted onward. Their determination paid off when they crossed into a clearing. The charcoaled soil with no vegetation was a clue they were getting closer. Every step they took, the ground deteriorated under them with each movement. The air was too smoky to breathe and hot enough to scorch the skin.

"Damn it to Lucifer! Are you sure this Power is worth it?" a tall female Power with short black and speckled white hair remarked. She continued coughing before pulling her full-face helmet down, muffling the rest of her unsavory curses.

Another Power leading the group lifted his face shield to speak, his face smudged with smoke and his sapphire blue eyes watering the minute the smoke and heat hit them. "Keep your face shield down! Thank the universe for Black Kyanite. It will provide protection from the heat. And yes, he is worth the trouble. We leave no Power behind!"

The imposing lead Power turned his attention to the air. He licked his finger and held it up in the heavy, opaque, grey smoke. He tasted it, rolling his tongue in his mouth, extrapolating what he could from the environment. "The air smells and tastes like a bonfire, mixed with animal skin. Many creatures perished in a quick incineration. We are close." He closed his shield with a flick of his wrist and gestured for the rest to move forward.

The wind changed enough for them to see the source of the smoke, a large, dark crater. The group of six Powers peered over the edge of the pit, searching for signs of life, but the abyss was dark, and a trail of smoke billowed from the gaping hole. A moan escaped it like a mouth releasing its death rattle. They moved away from their find, trying to escape the dark smoke following them like a panther stalking its prey.

Four of the Powers mumbled and argued about which of them was not going to explore the crater.

The tall female Power with short black and speckled white hair yelled, "He is probably dying, so what was the point?"

"I am not going in there!" Another female Power with short, teal hair sticking out in spikes underneath her helmet stated as she backed away, her hands up.

The lead Power with the blue eyes walked around, scanning the crater while the others bickered.

The final female Power with blue hair, whose wings were in no condition to make the jump into the crater, sat very still at its edge. The smoke did not bother her. It swirled around her and stopped inches from her body. Her aura kept the vapor at bay. Under her face shield she wore a black mask that hugged her face in swooping lines, mimicking the ocean waves. Legs crossed, she rested her hands on the tops of her thighs, palms up, and centered herself. It took only a second before her eyes flashed open, and her left eye glowed with a white incandescent light.

"He is alive. For now." Her voice sounded distant as if it echoed from the other side of the universe.

She closed her eyes and blinked, standing in one fluid movement, a concoction of poetry and athleticism. She lifted her chin to face her compatriots. They had stopped their squabbling, hitting each other on the shoulder with a flick of their wrist. The black- and white-haired Power stood with a teal-haired female posing with their hands on their hips, while the three males halted at attention with their hands behind their backs, indicating her message was clearly heard over their bickering.

The masked Power with blue hair knew her voice resonated when she spoke from her gifted state. However, the five Powers made no motion. They knew to never question their seer. "Well?" she asked.

The two females folded their arms, taking a defiant stance. The seer flexed and closed her right fist, as if feeling the itch to unleash her blade at their insolence. She would be damned if she would leave any Power to perish in a pit, but it would not be necessary.

The blue-eyed lead Power who had tested the air came from the side of the pit. While the others were busy quarreling, he formulated a plan. "Out of all of us, my wings are in the best condition. I will use them to slow my descent. You will fashion a harness to help pull the two of us up," he commanded. There was no room to question him, nor was he asking permission from any one of them.

They all touched their first two fingers to their Angelite discs—a customary Power Angel sign of respect.

He did the same in acknowledgement. He drew his blade as a precaution; it glowed a bright, royal blue, denoting he was of Archangel Michael's platoon. He opened his white- and-silver wilted wings, nodded to his brethren, and jumped into the cavity.

His wings slowed his drop, but the landing was harsh. He tucked and rolled, his body taking a beating as feathers scattered. He took a second to orient himself to the darkness and regain his balance. The smoke was thick. The light from his blade allowed him only a few feet of visibility before him. He raised his face shield to improve his vision, but the reek of burnt flesh nauseated him. He covered his mouth with his free hand to give him a chance to swallow the liquid steadily creeping up his throat. He felt the temperature change, the coolness a welcome relief as the heat dissipated, rising to the top. Probably looking to escape the smell.

He scanned the landscape as a figure came into focus. He moved in closer and amid the crater was the Power he searched for, mangled and broken.

He bowed his head and prayed over his comrade's body. Perhaps it was the sound of praying that bought him back from the brink of death, or maybe the anger did, but the injured Power stirred.

The rescuing Power grabbed his hand and whispered into his ear, "Yes, brother, we are here. We have come for you. We will take you home."

The inured Power opened his eyes, a slow blink, as he tried to bring the world into focus. *Home? They came back for me? Oh, they came back!*

He smiled and strained to speak. "I tried to get back. I did. I am so sorry. I nev—" He caught a glimpse of the angel's wilted wings, the cracked fissure in his disc—just like his. He laughed.

The rescuing Power stilled, his eyes wide. "What is it, brother? Why do you laugh?" The injured Power could hardly contain his laughter now.

The rescuing Power stroked the injured Power's forehead asking as he continued to hold his hand. "Have you gone mad with pain?"

"Brother, there is no home. You can't take me home, for we have no home," the injured Power said between strained laughs. He dropped the angel's hand, pushing it away. "Now go and leave me here to die." He turned his head from his would-be rescuer.

The rescuing Power stared. *Why is he speaking like this? It is blasphemous.* "No, you are just injured. You don't know what you are saying. The others are up top. We will get you out and find our way to the Shining Kingdom."

The injured Power grabbed the other angel with ferocity, pulling him close. His mental anguish allowed his body to push past his physical pain. "No, listen to me. I went back. They closed the gates. They won't let us back in." He gasped for air, shuddering and coughing, but held his rescuer's gaze. He needed him to understand the magnitude of what he was saying. "Didn't you notice the same fissure on our Angelite discs? Our wings are wilting and decaying off our bodies? They cut us off! They left us!" The angels' noses were inches apart.

The rescuing Power put all the puzzle pieces together, his eyes frantically shifting side to side. The bodies, with the discs cracked and their wings decaying. At first, some thought the kingdom had fallen, but none of the warning signs had come to pass. Commander Michael had gone to check. *Are we ignoring the obvious?*

His eyes focused back to the injured Power before him. But this Power had gone home. He watched him shoot skyward toward the gates and be sent back in a fiery ball of thunder. He paled. The injured one told the truth. He shook his head from side to side, closing his eyes, still not wanting to face the truth. "No! Commander Michael wouldn't leave us. No!"

The injured Power pulled his rescuer close to him. The raw, burnt tissue sloughed off against the other angel's armor as they embraced. His adrenaline fueled him. His lungs found breath.

"They left us?" the rescuing Power mumbled in between the falling tears, clutching for the other Power.

The injured Power held his rescuer as the angel crumbled to the ground under the emotional strain. The physical pain was nothing compared to the torture in the rescuing Power's heart.

The Power jerked away, endeavoring to pull himself together. He swallowed hard before he spoke. "Our discs were broken to disconnect us from the Shining Kingdom?"

"Yes, I believe so." The injured angel's throat was scratchy, his voice holding a bit of admonishment as if someone should apologize.

Without a word, the rescuing Power unsheathed his blade, and a bloodcurdling scream echoed up from the crater, slicing through the darkness.

Minutes later, the rescuing Power's gravelly voice yelled up to the others to send the harness down. The seer responded to his call; she moved, climbing about a quarter of the way down the crater on uneven rock to establish a secure lifeline for her brethren, while the others huddled motionless at the top, waiting and watching.

With blue liquid dripping from his forehead, the rescuing angel addressed the injured Power he had been sent to liberate. "Now what?" His voice was steady, but the left side of his mouth curved upward in more of a sneer as he spoke.

Weakness from their emotionally charged exchange settled in as the injured Power collapsed back on the rubble. Fatigue creased his face but he had a spark in his eyes. He was hurt but no longer alone. "I have a few ideas..." His breathing was labored. "We must talk about names."

The rescuing angel's right eyebrow arched as his lips parted and he mouthed the word before speaking aloud. "Names?"

The injured Power moaned and grimaced sitting up and squared his shoulders. The rescuing Power moved to assist him but the injured Power put his palm up to stop him. The rescuing Power sank into a crouch, leaning in to watch the injured Power. Anticipation charged the air between them. The injured Power took a deep, trembling breath. He had used up what little resolve adrenaline had afforded him comforting the young Power.

He blinked slowly and steadied himself. "Yes. My name is Jarvok. I was born in the Shining Kingdom's 4th

District under Archangel Gabriel's protection, and today I take back my name."

The other Power's eyes widened. His head jerked back. Then he smiled. But it was fleeting. His mouth dropped and his brows drew together as he lowered his chin. "Jarvok. I don't remember my name." He raised his eyes to meet Jarvok's and his shoulders tightened. Jarvok saw the panic building in the angel with no identity. Even through the smoke and darkness, Jarvok could see him clenching and unclenching his fists as his bottom lip trembled, ready to unearth a scream of frustration and terror.

Jarvok put his hands on the Power's shoulders and looked him in the eyes. "Choose your name." Jarvok dug his fingers into the angel's Black Kyanite armor. Small splits formed under his grip. His jaw clenched. He closed his eyes and inhaled. It was slow and controlled. He lifted his eyes to meet the angel's gaze. "Yesterday, I sacrificed everything—my last bit of Glory, my wings, and my dignity—to return to the Shining Kingdom, and for what?" Tears fell from his amber eyes, cutting through the soot and grime, but he did not falter. "You are better than what they told you, the lies they fed you. A day ago I would have said this was blasphemy. I would have met my Oblivion for the Shining Kingdom, but I was there, and they don't want us! As I lay with my skin on fire and my wings burned off, I say no more! I live for me and now, for you. Take back your name, take back your dignity, and I will stand with you, my brother. You are not alone."

The rescuing angel reached for Jarvok's wrist and squeezed.

Jarvok gave a smile. It was not one of happiness but of understanding. "You are no longer a slave to a cause you don't believe in. You are not being tricked into fighting a war that is not yours. You are not a number or a body. You matter! I will not abandon you, so what shall I call you?" Jarvok's stare filled with fire, determination, and empathy for the angel.

The angel never broke eye contact with Jarvok as he released his grip on Jarvok's wrist. His breathing slowed down. He nodded in comprehension, and his expression became placid. He raised his chin. "As of today, I am Zion," he whispered.

Jarvok shook his head. "No! Say it again with conviction!"

Zion stood from his crouch like a phoenix rising from the ashes. His wilted wings flashed to their former glory for an instant. "I am Zion!" he roared, his eyes blazed a glowing green.

Jarvok smiled. "Yes, you are Zion." Pride beamed from his broken body.

SIX:
What's In a Name?

T hough many moons had passed, the pain had only
dulled. Xi's ache was not visible. There were no scars
or wounds. Therefore, she had no right to cry over the
throbbing emptiness clutching at her heart, the twisting
pain whenever she glanced at the birds soaring above
her head, mocking her as they glided on the wind—her
lost friend.

All she could do was stave off the misery by helping
others. Assisting others propelled her forward on her
arduous journey as she crossed the beaches past the
Geburah Rocks toward the Epican Forest, all in service
to her kin.

Xi never forgot how it felt to be left behind. None of
them did. They tried returning to some semblance of life.
It was different, but it was theirs. She made sure the others
understood they had choices, not assignments. Each individual could select what element, flora, or fauna to protect. Many gravitated into clans with similar interests. She
helped facilitate these unions where she could. As they

adapted to their unorthodox lives, so did their elemental connection, growing more in sync with the center of their protection. Their bodies modified along with their new lifestyle.

Many of the Virtues chose to keep their angelic names, out of practicality more than nostalgia. Out of respect, she referred to her fellow Virtues as "Brother" or "Sister" unless they gave her permission to call them by name. Names were sacred to all angels. To be gifted with a name was a great honor. The only item that did not return or reinvent itself was their wings. It was particularly difficult for those who protected the air element. Xi had learned to ride air currents for short distances, hovering only a few feet off the ground. It was a far cry from being the wind, but Xi relished those brief moments, nonetheless.

While Xi acknowledged her persona died the day her wings did, she would not take another name. She swore she would wait until the day she could fly again of her own accord. However, she had her moments of self-doubt. She searched for something to ground her to this new life, and without a name, it was difficult to feel part of this new world.

Xi hadn't given other types of angels and their naming protocol much thought until she had discovered the grave-yard of armor while crossing the beach toward the far side of the forest after the night of the shooting star. At first, she wasn't sure what she had discovered. The mist had parted for her, revealing the profiles laying in perfect formation. The air was eerily quiet and still. When the sand hadn't crunched under her feet, she looked down and realized it was damp, stained blue with the blood of angels.

She closed her eyes and winced, biting her top lip. She'd wished she could fly. It felt wrong to walk on hallowed ground. Carefully making her way to the first formation, she'd squinted and tried to focus on the pile of driftwood and black, textured rock before her, unsure about what she was looking at. She hesitated before conceding to kneel on the sand, wrapping her long gown to pad her knees. She had unconsciously reached for the helmet before she caught her fingertips a breath away.

She'd gasped, wide-eyed at the hum of energy emanating from the black, jagged crystal. Flattening her hand in the air, she inhaled and exhaled, visualizing the rainbow wand laying deep inside of her, the colors lit up from red at the base of her spine to violet atop her head. Her chakras opened, ready to receive the energy and the information it carried.

She had avoided tapping into her chakras. The Virtues had all shared stories of their several failed attempts to contact Him through them; the signal went nowhere and received nothing. The process was exhausting. She had shut down hers down, afraid.

However, their magick and chakras were tools to be utilized. Trying to calm her heart and relax her mind, she closed her eyes and let the energy slip over her. It was warm, coiling up her arm like a thread on a bobbin, confirming it was the armor of the Power Brigade. Black Kyanite.

She jerked her hand back as if the Black Kyanite burned, bringing her fingertips to her lips. Her index finger lingered on her lip for a brief second as grief washed over her heart.

She let her eyes roam over the entire structure, drinking in its composition. The Black Kyanite helmet held an ominous presence. Its jagged crystal edges protruded to cover a Power's cheeks, providing the wearer with the illusion of angular facial features as not to give away the Power's gender. The dip in the brim covered their Angelite disc and made the Power appear as if they were scowling all the time. The helmet balanced on driftwood sticks, as the remaining pieces formed the torso and limbs. A large flat stone polished smooth from withstanding the worst of the ocean's waves was used to carve the Power's commanding Archangel Sigil into it. It was a beautiful way to honor their sacrifice.

She stood. There were rows of these arrangements, two hundred of these memorials by her assessment. It must have a taken a platoon days to do this. It had brought tears to her eyes. They died bravely in battle. The thought of a group of angry Powers stuck here on Earth with her and the rest of the Virtues was not a pleasant scenario. Powers were not known for their empathy. They were known for their prowess. Unfeeling and calculating angels trained to kill their target without remorse. If the Power Angels were locked out too, there was a chance the Virtues might become the focus of the Powers' anger at being separated from their Commanding Archangels. Without the Archangels to direct the brigade and remind them of their oaths to protect the Shining Kingdom and by default the Virtues, no one had the right to ask the Powers for further assistance. In fact, the Powers might come to view their oaths as void. Furthermore, they could have been looking for a way to prove it. This could lead to an altercation the Virtues were not equipped to deal with.

The thoughts distracted Xi from her long journey. She had been traveling for hours. It was her trip to visit the

Dryads, Virtues who had bonded with the trees. Their elder council members met during the phase of the waning moon. Xi made the journey to check in and discuss matters regarding their well-being and neighboring factions. Sometimes it was to put in place rules for dealing with the river nymphs who sang too loudly—no lyrical songs before sunrise. Other times, it was the young pixies playing hide-and-go-seek in their leaves—designated hide-and-seek times must be approved.

The entrance to their territory was silent. The thick canopy of sinuous branches blocked any sound from escaping to the outside. Birds didn't even fly overhead here. The thick brown branches intertwined, knitting a perfect image of two gigantic holding hands.

Her lips stretched into a soft smile, making her turquoise eyes shine. No matter how many times she saw this, it made her happy.

She closed her eyes and with her right palm facing up, she concentrated on her fourth chakra, the one associated with her heart. In her mind's eye she visualized the green, swirling vortex. The orb of energy opened into a twelve-point lotus flower. Xi exhaled as she sang, "Anahata," meaning unbeaten flow. She gave her energy permission to flow freely. The air above her right palm became thick, like sap from a tree.

She opened her eyes as her green lotus flower materialized. "You grace me with your presence. I am humbled."

Xi acknowledged the energy's company. She extended her hand. The green translucent lotus floated to the branches. The energy absorbed into the wooden barrier, traveling like blood through the veins, tracing every curve and bend. Xi waited and followed the emerald spark racing around with her eyes. The branches creaked as they released their grip from each other, granting her permission to enter.

Xi passed under the canopy and turned to watch the branches return to their embrace. The air was rich with the fragrance of leaves, moss, and the dampness from the rain. Trapped in the droplets was her favorite smell, clean and sweet, pure sunshine. As Xi moved, the leaves freed their perfume, unlocking it from the raindrops sitting on their surface. Taking a deep inhale, she closed her eyes, relishing the warm, amber scent of the sun's trapped rays floating into the air. She remembered that specific scent high above the treetops when she would fly and graze her hands along the sequoia trees in the summer. It was nice considering night had fallen.

Memories flickered behind Xi's eyes. She blinked and lifted her head, catching bits and pieces of the Dryads' conversation as their voices carried.

She cleared her throat and stepped forward, giving her customary greeting. "Merry meet, my ladies."

The talking abruptly stopped and the canopy of green leaves swayed as the branches parted. Xi stepped into the circle.

In melodic unison, the voices greeted her, "Merry meet, Xi."

The bark of their trunks morphed into various noses, eyes, and mouths of the Dryads. The sliver of moonlight left in the sky made it difficult to see the full idiosyncrasies of their expressions.

"Has the spring found you all well?" Her mouth curved into a smile.

The trees bobbed their branches, indicating yes.

"Is there anything I can do for you ladies?" Xi inquired.

The Dryads remained hushed as an elder representative spoke for them, an oak tree whose bark swirled like water, dappled with lichen in different shades of green and gray. She wore them like badges of honor. Her branches reached and twirled skyward, covered in a dressing of lush, green leaves that were her crowning glory. Her loud voice had a hollow quality like wind blowing through a cave. "Dear Xi, each month you travel here to assist us in settling petty squabbles and other such nonsense."

Xi curtsied. "It is my honor to assist you." She nodded, her eyes glistening.

The elder Dryad continued, "It is time we return the favor, my dear Xi." The pattern of bark emulating an eyebrow arched. "Since the night of the shooting star, you have taken each Virtue into your heart and looked after them. You have made this unbearable situation a little better. You gave hope to the hopeless."

Xi dropped her gaze and heat flushed her cheeks, humbled by the eldest Dryad's words.

Virtues began to pour out from each crevice and corner, the brilliance of their torches illuminating. The forest came alive with light and festivities. The Virtues all circled Xi.

She looked around at the activity, her eyes shifting side to side. Bewildered, she turned back toward the Dryads, who tipped their branches. Above her head the high-pitched buzz of pixie wings sounded, like a symphony of hyperactive crickets. They carried a circlet of purple pansy flowers. Xi ducked, not sure what was happening. The young pixies giggled and held the circlet, hovering in place waiting.

The elder Dryad's voice reverberated. "May I present your queen. She gave us hope where there was none, light when there were only shadows. She is no longer Xi. Her name is Queen Aurora. The queen of the dawn. Queen of a new beginning. Long live our queen."

Every Virtue bowed as they chanted, "Queen Aurora. Long live the queen!" The pixies placed the circlet of flowers on Queen Aurora's crimson hair and bowed.

Aurora stood, paralyzed by the events. *Queen?* Her body shook and her mouth fell open. *I can't be a queen. I don't know anything about being a queen. I don't want to rule anyone.*

She gazed upon their hopeful faces. Their eyes held the light of a better future. Aurora loved these creatures. Abandonment was not in her vocabulary. The night of the shooting star replayed in her mind. She watched it climb and fall. She promised to give her kin hope and faith. This was her opportunity to fulfill that promise as their queen and friend. She clenched her fists to stop her fidgeting.

As a queen, she could keep her word. No one would hurt them. She could protect them.

Aurora? She repeated her name. Mouthing it a few times, biting her bottom lip, she wrung her hands and pulled at her fingers. The plan was to name herself when she could fly again but being given a name out of love meant so much more. It was such a gift, a true gift. *I can do this. They believe in me.*

Aurora gave them all one last look, scanning the surrounding group. She tightened her mouth. It quirked a bit to the left as her resolve set in. Bowing her head, tears slowly rolled down her cheeks. She stood tall and raised her chin. "I am honored, and I will serve as your queen in a righteous and loving manner. We will rebuild a free society with hope and faith."

Thunderous applause erupted.

Aurora raised her hands to her mouth, trying to cover her excitement, disbelief and her beaming smile. Every creature who witnessed her words leaped to their feet, cheering for their new queen.

Aurora walked up to each Dryad and hugged them. "I will do my best to live up to the tribute you have given me tonight," she said emphatically.

The eldest Dryad smiled. "My queen, you earned this. Look, dawn is upon us." The Dryad pointed with a branch to the break in the sky, where the navy blue of night faded and the early morning rays reached their arms out to the world. The Dryad gazed at her queen and said in a voice full of wisdom and newfound joy, "You see, it is a new day. You have brought with you the dawn, just as your name-sake foretold."

Aurora watched the morning light chase away the last remnants of the night. She took in the sight laid out before them. Hope had arrived on the beams of sunshine once again. This time she would meet the day wearing a crown and bearing a new name.

Her expression relaxed as she wondered, *what will the light deliver to me next?*

SEVEN:
WINGS

A urora sat at the shore. The wind was stronger by the sea. It reminded her of flying. She loved to close her eyes and raise her face to the warm rays of sunlight. If she concentrated, she could lose herself for a few precious seconds and recall the sensations of the wind, the salty taste of the damp air on her lips, the musky scent of the sea, and the sound of the rushing wind as it whipped by her. It called to her heart like a childhood lullaby, comforting and warm.

A splash of cool saltwater on her face and the presence of being watched brought her crashing back to her reality.

Aurora opened her eyes. Her friend Serena pulled herself up onto the shore by her elbows.

Serena was a mermaid, a term she invented. Serena had been an Oceanic Virtue before. Therefore, it was a natural for her to be taken with the sea and continue to protect the aquatic life dwelling there. The rest of her faction of Virtues followed suit, changing their appearance as well, living in the sea after they were cut off, calling themselves

Merfolk. Serena had adopted a tail, a rainbow one, the only mermaid with a rainbow tail. Aurora's friend's sense of whimsy always brought a smile to her face.

"My queen. I would curtsy, but since I no longer have legs..." Serena said with a crook of her eyebrow and a sardonic smile.

Aurora rolled her eyes. "Oh, please, you wouldn't curtsy even if you did," she retorted, matching Serena's wit and patting the wet sand beside her. "Please, join me."

The two friends enjoyed the peace, letting the breeze play with their hair. Their strands mixed together, Aurora's crimson red tangled with Serena's gold. It looked like a flurry of flames behind the two as the wind picked up. The sun's rays touched down, basking on their luminescent skin. The waves rolled in, each one as strong and bold as the last. The surf rushed up around their lower halves, tickling and cooling their bodies while they watched the waves play their game of catch and release with the shore. Their teasing gave way to silence between the two.

Finally, Serena broke the spell, never breaking her gaze with the horizon. "Do you think He knows?"

Aurora had waited for the inevitable question, glad in a way her friend had brought it up and not anyone else. She sighed, her shoulders slumped, and a line formed on her forehead. "I'm sure He does." Aurora did not break her gaze either as she attempted to sound detached.

Serena looked at her friend. Aurora's brow was furrowed, her lips tight as she stared out at the crystal-blue ocean. Serena bit her bottom lip and her tail tapped on the wet sand. The mermaid timed her tail so it was making the loudest possible thwack on the compact sand in between the incoming waves.

Aurora remained stoic for the moment, but the sound of Serena's wet tail had Aurora at her breaking point. "I don't have to be a mind reader to know you have more to say, Serena. Besides, the incessant tail-tapping isn't subtle, and chewing on your bottom lip was always a dead give-away, so out with it," she scolded. Her back teeth clenched. She was more than just a little annoyed.

The mermaid rolled onto her stomach, propping herself onto her elbows as she took a deep breath. She doodled in the sand before flipping onto her back and twirling her long, blonde hair around her fingers. She changed position for the third time, onto her side, propping her temple on her fist as her elbow dug into the sand, and wriggled her nose.

The constant repositioning wore on Aurora's last nerve. She closed her eyes, waiting for Serena's commentary, trying desperately not to lose her temper.

After a few moments that felt like an eternity, Serena spoke in a fast deluge of questions. "So you think He is upset you are the queen? Are you afraid He will punish us or you? I mean, technically, we are worshipping you, and that's strictly forbidden. I mean...to worship another. Not that we idolize you... Well, you know... I..." Serena fumbled over her words.

Aurora's anger built until she couldn't control it anymore. *I want to fly away...but I can't because He took that away from me.* She wanted Serena to stop talking, wanted her to be quiet. She longed to go home, to stop being queen, to make the world stop for a second. But most of all she wanted to ask Him, *why?*

It all bubbled to the surface and Aurora yelled, "Be quiet! Stop! Just stop!"

The mermaid looked at her friend with wide eyes and mouth open, her beautiful face frozen in a state of shock. Because in the hundreds of years they had known each other, her best friend had never yelled at her, or it could have been her friend hovered twenty feet above the ground with what appeared to be wings on her back.

"Um...Aurora?" Serena said, speaking to Aurora like a child on the verge of a tantrum.

Aurora's eyes were shut so tight the crinkles were almost red from trying to regain her composure. The anger mixed with hurt, frustration, and something else Aurora wasn't sure of. "No, listen to me. I—"

Aurora opened her eyes to see her friend looking up at her in astonishment. *How did I get up here? And what is on my back?*

She slowly turned her head, fear pulsing through her veins, mixed with a touch of anticipation. Time was measured by the thrum of her heartbeat whooshing in her ears. She held her breath, but just as her chin passed her shoulder, something snapped through her like an electric shock. She fell to the earth, much like the feather she had dropped off the mountain so long ago.

Aurora plummeted twenty feet. Serena rolled out of the way to avoid being hit. Aurora landed with a thud on the wet sand.

Serena crawled over to her, elbows digging into the earth, becoming raw and pink as she dragged her finned body to her friend's side. She brushed the sand off her friend as best she could, scanning Aurora for signs of injuries. "Aurora, Aurora!" she pleaded until her friend opened her eyes.

Aurora briefly looked around, her eyes moving wildly. "Please, tell me...was it a dream?" she said in a low, trembling voice.

"No, it wasn't," Serena said, her shoulders relaxing. "You had wings again. They were different, but they were wings." Her face beamed.

Aurora's eyes were glassy with unshed tears. "You saw them? Tell me—what did they look like?"

Serena briefly contemplated, then said, "Like nothing I have ever seen in my days, Aurora. They were translucent. No feathers, just colors swirling as if the wind was contained in the shape of wings, held by sheer will. Your will, my queen. They were magnificent. By all the elements, you are a queen, and you deserve to be worshipped." Serena hugged Aurora.

Aurora broke the embrace and pushed her friend away. "No, Serena. I was just about to tell you I miss Him. I want to go home too. I want to know why He left us. I don't think I can keep this up. I'm not sure I am fit to rule—"

Serena placed a finger on her friend's lips. "You haven't grieved for your loss. The night of the shooting star, you immediately began taking care of all of us. We all thought that star would return home. Thus, we all were, but that did not happen. He left you, too. He left all of us, but we had you." She placed her hands on each side of Aurora's head, holding her steady to look into her eyes. "We all coped because of you. It is why we made you queen, and now you have to deal with knowing He is watching and judging. I hate to think of it as a cruel joke." Serena's eyes filled with tears. "I don't envy you, Aurora. He knows you wear the crown and why. I would like to think this is all part of some grand scheme of His."

Serena moved her hands from her friend's head to her hands and squeezed them, trying to ground her to the present. She knew her friend all too well. Aurora tended to get lost in her mind.

Aurora's eyes flicked up to meet Serena's and Aurora exhaled.

"I know when He locked us out it was hardest on you. I didn't lose the ocean, but you lost the wind," Serena said.

The two friends sat on the sand and cried together. They mourned the past and what had been lost, but in the back of Aurora's mind, she knew something had been found today, as well. Aurora's anger dissolved much the same way the sea erased her footprints on the sand where it met the shore. Each wave ran up along the sand, starting something new while helping to forget what had been there a second ago.

The sun began setting when the two parted ways. They embraced but didn't speak. There was nothing left to say. Aurora brushed the sand off and watched her friend disappear beneath the waves.

"My dear Serena, what would I ever do without you?" She blew a kiss.

Aurora turned to the dunes and thought about the day. She so badly wanted to try to fly again, but the possibility of failure felt like an anchor around her ankle. Heavy. She was afraid her rage had fueled her flight. If it was an emotional manifestation, it frightened her even more. Outbursts like rage and jealousy were what had helped Lucifer corrupt many angels. She couldn't afford it as queen. She would have to sacrifice her wind for the good of her kin.

It was what being a ruler was about.

EIGHT:
LEARNING CURVE

500 YEARS SINCE THE SHOOTING STAR

It took Aurora many moons and several solar eclipses to grow into her rule. This translated into a few centuries by others' standards. She worked toward becoming a strong queen. She strived for righteousness and fairness. She searched for her kin, including the ones who had run away, wishing to disappear. It took time, but Aurora had won their trust and brought many of them back into the fold.

The Oberons and Selkies were the hardest to win back. Each one had bonded with their respective wards. The Oberons were guardians of the Polar Bears, taking the shape of the great bears except for their leader Valemon. Valemon loved to meet Queen Aurora as his handsome self, not his polar bear beast. Valemon was tall and built like a boulder, square and strong, his wispy white, blond hair kept long with dark brown braids on each side. His sun-kissed complexion was dusted with iridescent highlighter, creating a striking contrast to his espresso eyes. Valemon knew he was handsome, but he had the temper of his polar bear ward.

With each meeting, he attempted to charm Aurora. "My dear queen, how is it that you look lovelier than the last time we met?" Other such compliments flooded from his full lips. However, Aurora never gave into his charms.

The Selkies protected the seals. The Selkies only changed into seals when they entered the water. Otherwise, their oversized, dark eyes were their only distinguishing feature. Leonis was their leader. Her blue hair and faint, blue water marking, a long V-shape around each eye and tracking down each cheek but not crossing her nose denoted her status.

Leonis did not waste empty compliments on the queen as she said, "Aurora, Valemon is a polar bear, our natural enemy. My ward's enemy is my enemy. Why should I join you and him?"

The adversarial relationship between the two natural predators and prey made Aurora's job difficult. Just as she made headway with one, such as getting Valemon to back off the charm, Leonis would shut down. If one side wanted to be part of Aurora's plan, the other did not. There were long, drawn out, diplomatic discussions between the queen and each side's leaders. Aurora constantly found herself weighing in on territorial disputes between the two factions. Aurora had to draw boundary lines between the two and settle their territory to the North. Eventually the two came to an understanding, though it was precarious. With Valemon making it clear he would be on guard "I will abide and join Queen Aurora, but the Selkies must stay out of the waters during the cooler weather and migrate south."

"The Selkies will migrate south but in the cooler weather, but during the warmer times, we have the water bear!" Leonis shot back, her dark eyes looking like the sea at midnight.

Aurora rubbed her temples. "It is settled, but both of you be warned! I will not tolerate dishonesty." Aurora knew these kin would be at odds and require structure for the foreseeable future.

If the Oberons and Selkies hadn't tested Aurora's diplomatic skills, then the Keratas, a small group of miniature ponies gifted with a single, clear quartz horn that acted as a magick amplifier, then no one could. The Oberons and Selkies' problem was built on a predator and prey issue; the Keratas were just pains in the asses feeling they were powerful enough and did not want to be ruled. They were a bit egotistical and enjoyed their uniqueness, equating it to entitlement.

Aurora needed to demonstrate a point to their leader Lolita.

"You are actually quite vulnerable, Lolita," Aurora said.

The small, white pony shook her silver mane and pranced about, mocking the new queen. "And how do you figure that, Aurora? We can amplify magick. If a clan wants their magick boosted, they must pay our fees. We have a service you want." Lolita stopped her prancing to cock her head and pose.

Aurora smirked and strode over to the pony just enough to demonstrate their size difference. "My dear Lolita, who stops me from just picking you up, taking you with me, and forcing you to amplify my magick? I only need your horn, not you." Aurora folded her arms.

Lolita backed up and reared. "How dare you threaten me!"

"I am not threatening you, Lolita. I am simply proving a point. Another could easily come and take your horns. It is not a proven fact you are needed to amplify. Yes, it helps, but your horns will still do the trick, Lolita. We both know magick is about intent. It is best if you are alive, but your horns will work with or without you attached. Join me. As part of the Court of Light, you will be under my protection. The factions will be united under one governing body. No one will attempt to overthrow one another or look to gain an advantage." Aurora paused. "However, if you are on your own, I cannot guarantee you might not be sought out for obvious reasons. I have chartered peace with the Oberon and Selkies." Aurora quirked her brow at the pony.

The pony paced and circled the red-haired queen, her horn gleaming in the light. "I do not like being intimidated into submission."

"And I do not like doing it, but, Lolita, as queen...I must protect my kin in any way possible. A soft hand does not always make for the best ruler. There are times I must be hard if it is for my kin's own good. I will not abandon their well-being." Aurora's eyes locked with Lolita's.

The pony paused when Aurora spoke the word *abandon*. Her eyes gleamed as her horn twinkled, a pulse of energy running through it. Every creature had a scar from the Abandonment. Aurora had picked at Lolita's. "You are wise, Aurora. We may not agree on your methodology, but I know your heart is in the right place. The Keratas will join you."

"Thank you, Lolita." Aurora nodded her head at the pony. "I will do my very best to serve you well."

Once Aurora found all of her kin, she took time to build a court in which all Fae were welcome, the Court of Light. Queen Aurora accomplished this with the help of her advisors, a group of four bishops, each representing an element: earth, wind, water, and fire. They held no loyalty to their respective factions, only to the Fae kin as a collective and to act as advisors to their queen. Aurora picked her first bishop, a Virtue named Ingor. He was the group leader of Virtues assigned with the task of guarding the smoking mountain, a Basaltic volcano in the far desert lands. Aurora trusted Ingor's logic and pragmatism. Together, they sought out the rest of the bishops and began to determine how to structure a fair political system.

Next was the infrastructure of power, starting with the Royal Houses. The Royal Houses had a direct connection to one of the four elements—earth, air, water, or fire—and were the guardians of them. Their House names reflected their respective elements. A lady or lord led the House. They would come to court and deal with any political matters for the House. Aurora went further, renaming the tribes to factions, by Royal Decree, adopting names defined by their respective objects of protection or their wards. The faction was a smaller group of Fae kin who shared the same bloodline, elemental gifts, flora and/or fauna wards. A House could be a combination of more than one faction under one element. Factions were connected to an element through their ward but those who did not hold a straightforward bond with the element were called "secondary houses."

Lady Danaus was such a secondary house leader. Her House Papilionem was guardian to the Butterflies. Therefore, her faction Viceroy was connected through the element air because of her wards, but she herself did not have an uninterrupted link to the element. The leaders of their factions would go to their respective elemental Royal Houses to voice grievances and cast votes. It was not perfect but it was a start. Gone was any trace of their old life.

Bishop Ingor took a long inhale as he finished his reading. He glanced into her eyes, searching for approval.

"It reads like a story, Ingor, and I see you managed to work yourself in." She smirked.

"Well, Your Grace, someone should be keeping documentation of the beginning of this journey. Besides this is all new to us. We have been Virtues for so long, dictated to. You are creating something complex and new." He waved his finger at her.

Aurora sat on a rock. "You are correct, Bishop Ingor. This is more complicated than I thought it would be. The systems, rules, and where will we live? We should have a home, one where all are welcomed." The queen glanced at the landscape, the trees' branches swaying in the breeze. The mountain peeking over the treetops caught her attention as if beckoning her forward.

"Yes, we do. It is a good thought, my queen," Ingor said as he reviewed his parchment. "I will even make a chart of the houses just to explain it better."

Aurora kept her distance on the snowcapped mountain peak and nodded, biting her lip, "Go ahead, Bishop. I have one last piece of my Royal Court to settle."

A friend I pushed away after the Abandonment. The last part she thought, wanting to keep it from Ingor.

ROYAL HOUSE

House	Element	Representative	Faction
Apsaras	Air	Lady Devas	Pixies
Hathor	Earth	Lady Sekhmet	Apolline
Oceania	Water	Lady Serena	Merfolk
Acthnici	Fire	Lord Oromasis	Will-O-the-Wisps

NINE:
MEMORIES IN THE WIND

Aurora found herself at the base of the mountain where she attempted to confront her Creator so many moons ago. The winds shifted, urging her forward, yet she refused to move. She breathed in the crisp air and rolled her neck. The tension did not leave. Instead it settled like a cloak around her. This place was the site of so many failures for her as she glanced at the jagged rocks protruding from the cave opening, casting long, fang-like shadows on the glistening, pristine snow.

The breeze swirled, carrying white powder from the snowcapped ledges and surrounding trees. The glittering and shimmering particles hung in the air, dancing about. Aurora tilted her head. Her skin prickled with energy as the snow shaped faint, ghostly outlines of silhouettes before her eyes.

Tall, lithe creatures with large wings formed, the scene depicting when their Creator dropped all the Virtues off on this planet. Their dancing and singing rang in her ears. She remembered how her skin smelled after flying in the

dawn's rays. She wanted to look away but couldn't. The feeling of joy was overwhelming. Things were so simple, yet there was a sense of disconnect too. Scrutinizing the outline of Virtues, Aurora realized she couldn't have named more than a few of the Virtues that day and now she could name everyone. She knew who was stuck here with her on this planet, but the day she arrived she'd only known a handful, even though they had been Virtues together for as long as she could remember. Her brow crinkled and the joy that had been there was dissolving much like the snow outlines. The memories continued their dance. They didn't care how much her situation had changed, that she was now queen or that she went by a new name.

The breeze changed direction. The sparkle of the particles shone in the sunlight as four figures appeared—a tall one with the largest wings, two others of equal height, and one smaller figure. The snow suspended in this stance as if waiting for her to make its acquaintance.

Aurora dropped her head. "Desdemona," she whispered as her gaze zeroed in on the smallest one.

The scene played out before her eyes the day Archangel Gabriel delivered Desdemona to Earth. Desdemona had started life as a Power and became the only Power to ever exalt to a Virtue. She was the Virtue's protector—their only one, at that. All the Virtues were due to greet her but they all deemed themselves "too busy." In reality, they blatantly said they would not welcome the former Power, as none of them considered her a "real" Virtue. Many of the Virtues looked down upon Desdemona because of lineage, as if she was beneath them. Aurora recalled having to drag Serena along with her. She had befriended Desdemona, and the two became close. When the Virtues were abandoned, each of them dealt with it in their own way. Aurora went through a dark time and Desdemona bore the brunt of it.

"Archangel Gabriel, I am most humbled by your personal delivery to the newest member of our ranks. How may I be of service?" Their conversation reverberated in her head.

"Virtue Xi. Guardian of the element Air. Merry meet? Where are your brothers and sisters?" The Archangel was strict in his tone. She smiled as even her memories referred to her old angelic name "Xi."

"They are busy with our Father's wishes. Virtue Serena and I are present to be of any assistance you may need." Xi pulled at Serena's robe sleeve, forcing her to step closer.

"Yes, I can see Virtue Serena's enthusiasm." He looked down at the other Virtue. "No matter." He waved his hand. "May I present the newest member of your rank and the Virtues' guardian, Virtue Angel Desdemona." He pushed the smaller angel forward, his hand guiding her on her back.

Aurora remembered her short hair, the color of a raven's wings with bangs, their tips the same as Xi's crimson tresses. She was dressed in a long, blue gown from her exaltation ceremony. She kept pulling at the collar.

"Xi, since you are the only Virtue to show, it is up to you to acclimate her." He handed Xi a rolled up gilded scroll. "Her exaltation papers and responsibilities are listed. Desdemona was an excellent Power. She is very skilled and will protect the Virtues." Gabriel pivoted to leave.

"Archangel Gabriel, pardon me, but why do we need a protector?"

"Why? Because, my dear Xi, you are not trained to fight, and there is a war going on. My Powers cannot stop to come to your aid every time you need them. I think Father made a mistake not training you to fight. The Power Brigade is bound to protect you, and they will serve as they are commanded, but you must be self-sufficient, dear Xi. You have one of the best Powers there is. Learn from her." Gabriel turned and placed a chaste kiss on Desdemona's forehead, over her Angelite scar. "Thank you, Virtue Desdemona. Until we meet again."

Desdemona said nothing. Her eyes reflected with the tears she held back as she watched him take off. She turned to the other strange Virtues, pulling again at the collar of her dress.

"She's all yours, Xi. I am out of here. But for Father's sake, get her some clothes," Serena said before she disappeared.

Xi looked at the figure. *She's right.* The new Virtue needed clothes. "Let's get you out of that gown."

"What?" Desdemona replied.

"My friend Serena always told me clothes make the angel. You cannot do your job if you don't like what you are wearing. If you pull at that collar one more time, you are going to rip it. Let's find you something to wear. I am thinking pants are more your style. Come on."

"But it's against protocol."

"This isn't the Power Brigade, Desdemona. You are a Virtue. Besides, I won't tell if you won't."

The snow swirled and the voices in Aurora's head became a spin of conversations and laughter the two shared over the time they spent on Earth bonding as Virtues.

A swirl of the light wind changed the snow framing into two shapes.

Their postures said it all—they were arguing. This was the memory Aurora had been dreading. She knew which outline was hers and which was Desdemona. The cutting words resounded in her head as the snowflakes waved and skipped, acting out her shameful behavior while her mind added the dialogue. Her figure loomed over her friend and protector, her arms flailing about, making dismissive gestures.

"I don't understand, Xi. Why must you go alone?"

"Because it is my right as a true Virtue. I do not owe you of all angels an explanation. Now go." Xi's eyes burned as she pointed in the opposite direction of where she was headed.

"Me of all angels? What is that supposed to mean?" Desdemona narrowed her gaze.

Xi stepped closer to the other angel, her hands on her hips. "You know precisely what I mean. I have something to do, and I do not need or want a pet on my journey. You are not my responsibility. You aren't even a real Virtue. Leave me, Desdemona."

The contours and forms shifted, but Aurora was aware of how the rest of the exchange played out, the vitriol she'd spewed. All Desdemona had sought was to support her, see she made it to the top of the mountain, make sure she was safe. However, Aurora would not allow her friend to witness her petulance. She was broken and yearned to wallow in her self-pity alone. She wanted to grieve in peace, to feel justified in her defiance of their Father. To have a witness was too much. The worst part, the battle raging deep in her aura, Aurora had not decided if she would be coming back. Oblivion's edge was closer than it had ever been before, and she did not wish for anyone who might hinder her. If she wanted death, it was her choice.

Aurora left Desdemona at the base of the mountain with the rest of her compassion. The pain and hurt blinding her as well as acting as her only companion up the mountain.

Aurora closed her eyes, her bottom lip trembling. When she opened them, one sparkling snow ghost remained—Desdemona, on her knees with her hands covering her face.

The breeze blew, and inch by inch, the memory slowly disintegrated but not before the snow outline lifted her head to face Aurora. With one final gust the snow swirled upwards and disappeared.

Aurora gazed up at the mountain. She shielded her face with her hand. The gleam of the jagged, snowcapped points glittered like crystal. A soft smile curled her lips at the juxtaposition of the play of light and dark.

"There is light and dark in everything, even in our not-so-proud moments. I did not choose Oblivion that day. I chose a new path, and now I must share it."

TEN:
REUNION

D iscovering Desdemona had chosen to remain in the cold and isolation did not surprise Aurora. The seclusion of the mountain was fitting for the former Power who had always felt like an outsider. Yet she was more powerful than most of the Virtues put together. Desdemona was a force to be reckoned with. Aurora suspected many Virtues used the excuse of Desdemona's lineage to treat her poorly when in truth they were afraid of her.

The mysterious mountain suited Desdemona. Aurora gazed upon the dark, deep cavern hole, the sweet tang of ash permeating through the air. Desdemona had a fire going.

Aurora entered with trepidation, hugging the wall, taking careful, slow steps. She called Desdemona's name as she traveled down the cold, bleak corridor. There was no answer. The light grew brighter, and she saw a body hunched over the blaze covered in fur pelts.

"I was wondering when you might return. I'm guessing you need something?" Her voice was husky and smooth. She never turned around to acknowledge her visitor.

Aurora swallowed. "Hello, Desdemona." She lingered in the entryway, waiting for a formal invitation. When the situation did not present itself she continued inside the dwelling.

Various animal pelts lined the floor. Branches were set up as drying racks for the meat she was preserving, while a circular wooden wheel was suspended from above with lavender, thyme, lemon balm, and rosemary hanging in different stages of preparation. Rudimentary stone pillars held small mixtures of white sage burning in the corners to clear the room of any unwanted energies.

Aurora inhaled deeply, taking in the sweet, earthy scent of the sage. "What? No, no, not like that. What I need is to apologize to you, Desdemona."

The figure in fur stood and spun in a motion of bone-less grace, throwing her hood off. Desdemona's grey eyes sparkled against the orange illumination of the bonfire. Her ebony bangs with their deep-red tips rustled, showing a hint of her Angelite disc scar. Her braid was down to the nape of her neck now. Aurora remembered when her hair grazed her jawline. Desdemona stood shorter than Aurora, though with her lean, muscular build and the way she carried herself, the smaller angel appeared to be ten feet tall.

"Apologize?" A sneer curled on the right side of Desdemona's lips.

"Yes, Desdemona, I owe you an apology. I was cruel to you that day. I want you to come with me, back with the others." She extended her hand in a gesture of authenticity.

Desdemona glanced from the hand back to the Virtue it belonged to, shaking her head. "Why? You need someone to carry something, or perhaps you want me to act as a footstool for you and the other Virtues to rest your tired feet upon? No, thank you." Desdemona faced the fire, dismissing her guest.

Aurora sighed. "Desdemona, they made me queen. I want you to come with me and be treated as an equal. You are not beneath anyone. I am so sorry for what I said. I was hurt and—that is no excuse for my behavior. I am sorry, Desdemona, for saying you weren't a real angel." Aurora closed her eyes tightly as she recanted her words.

Desdemona shook her head as Aurora spoke. "You said I was a disposable body to be used as a real Virtue saw fit and you no longer needed me. Now you have a change of heart because they deemed you queen? Instantly I am equal? Because I have something you want." She turned her back to her visitor.

"Desdemona, I am trying. Please, I want you to hold a high place in my court. You are extraordinary, the best warrior I have ever known—Virtue or Power. I want you by my side. I value you, and I apologize for making you feel like I did not. You will have free rein to train the guards as you see fit." Aurora's voice had an enticing lilt to it.

Desdemona's eye flicked to the side as her mouth quirked upon hearing the last part of Aurora's offer. "Control over the guards? To arrange them as I please?"

"Yes."

"You promise? No interference." Desdemona's tongue rolled around her inner cheeks as she contemplated the offer.

"You have my word." Aurora's head leaned in, anticipation hanging in the air.

Desdemona faced Aurora, her index finger to her lip as she paced. "You will never speak to me like that again. I will also get a place of honor in the court?"

"From the bottom of my heart, Desdemona, I wish I could take back my callous words. I am sorry. I will never speak to you like that again. You will have a place of honor and respect in my court."

Desdemona closed the gap between them, bringing her index and middle finger to her forehead in the Power Angel show of respect. "I accept."

Aurora smiled. She placed her right hand over her heart in a fist and bowed her head. "I have done away the titles of Virtue and Power, along with the old traditions. We will start anew. I am Aurora, Queen of the Court of Light. I am Fae." She repeated the bow with her hand over her heart again, urging Desdemona to follow.

Desdemona tilted her head sideways and pursed her lips, mimicking Aurora's bow. "I am Desdemona. I will serve the Court of Light. I am Fae. What is Fae?"

"We are Fae. The Fellowship Aegis of Earth. Fellowship as in society, aegis meaning protectors or defenders, and Earth is self-explanatory."

"The society of defenders of Earth. Hmm...I like that. I enjoy being a protector." Desdemona's eyes glinted in the firelight.

"I am glad. I thought you might." Aurora gave her a wink. "I want to erase the lines of entitlement. No Fae should feel obligated by their past. I believe it is fitting since our love of the Earth, elements, and creatures is what helped us through this hardship. You, dear Desdemona, are Captain of the Royal Guards of the Court of Light. You are responsible for the safety of all Fae."

Desdemona's eyes widened, and she dropped to her knees, bowing her head. Aurora pulled her up.

"No, you do not kneel to me or anyone ever again!," Aurora said. "Blind faith is what led us here. Never again. Loyalty to the kin, not to a crown."

Desdemona straightened, pulling her shoulders back. "Thank you."

"You deserve this," Aurora said.

"No, not the title. Though I am the best suited for the job. I mean...thank you for the apology. I am not aware of another Virtue Fae who would apologize to me. To humble themselves by admitting their mistake is the sign of a fair and just ruler." Desdemona gave a small curve of her lips.

"Together, we will do more than survive. Come, Captain Desdemona, we have a kingdom to create."

Surveying the meadow with Desdemona by her side, Aurora lifted her chin and sighed. "Yes, this will do nicely."

Desdemona placed her hands on her hips, smiling brightly. "The palace will be in the meadow near the mountain where you rescinded your faith and loyalty." She looked at her queen and broke her usual stoic demeanor and grabbed her shoulders. "It's perfect!"

"An appropriate reminder I will one day soar above that very mountain." Aurora pointed at it.

"It's practical, close enough to the sea with water channels for the Merfolk," Desdemona said, taking a more logical approach. "The Epican forest was near for the Dryads, and the cave dwellers could easily configure a tunnel system given the caverns below the mountain."

Aurora's eyes slid to Desdemona's. "Told you this will do nicely." Her arms spread wide.

ELEVEN:
GIRL TALK

Queen Aurora strolled along the shoreline, waiting for Serena. Her royal duties had kept her busy in the last few weeks. She missed the morning talks with her best friend. Serena had been elevated to a Lady by Aurora, and head of the water Fae factions. Now, when she saw Serena, it was usually regarding Fae business. They both made a concerted effort to keep their morning talks about girl stuff which gave her great pleasure.

Here at the ocean, there were no crowns, no formalities. Only two best friends, laughing and loving their time together. Aurora closed her eyes and lifted her chin skyward. Her hair blew back, and the breeze caressed her skin. She enjoyed how it slipped over her body like ribbons. It reminded her of flying.

A cool splash of sea spray caught her in the face. Aurora opened her eyes with a smile, knowing who she would find. Serena lay on her stomach in the sand as the waves washed up on her rainbow-scaled tail, and the sun shone down on

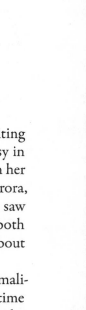

it. Aurora had to shield her eyes from the bright kaleido-scope of hues reflected from the mermaid's tail.

Just below Serena's waist was an umbrae of rain-bow-patterned scales initiated with tones of scarlet and cherry-red, slowly dissipating into ginger before exploding into indigo and sapphire-blue fins. Serena's tail was her pride and joy, second only to her hair, which skimmed the top of her waist. It was golden-blonde and reminded Aurora of a sunset. Sometimes, she wanted Aurora to braid it while they sat together on the beach.

Serena's skin was the most interesting part of her, even if Serena didn't think so. It was luminescent like all Fae, but it had a blue tinge. Embedded in the luminescence a water reflection pattern shimmered. The water impres-sion morphed based upon the actual sun's reflection in the water Serena swam in. Much like a chameleon, to blend into her surroundings. Until Aurora had brought it to her attention, Serena had been oblivious to this ability. Aurora often teased Serena that she only played at being unaware of certain things. For Lady Serena was far from unmindful.

Aurora ran to her friend as she lay in the surf. Serena pulled herself farther up onto the shore and rolled onto her back, half her tail stroked by the gentle surf. Aurora gave her friend a hug and joined her, rolling up her dress and placing her legs in the surf. The two friends gazed out into the horizon.

Tension began to grow, and Serena flapped her tail side to side.

Aurora anticipated her friend's question as they watched seagulls fly overhead. "No, I still haven't flown since that day," Aurora said on the end of an exhale, trying not to sound disappointed.

Serena wiggled her nose, then tapped her fins. "Have you tried?"

"No. Too much going on. Kind of busy being a queen and all. You know, ruling a kingdom." She smiled and placed her right leg over Serena's tapping fins. "Can we stop with the fishy fidgeting?" Aurora scrunched up her face to the side.

Serena smiled. "Oh, is that a royal command?" Serena pouted and batted her eyes before splashing Aurora.

"Okay, got it. I'll take my invisible crown off." Aurora blushed, embarrassed. After all, Serena was just being a friend.

Serena hugged her friend's shoulders from the back, playfully planting a wet, sloppy kiss on Aurora's cheek. "No. Every gal should wear an invisible crown all the time. Even you, Rory." She placed her cheek against her friend's head.

Aurora put her hand over Serena's and leaned into her, closing her eyes and allowing her body to fall back into an embrace.

The two Fae sat on the beach, exchanging quips and laughs for hours. The stress of Aurora's royal responsibilities lifted until a figure on the dune ran toward them.

Aurora felt the tension pulsate through the air and crash back into her, like the waves hitting into the shore.

TWELVE:
HOLD MY HAND

"**Y**our Majesty! Your Majesty!" A four-foot-tall figure with pale-green luminescent skin waved his arms. A long navy-blue beard and a handlebar-style mustache made a stark contrast against his bald head covered with dark-green tattoos. His small, stocky body hid the power contained in his stature. Iridescent bracers on his large forearms indicated his faction.

He was a Spelaion. They were a cave-dwelling Fae who mined in the caverns, utilizing an acid-based liquid their bodies produced. This liquid enabled them to fashion gorgeous structures from the minerals underground. The bracers tapped into this reservoir of acid, allowing him to mine with his bare hands. Only the Spelaions wore them. The bracers were not just ornamental; these cuffs were deadly. Not only did they control acid flow for work, but they also gave them the ability to shoot the liquid at an enemy up to ten feet.

"Your Majesty! Please, you must come quickly!" the gnome said.

Spelaion never traveled from their caves, much less to the ocean.

Serena tilted her head at Aurora and shrugged.

Aurora's brows knitted together, correcting him at his formality was not proper given his emotional state, her mouth tightened. She folded her arms across her chest in anticipation.

The gnome gave a hurried bow, a blush covering his cheeks as he did. He seemed embarrassed he had forgotten his manners.

"What is your name?" Aurora asked softly, trying to calm him down as best she could. The gnome backed up, staring at Serena. Clearly, he had not seen a mermaid before.

Aurora glanced at Serena and back to the gnome. "Sir, your name?" she soothingly prodded.

The gnome shook his head. "I am Aster of the Spelaion Faction. Your Majesty, please, you must hurry. We have found something, and no one knows what to make of it. The Dryads told me to find you. I'm assigned with the important task of escorting you to them." His voice rose with each word.

Aurora was surprised the Dryads had asked for her. Usually they could handle things. "Take me with you at once, Aster."

Waving goodbye to Serena, Aurora followed the Spelaion from the beach. Aster kept looking over his shoulder at the Finned Fae. Serena gave the gnome a flirty wink as they scampered up the dune.

Aster led Aurora to two white deer in the dunes—a big one with large, white antlers and smaller one with a trail of sapphire-blue, bristly fur trailing down its neck and white, glistening antlers.

Aster jumped onto the back of the smaller one and Aurora took the other. The two Fae sped off toward the Epican Forest. Their journey would have taken days on foot but took only hours on the back of the deer. The landscape blurred around her as they traveled deep into the forest. The deer took the uneven terrain without trouble, leaping and prancing over fallen trees, small streams, and rocks, kicking up the damp smell of the earth. Their hooves dug into the ground and drove them forward.

The entrance to the Dryad territory was open in anticipation of Aurora and Aster's arrival.

Aurora heard the commotion before she dismounted her deer. She gave the animal a grateful stroke along his neck and made her way with Aster toward the voices. As they approached, Aurora could see it was a meeting of the minds. The Dryads were not alone. The pixies flittered about in their frenetic manner. The high-pitched buzzing of their wings denoted their anxiety, and a few larger pixies without wings stepped out to take their places. They were joined by a few of Aster's Spelaion faction members. The white deer they had ridden even had their representatives present, and an elder from the Dryad faction was attempting to call some kind of order to the chaos, though no one listened to her.

Aster made his way ahead of Aurora to the center of the activity. He climbed onto a pile of granite rocks, allowing him to see over the group. He cleared his throat. However, it did not even garner a blink from anyone. Aster put his fingers in his mouth and released an ear-piercing whistle.

The gaggle of Fae stopped and looked up.

"May I present Queen Aurora," Aster announced with a sweeping bow.

Aurora gave a shy smile at the earth gnome before she met everyone's eyes and moved past Aster into the center of the craziness. "Merry meet, my friends. What seems to be the problem?"

Everyone spoke at once, making their words indecipherable.

Aurora shook her head and backed away from the clamor. She placed her hands up, trying to quiet the crowd. "Wait, wait, please. I can't understand you." But no one listened.

Aster climbed atop his deer this time and whistled again, louder than the one before.

Aurora looked up at him.

He winked at his queen. "Shut up! Your queen only has two ears. She can't listen to all of you at once! Have some respect!" Aster smiled as he tipped his head. His green skin gleamed in the light streaming through the breaks in the forest. "Your Majesty."

Aurora mouthed "Thank you" to Aster and turned back to the group of Fae standing before her.

They were scared, looking to her for answers.

She took a breath. "I will hear from each faction. Please pick one representative to speak on your faction's behalf. Wait until I call upon you to speak. I promise I will listen to each representative. First, I would like to hear from the Dryads. Please, tell me what is going on." Aurora tried to sound authoritative and compassionate at the same time. She glanced at Aster, who nodded as if for encouragement. Aurora took her seat on a nearby rock formation, awaiting the Dryads' representative.

The elder Dryad Lady Fernia spoke. "Thank you, Queen Aurora. It was brought to our attention by the

Spelaions they have discovered what appear to be pictures of their caves." Lady Fernia bent a large branch downward, her leaves rustling as birds flew off, to signify she was done with her statement.

Aurora raised her right hand to her chin, cupping it as her eyebrows drew together. "Pictures? The Spelaions discovered these? I would like to hear from the Spelaions next," she said with a graceful motion of her hand before returning it to her chin.

A Spelaion, older than Aster, stepped forward and bowed. He shared Aster's stocky build and green skin, but his beard was not just green; it was a rainbow of every shade of green from the light celadon to the deepest fir tree, with flecks of gold scattered throughout.

Aurora recognized him immediately. "Merry meet, Malascola, leader of the Spelaion Faction. Was it you who found these pictures in your caves?"

"Yes, Your Grace. I was leaving to go hunt when I came across this..." Malascola motioned and four Spelaions, matching his height and tattoos, struggled to bring forth a piece of orange-hued limestone approximately four feet by four feet. They had carved it from the cave wall.

Carefully, they leaned it against the rocks for Aurora to inspect. On the rock face were several left-handed prints outlined in red and brown paint. Aurora walked over and put her own left hand up to the rock pictures. The hands were too small to be Fae.

"Thank you, Malascola. Do you have any further details to add?"

"Yes. Members of the Aubane faction reported seeing the owners of these hands after a few of their young were killed by these unknown creatures. The Aubane members who escaped said the creatures ambushed them in a ravine."

There were gasps at Malascola's revelation of any Fae being hunted.

One of the pixies reached for the small branch of the Dryad she stood beside upon hearing the news the white deer were being hunted. Her eyes wide, the pixie held the blossoming branch like a child holding her mother's hand.

Malascola turned toward a large, white stag. His elongated neck was majestic and his black eyes appeared limitless like a midnight sky. They were dark, but like the sky, they held the light of a thousand stars behind them. His glistening, snow-white antler tips were dusted with gold that glittered as he made his way through the group.

The other white deer bowed their graceful necks as he pranced forward.

"Your Grace, I am Theadova of the Aubane Faction. I come with disturbing news. I have seen the owners of these hands. They look like you, only smaller and primitive in their language skills. They have hunted my younger ones who have not yet turned white or whose antlers have not fully grown. I believe they want their meat for food and their fur for warmth. However, when they see any of my faction who are mature, they fall to their knees, praising them. I have ordered my kin to stay in hiding until I spoke with you." The stag stepped back and arched his head down, awaiting Queen Aurora's answer.

Aurora reached back to steady herself on a slanted piece of flagstone. She slowly sat down, squeezing her eyes shut. Her kin had to hide in fear from harm.

"You have done well by your kin, Theadova. Until we know what we are dealing with, I feel it is best for us to act with caution around these creatures. You will all come to the Court of Light. I offer you and all Fae sanctuary. While I consult with my bishops, I will call a representative of each faction to a meeting where we will come together and deal with this issue as a whole. Are we in agreement?" Aurora squared her shoulders. As much as this sounded like a request, it was a command.

There was much chatter and noise, but the consensus was of cooperation.

Aurora smiled. "Very well. Malascola, since your kin were integral in the construction of the palace, please direct the others who are not familiar with the way to the palace? I will spread the word of sanctuary and send out my invite to the other factions. Oh, Malascola, may I take the hand painting with me?"

Malascola lifted an eyebrow. "My queen. It would take many of us to carry it such a distance—"

Aurora's smile reached all the way to her eyes. She placed her hand to her mouth to hide her misplaced excitement. She closed her eyes and concentrated. A bead of sweat appeared on her brow. Her chakras aligned and she raised her right wrist in a graceful gesture, palm facing up, and beckoned with her index finger. The rock lifted and floated toward her.

Aurora opened her eyes. She did not wipe at her brow. Everyone stared in amazement at the levitating stone and back at their queen with newfound respect. Her mouth was soft and upturned with self-satisfaction. She straightened her shoulders and tossed her hair back, allowing her long, red tresses to wave behind her like a cape.

"No need. I can carry it myself. I shall see you at the palace. Theadova, may I bother one of your kin for a ride home?"

Theadova gently bent his neck, trying not to stare at the hovering stone. "Your Grace, it would be my honor to carry you home. My faction will follow you."

Aurora bowed in response and mounted the large white stag. "To the palace where all are welcome."

She gave a rallying cry, and Theadova took off with a herd of white deer at his back, their thunderous hooves echoing through the forest.

THIRTEEN:
THE COURT OF LIGHT

A urora had started construction on the Court of Light palace during the summer solstice. She hoped to have it complete by the next summer cycle. For now, certain parts were livable, and it was lovely, large Selenite crystal towers to the west and a spiraling Rose Quartz atrium sat at the apex with colorful crystal mosaic tile roofing being placed. The mosaic colors reflected their rainbow hues off the other structures.

Malascola's faction had been crucial in several engineering and designing aspects of the citadel. Without the Spelaions, the speed and intricacy of work would not have been possible.

As Theadova and Aurora came upon the palace, Theadova stopped short, almost bucking Aurora. "I apologize, Your Grace. I haven't seen it since you began construction. It's wonderful," he said with wild-eyed wonderment.

Aurora dismounted. She could walk the rest of the way. It was disrespectful to ride her guest into the gates. "Yes, it is, and it is your home, Theadova. It is home for all the

Fae. It is why I built it, a place for protection and serenity. Come, let us get everyone a drink after our long journey."

Aurora led Theadova and the rest of the Aubane faction through the Palace's Hematite entryway. The courtyard buzzed with work, hammering, carrying of materials, and the clanging of crystals, but it all came to a halt when the queen entered. Aurora graciously smiled and continued on her way, making a concentrated effort to point out every Fae working and personally greet them with a wave or a compliment. It was clear to any onlooker she was well-liked by everyone she came in contact with.

Bishop Ingor rushed to greet the queen. He was shorter than Aurora but very lean. He was of the Salamander Faction and a fire elemental. He had deep auburn hair with glints of orange highlights toward the ends resembling a smoldering fire. He wore his hair in a low ponytail that hung to his upper back. The distinguishing features of the Salamander Faction were their red eyes with yellow pupils. His long face, aquiline nose, thin mouth, and high cheekbones gave him a lizard-like quality, a common trait among the Salamanders.

"Merry meet, my queen," he said as he looked at the ocean of white deer magnificence following her. "I see we have guests." Bishop Ingor cocked his head as if to say "Care to share?" Aurora stepped aside, allowing the bishop to take in the vision of the Aubane faction standing before him.

Aurora presented Theadova to him. The two exchanged pleasantries and Aurora asked a water undine gliding by to arrange refreshments for her guests. Aurora gave Bishop Ingor a serious look. "We must prepare for more guests at the palace. Please see to it and have the other bishops meet me in the West Tower right away. We have much to discuss."

The levitating stone cut through the crowd of deer. Bishop Ingor opened his mouth to speak but Aurora held her hand up. "Not here. In the West Tower." She abruptly turned away from her bishop to face the white stag. "Theadova, I will let you rest after the long journey. Let me consult with the bishops, and we will meet later before the moon rises. I think it is important for them to hear your story as well." Aurora smiled reassuringly at the white stag.

Theadova bowed. "Thank you, my queen."

Bishop Ingor was either wringing his hands or pulling at the ginger-glinted ends of his ponytail. His nervous energy sparked off him. However, Aurora would not entertain him until they were safely behind closed doors.

"Gather the others and we will speak. This is much worse than we imagined. His prophecy has come true. They are here, and in his likeness, just as he promised." Her right eye twitched with her statement as a twinge of anger welled up in her.

The West Tower was modest, but it was structurally sound. The Great Hall was in the final stages of construction, but her meeting quarters off the Great Hall were finished. Queen Aurora sat at a table of teak, her chair was larger than the others with a septagram on top. While the room itself was finished structurally, the decor was still sparse. A clover window to the east was bare of window coverings.

"My queen, when will Malascola begin the fresco in your quarters?"

Aurora glanced at the room, pursing her lips. "I guess the room is a bit stark."

"It needs to look a bit more...fitting for a queen," Ingor added.

"Ask him to put this on his list Ingor perhaps we could spruce it up a bit." She nodded as they waited for the other three bishops to arrive.

A moment later, Bishop Geddes and Bishop Ward filed in. "Merry meet," they said in unison. Aurora nodded and they all took their seats.

The four of them stared at the empty chair, Bishop Geddes exhaling in agitation.

"Will Bishop Caer be gracing us with his presence?" Bishop Ward said with a snort.

Aurora was not in the mood for such antics. This was far too serious a matter. "I remember a certain young bishop who was late to his own coronation ceremony because...what was the excuse? Oh, I remember. He was discussing the philosophical ways of salmon migration with the River Nymphs." She eyed Bishop Ward, almost daring him to speak.

He glanced down and blushed.

There was a commotion outside of the room, someone running and tripping up the stairs. Bishop Caer stumbled in the room. Breathing hard and his uniform disheveled, he tried to unwind his cape tied around his right arm.

"M-m-erry meet, Your Grace. Bishops." Bishop Caer had only recently been awarded his title, and he was still getting used to his responsibilities.

Aurora nodded in acknowledgement, but he appeared traumatized. This was not just his usually tardiness.

"Bishop Caer, what seems to be troubling you?" She lifted an eyebrow.

"Power... Power Angel, I saw one..." His hands visibly shook.

Bishop Geddes stood up. "Impossible. We haven't seen one! You are imagining things!" He waved a dismissive hand. "Let us continue on why we are here."

Aurora would not allow anyone to be treated as such. Caer was obviously scared by something and no one would tell him otherwise in her presence. "Bishop Geddes, that is enough!" A gust of wind across the table garnered a look of surprise from everyone. "Bishop Caer, explain what you saw, please."

Bishop Caer glanced at the other bishops, who averted their eyes. He gripped his cape within an inch of its life.

Aurora spoke softly to him. "Bishop Caer. I believe you saw something, please tell me."

Bishop Caer gulped. The bob of his throat looked painful as he swallowed one more time before he spoke. His eyes focused over Aurora's shoulder. He skewed his head, his eyes glazed over as if pulling the memory back to life. "I was walking back from the Dryads. I paused at the ocean to meditate and I—when I heard your call that we were meeting. I promised you to take a bouquet of flowers to the Power Memorial. I did not want to break my word, so I stopped there on my way back. When I came upon the blue-stained sand before the first row of armor markers, I saw a figure in the distance, so I hid. He was large with white hair, and his face was covered with Black Kyanite armor, but the armor was melted onto him. It continued onto half of his arm and shoulder. The armor was...part of him. I've never seen anything like it." Bishop Caer gave a slight shake of his head, then focused his attention on his queen.

"He went to an armor marker and dropped to his knees, unsheathed his Elestial blade and mumbled as he drew on the marker. He did it to two more graves before he walked away. I waited until I was positive he was gone. I wanted to see what he had done to them, and I think he gave them... names." Bishop Caer dropped his gaze to the table.

Everyone stared at him in frozen silence. They turned toward their queen.

Aurora managed to look calm, though she was anything but as she hid her trembling hands underneath the table. "I see. One problem at a time, gentlefae. Bishop Caer, thank you for the information. You are right to be concerned, and we must move strategically. As of now we have more pressing issues to deal with than one Power."

"But—" Bishop Ward tried to press while Bishop Geddes kicked the bishop's shin under the table, causing him to squeal.

Aurora eyed Bishop Ward who took Geddes's hint. "Nothing, Your Grace. My apologies."

Aurora waved her wrist, and the large slab of rock silently moved from the floor, then hovered over the table. She circled her wrist and the chunk stood vertical.

The bishops gasped at the handprints displayed on the rock wedge.

Bishop Ward's story evaporated like the morning mist.

"Yes, I believe we all know what these represent. He made good on His word. He populated the Earth in His likeness, just as He said He would."

Bishop Ingor piped up, "Could the hand paintings be from the Power Bishop Caer spoke of?" A fleeting spark of desperate hope crossed his eyes.

Aurora shook her head. "No. Do not be naive," she whispered, her agitation growing like a slow boil. "Look at them, Ingor! They are not Fae. They are too large to be pixie and too small to be any other Fae." She pointed at the rock, her eyes flashing from their turquoise-blue to an almost jade-green. She closed her eyes, tightened her mouth, balled her fists up, and released them slowly as she reopened her eyes. "Theadova and his kin have actually seen them. Unfortunately, they have hunted the Aubane's younger kin. That's why I invited the entire Aubane faction here, for safety." Aurora's voice was quiet.

She began to wander around the room, yet it was in a deliberate pattern, one foot in front of the other, like walking a thin, invisible thread only she could see, her eyes cast down, her breathing calming. She raised her head as she swept her long, white gown behind her, unaware of the sand, grass, dirt, and other stains from her day. Yet despite the grime marring her dress, it somehow made her appear even more regal. Her right arm tossed the fabric rustling it, her chin tipped up.

"These are the beings we were preparing the planet for, so long ago. Our first priority are the Fae's safety. I have called a meeting for tomorrow with all the faction heads. Please make sure they are aware, and we have room."

Bishop Geddes frantically looked left and right. "Your Grace, when you say in His likeness, are you saying what I think you are?" He cast a glance over his shoulder as if someone might be listening right behind him.

Aurora looked at Bishop Geddes with a sense of empathy and pity. She needed her advisors to be strong, but perhaps this was too much for him. "Yes, humans. His children of Earth have finally come to fruition. He may have been many things, but our Creator was never a liar."

FOURTEEN:
THE CROWN MAKES IT REAL

A urora's first true test as a queen was the invitation she extended for the lords and ladies of the Royal Houses and the leaders of all the Fae factions to come to the Court of Light to discuss the mysterious hand paintings discovered by the Spelaions. The "creatures" hunting the Aubane faction needed to be talked about too. Aurora and her bishops knew these "creatures" were, in fact, primitive humans and they were not surprised by their appearance.

How can I tell the other factions without alarming them? The Court of Light was beginning to mature. They all had started to accept themselves as truly Fae. The appearance of the humans could reverse their progress. Many still held out hope their Creator would return for them. She did not want them to see this as a false sign.

They had spent the afternoon poring over what remained of their Virtue texts and consulting with their new Oracle Reva. Reva was of the Sphaeram faction. Her mother and father were both Virtues but she was born of the Earth, meaning she was not made by their Creator. Her

gift of sight was extremely limited, but they all hoped it would strengthen in time as all Virtue Oracles' had. Reva had encouraged her queen to above all else be honest with her kin.

Aurora agreed, but she had never spoken in front of her entire kingdom. She had always dealt with the factions in their own territories or in smaller groups. This was the first time they were all in one place.

She searched the crowd from behind the Great Hall's immense curtains, then quickly made her way back to her private chamber, her heart lodged in her throat. She closed the door and paced the crystal floor. Being queen in the crystal palace was different than when she visited the Dryads or spoke with Serena. This was commanding a kingdom.

A knock on the door shook her out of her spiral of self-doubt. "Come in," she said, happy for the distraction.

Hogal, her metal worker, peered around the corner of the door, his wiry salt-and-pepper hair sticking out from beneath his red cap.

"Me Majesty?" he asked.

Aurora's face lit up upon seeing Hogal, followed by his apprentice Marco. Marco had just been made apprentice and thus Hogal's new shadow too. He had Hogal's same leathery complexion, but Marco's hair was deep eggplant slicked back into a low ponytail with gold ribbons evenly spaced down the length. It was topped off with a gold cap, demonstrating his apprenticeship level.

"Marco, congratulations on your promotion. You have a wonderful mentor," Aurora said.

Both gnomes blushed at the attention from their queen.

"But what brings you here?"

Hogal elbowed Marco at Queen Aurora's inquisition and eventually used his foot to push the younger gnome forward. Marco was painfully bashful and hesitant to speak to Aurora. His large, aubergine eyes with their gold flecks shined as he gazed up at his queen, struggling to find his voice.

Hogal released a huff and rolled his eyes. "Me Majesty, Marco has a gift for you." The older gnome gestured to Marco, miming the action. Finally, he spoke. "Go on...I's said, give it to her!"

Aurora, sensing Marco's apprehension, knelt down and smiled, trying to be as open and accommodating as possible.

Marco inched forward and pulled a rich gold velvet pouch from behind his back. He handed it to Aurora with a coy smile, unable to meet her gaze.

"Thank you," she said with a gracious grin.

Marco bowed and scampered back to Hogal, practically hiding behind his mentor. Hogal gave a careless shrug of his shoulders at Marco and both gnomes turned their attention back to their queen.

Aurora carefully untied the satin ribbons closing the pouch and gasped as she pulled out the gift. A gold circlet crown, with every Fae faction's symbol intricately laid into the crown's band. The center of the crown was the septagram with the Angelite disc Serena had given her set into it. It was beautiful. Aurora held it delicately above her head, inspecting it from every angle. She ran her fingertips over each faction's symbol, felt the markings of her kin's namesakes. It was such a generous and sweet gift.

"It be his apprentice test. Marco did most of the work, but I's worked on it with him. Marco dids the designs."

Hogal had a glint of pride in his eye, making Aurora smile almost as much as the gift had.

Touched by their kind gesture, she wiped at her tears.

Marco took that moment and found his voice. "Does Me Majesty likes it?" His voice was small but full of courage. Large, bright eyes glimmered with hues of deep purple and black, sincerity in their depths. His eyebrows rose, knitting together.

"I love it, Marco. It's glorious! Thank you so very much!" She hugged him, holding him close and squeezing him.

Hogal cleared his throat. "Its was mines idea. Yous dids not have a crown. What's a queen without hers crown?"

Aurora glowed as she walked over and hugged him, but Hogal backed up, feigning disapproval at the display of affection. "Nons of that huggy stuff." But his fight was just for show. He melted into her as soon as she put her arms around him.

Aurora stood up and put her crown on. "Well, how does it look?"

Both gnomes burst with delight. "Perfect!" They jumped up and down in unison.

"Thank you, my friends. I guess now I really am ready to face the factions as their true queen. I have a crown to prove it." She winked and fixed her hair, crown in tow. She was as ready as she was ever going to be.

FIFTEEN:
JUST BREATHE

A quick rap on the wooden door to the queen's private chambers announced Desdemona's arrival. "Your Grace? They are ready for you." Her voice was low but authoritative.

Aurora opened the door and Desdemona eyed the gold crown. Her left eyebrow rose in a sharp arc, and she briefly pursed her lips, taking in her queen's new accessory.

The two gnomes peered around the corner, gauging the captain of the Royal Guard's response.

"Nice touch," Desdemona said with an approving glance, stepping aside to let her queen pass. Desdemona lingered on the two gnomes for a second with a ghost of a smile.

The gnomes high-fived each other once their queen and her guard were out of sight.

The two Fae walked silently down a short corridor toward the Great Hall. Stained glass illuminated their way, prismatic colors playing hopscotch over the crystal floors,

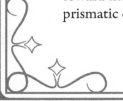

always managing to stay one step ahead of them. The loud chatter could be heard the minute they rounded the corner.

Aurora's heart beat faster and faster. She unfolded her hands and delicately stroked the septagram on her crown for comfort. *How many are there since last I checked?*

Her question was silently answered as she rounded the corner. A sea of Fae filled the yet unfinished Great Hall. Her heart went from beating a thousand times a minute to stopping all together. An inaudible "Wow" escaped her lips.

Desdemona, ever vigilant, said, "Just breathe, my queen. I've got your back." Her eyes conveyed reassurance as her lips gently curved up. Desdemona took to the make-shift platform, constructed only hours before. Her black boots clicked and clacked as she strode languidly across the platform. Though diminutive in size, Desdemona walked as if she had thunder in each step. "Silence!" She paused until she was satisfied the crowd was paying attention. "May I present Queen Aurora." Desdemona's voice boomed and commanded.

How can I possibly follow that? Desdemona acts more like a leader than I do...

There was no time for such thoughts. The crowd quieted, their attention directed toward the platform as they awaited their queen.

Desdemona unsheathed one of her Harbinger swords and gently ran her hands over the blade in a soft caress. All eyes of the crowd concentrated on her, and with a swift downward stroke, she sheathed it in a dramatic motion. Clearly, she was unhappy. Desdemona glowered at the standing group and gave a dramatic eye gesture downward.

Aurora started to step, but Desdemona subtly placed her hand out, holding the queen in her place. Aurora was puzzled until she witnessed Desdemona's satisfactory lip curl as the crowd took the hint and bowed their heads, placing their right hands over their hearts in the customary Fae sign of respect. Aurora swallowed, uncomfortable with all the focus directed at her, and made her way out onto the platform.

Aurora hoped each step would give her some confidence. Her four bishops closely followed behind her and Reva the Oracle joined them from the right. Aurora inhaled and felt for her crown, holding it in place so it would not slip off as she bowed back to the crowd. She thought of the gnomes' sweet gift and their belief in her.

I can do this. I have to.

Aurora raised her arms. "Merry meet, my friends."

The crowd responded, "Merry meet."

Aurora tucked a stray hair behind her ear, trying not to fidget nervously. "Thank you for coming. I have invited you today to address the rumors regarding the hand paintings and the creature sightings many of you have either heard about or seen. We all must remain calm and not give in to hysteria." She glanced at Desdemona who gave her queen a nod of encouragement.

The pause was all the crowd needed to begin bombarding her with questions. "What are they?" one voice yelled.

Another called out, "Did they really kill a young member of the Aubane faction?"

The room erupted into unintelligible questions from every direction.

Bishop Geddes took the lead. "My Fae kin, please quiet down. This is to be a civilized discussion. No, of course not.

They didn't kill anything. No, we don't know what they are. Shut up!" His bellowing anything but civilized.

Aurora was annoyed with Bishop Geddes's tone and his blatant lies. The humans had killed a member of the Aubane faction, and they did know what they were. She wanted transparency. They had discussed this earlier today. "Enough!" she said, mimicking Desdemona's tone. "Bishop Geddes, stand down."

Aurora settled her gaze on her bishops. Bishop Geddes stepped back, his head hung low in reproach.

"Please, my fellow Fae, I know what these creatures are—" Queen Aurora tried to explain.

More questions and calls erupted from the crowd, interrupting their queen. "What are they? Please tell us!"

"Your Grace, what are they?" rebounded throughout the gigantic hall.

Aurora had planned to hear the factions out, listen to their encounters, and let them have a voice. However, as much as she wanted this to be a benevolent monarchy, they needed a strong, clear leader. A benevolent dictator would have to do. The next revelation would rock many of them to their core. She could either soften the blow or make it quick.

"I will share all I know, but I will not shout over you or be interrupted, nor will I coddle you. I know you are all strong Fae, and I need you to be that Fae right now. Understood?" Aurora said, her eyes fixated on the crowd.

A few Fae nodded.

She nodded back.

A few answered her. "Yes, Your Grace." A few more responded until the entire hall rang out with a resounding, "Yes, Your Grace."

Aurora smiled. "Very well. These hand paintings were made by humans." She didn't wait for the hysteria to set in. She pressed on. "I will not have you live in fear of humans. For those of us who began a lifetime ago as Virtues, we knew this day would come. It was why we were here to begin with." She paused, choosing her words carefully.

The crowd took the opening. "But we weren't supposed to be here when they came," a voice called from the back.

"Maybe He's coming back for us!" another yelled with a sense of excitement.

This is what I was afraid of.

"No!" A gust of wind exploded from behind the queen, the wave rumbling forward over the hall as she raised her arms in protest. The mere mention of the idea of Him coming back for them caused rage to boil and churn inside of her. The hall had become deathly silent after Aurora's power display. "We will not look to a false savior. No one is coming for us. We are Fae. We protect the flora, the fauna, the Earth herself, and all that inhabit her. Including now these humans. But most of all, we protect one another." Her voice thundered with her last statement. The hall broke out into applause. Aurora elevated her hands to calm them and they obeyed. She had their attention and trust. She took a breath. "These humans need guidance. They are primitive. They too have been abandoned on this Earth. Left to fend for themselves. They do not know how to work with the Earth, how to respect nature. We will guide them and show them how to be one with their environment. We know what it is like to be neglected by our Creator with no direction. Think how these naive humans must feel. Alone and misunderstood."

Mumbles and chatter of understanding moved through the crowd.

"It is our duty as Fae to help them. My kin, I promise you as your queen, your well-being is still and will always be my first priority."

That sealed the deal. Aurora had won over the crowd. Cheers deafened all present.

Aurora spoke above the noise. "I will make the first move and contact the humans. I will lead by example. I ask for your cooperation. Please stay within the Court of Light palace. It is your home. Once I return from my meeting, I will brief you with my findings."

This time the crowd bowed without prompting from Desdemona, following with the chant, "Long live the queen!"

Aurora smiled and swiftly exited the Great Hall with the grace of an experienced monarch.

Aurora didn't wait for Desdemona to escort her back to her private chambers. She held the crown on her head as she picked up speed, sprinting down the corridor. She threw the doors to her chambers open, slamming them shut behind her. Sinking to the floor, she held her head and cried. The cool, crystal floor was smooth, hard, and uncomfortable, a fair comparison to how she felt as queen in the moment. She had no idea what she was doing.

What had she just said or done? Was her plan even correct?

She was so afraid of leading her kin down the wrong path. What if they had chosen the wrong Fae to lead them?

Her crown slipped down and she removed it. Aurora stared at it, running her fingers over the fissure in the Angelite disc. The shallow crack ran through the gold sigil of an archangel she would never see again from a home she was not allowed to return to. She picked at the break with her fingernail. Bits of crystal flaked off. She rubbed the grit between the pads of her fingers. She leaned her head back in resignation, bumping it a few times on the door, hoping it would knock some sense into her.

She took a deep breath and glanced again at the crown and the crystal disc cradled in the center. The pale blue shimmered and caught the light as if it were winking at the queen. Serena swore it was from the Power she had met the night of the shooting star. Serena insisted the mysterious Power was the shooting star they had all witnessed, trying to reach the Shining Kingdom. She had given Aurora the Angelite disc the day of her official coronation as queen of the Court of Light. It acted as a reminder even the lowliest moments could make for extraordinary changes.

Leave it to Serena to give me a smack on my ass when I need it.

Aurora stared at the crown and all the details, how it shimmered and shined. "Serena will just die when she sees you!" She smiled at the inanimate object.

SIXTEEN:
Best of Intentions

The next day Aurora met with Desdemona, Reva, Theadova, and her bishops to discuss her plans to act as emissary to the humans and establish a dialogue with them. She needed to stuff all her self-doubt down deep inside. Just as she had asked her Fae kin to be brave, she needed to do the same. Lead by example was what she had said.

Aurora had her breakdown last night. She now wore a crown atop her head, but it ran straight to her heart and anchored into her soul. The image gave her strength.

Aurora's priority in conversing with the humans was to arrange the Aubane faction's safety. She would not tolerate the hunting of any Fae, much less their younger faction members. She meant what she'd said—her kin's well-being was her main concern.

Everyone had opinions on how to handle the humans but no one had a concise plan. Instead, the bishops bickered and lectured her on protocol. Aurora didn't much care about the past. She wanted to move forward, toward

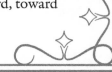

the future. She exhaled, listening to strings of nonsensical rants of advice from the bishops, which she equated to pouring water into a cup with a hole. No matter how much energy was dispensed into the cup, it would never be filled.

Aurora had had enough. She raised her hand to her forehead, wincing at the sound of Bishop Geddes's droning voice. "I will not make this an issue of formalities." Annoyance rang in her voice. "I am simply going to speak with them on my own. Theadova, can you take me to the last place you saw the humans?"

The room silenced quickly as all eyes focused on the queen.

Theadova's eyes shifted side to side. His ears twitched as everyone waited for him to answer Queen Aurora. He ran his tongue over his lips and swallowed hard. "If that is your wish, of course I will, Your Grace. I know where their village is." His short tail flicked up at the rising anxiety with his agreement to her request.

Aurora sighed. Her eyebrows returned to a more neutral position, and her mouth softened with the knowledge of Theadova's cooperation. "It is settled. I will ride tomorrow to act as an emissary to the humans."

Her determined glare had the bishops exchanging uncomfortable side glances at one another. Bishop Geddes bit his cheek. Aurora knew Bishop Geddes did not agree with her plan. He'd proven it by his little display, but he did not wear the crown. She did. She would deal with him later.

SEVENTEEN:
The Road To Hell Is Paved...

T he next morning, Theadova and Aurora set out to meet the humans. Desdemona escorted her to the back gate. Her stride was not its usual stealthy glide but more of a stomp.

"I know you aren't happy with this, but I must do this alone," Aurora said as they walked, sensing her captain's frustration with her decision.

"I have heard that statement before," Desdemona said. Aurora rubbed her temples. Desdemona caught her queen's gesture from the corner of her eye and winced at her flippant commentary. "I am just worried for you, my queen. I cannot protect you from here."

Aurora paused to face her loyal protector. "Thank you, Desdemona. I appreciate your sentiment. I told you when you vowed your loyalty, I wanted you to protect the Fae, not me. I do not want blind loyalty. I want to earn loyalty and respect. We all know what happens when we are forced to have blind faith in one leader. We believe them infallible, and they disappoint us. I made you swear loyalty to the Fae kin, not the Fae crown. I need you to protect the Fae while I am gone."

"I have pondered your oath, and I find it has faults."

Aurora quirked her brow. "Such as?"

"How can I have loyalty to the kin but not to the crown? Yet I must protect you? It doesn't make sense." Desdemona faced her queen, her hands behind her back.

Aurora smirked. "I understand your question, and I applaud your candor. Furthermore, the idea that you took the time to examine the oath only reinforces my decision to choose you."

Desdemona shook her head. "Your Grace?"

Aurora placed her hand on her captain's shoulder. "Loyalty to the kin, not to the crown, means I want to earn your loyalty. Do not give it to me or anyone simply because of a piece of jewelry. Let their actions speak for them, not a title. Place those you cherish along with what your heart tells you is correct above all else, regardless of if they wear a crown. I want you to be the one to keep a watchful eye over the Court of Light. Let all that the light touches forbid the day when a Fae who rules allows their own thirst for power to endanger the well-being of all of us. You must step in. You are the only one strong enough. Let your oath guide you, dear Desdemona. In the meantime, give me the opportunity to earn your respect and loyalty. Protect me as you see fit. I do not ask you to lay down your light for me. I only hope to deserve your trustworthiness. It is a precious gift from a Fae such as yourself."

Desdemona acquiesced to her queen, blinking back tears.

Aurora knew better than to point out Desdemona's emotions. "Theadova and I shall return by tomorrow eve.

Please be sure all stay in the palace until I have negotiated their safety. I told the bishops to keep the heads of the factions abreast of my progress."

Desdemona stood tall and straight, nodding at her queen's instructions. She watched with a fixed scrutinizing glare as Aurora mounted Theadova. The white stag made eye contact with the former warrior angel. The air grew tense and thick between them. Desdemona's steely grey eyes bored into Theadova's large black gaze. A warning to the leader of the Aubane faction. He was the queen's protector and Desdemona would hold him accountable. Theadova gave a subtle tilt of his chin before he and the queen slipped out the back gates.

Aurora had never been one for fanfare. The two of them disappeared over the forest hills in the early morning light without any Fae being the wiser. Desdemona stayed, keeping watch, still wishing her queen had allowed her to accompany the two. She could not shake the feeling this was not going to be as easy as her queen thought.

Slowly, the forest came alive with the sounds echoing in morning. Bugs zipped by their ears, birds hummed their song and the wind sang in the leaves. As the woods woke up to greet them, Aurora used nature's music as the backdrop to her thoughts.

Theadova and Aurora traveled for hours. Theadova talked about the many scenarios they might encounter with the humans. Aurora was honest with Theadova about her fears as a queen. He listened and shared his own experiences as the leader of his faction. Aurora contemplated if she had known Theadova in his original Virtue Angel form. She wondered what he looked like before he bonded with his ward. She could not recall a Virtue by his name.

Of course, that meant nothing. The Virtues had been closed off from the Powers and each other.

Stopping at a small clear stream, Aurora stroked his neck. "I am sorry, Theadova."

"For what?" the white deer retorted, pausing halfway through his drink. "For not taking the time to get to know you before all of this."

She gestured with her arms open at her side.

The deer glanced around, his tail twitching along with his ears as he searched for signs of danger, attempting to make sense of the queen's remarks. "I beg your pardon, Your Grace?"

Aurora shook her head, briefly placing her fingers on her forehead to gather her thoughts. "I mean, I apologize it took such extreme circumstances for me to talk to you. It should not have been this way. It is a shame we must learn these lessons under such harsh conditions. You are a kind leader to your kin, and I am honored to know you and for you to assist me. Thank you. I should have taken the time before—"

"Please, Your Grace. You searched us all out and united us under one banner. I am honored. Let us not converse of the past but look to the future. Speaking of which, we have still more traveling to do. We must be on our way."

The sun had risen to the sky's highest point when the two travelers reached their destination. Swirls of smoke hovered over the tree line, dissipating into small coils of light grey until it was nothing more than a thin mist in the upper atmosphere. The sweet tang of oak and ash rode on the breeze.

"We are near, Your Grace," Theadova whispered.

Aurora dismounted, choosing to walk now.

"Their village is just over the mound. We must tread carefully. These woods are their hunting grounds." Theadova's eyes darted side to side, his hackles up, his ears swiveled and flicked.

She couldn't blame him. He had seen his younger members hunted down and killed by these humans.

"The quicker we make it to the village, the sooner we can put this to an end."

The two Fae quickened their pace, heading toward the plumes of smoke. They came upon the village. The humans milled about their daily chores. Their hair was long and unkempt. They used mostly animal skins as clothes. The women prepped food and carried water baskets, while men took mammoth tusks and fashioned them as weapons. Others helped a man repair his family's one-room dwelling, hoisting animal skins over the holes. Children played with one another, running in and out of huts. Their lifestyle—simple and easy. *Is this what their Creator intended for them?*

Theadova spotted the head of the village. "There, that is him," he whispered, gesturing with his head to an older man with a headdress made of bone, teeth, and brown-speckled feathers. He carried a large, carved walking stick, decorated with bones. The villagers nodded as he walked by. "I think it would be best if you rode me into the village, Your Grace."

Aurora had wanted to walk in, but Theadova was shrewd. If these humans thought of him as a sacred creature, riding him would garner their respect. She mounted him and took a deep breath as he charged into the village.

Theadova understood drama. He streaked into the center of the humans' gathering, skidding to a halt before the head of the clan. "Hold on!" Theadova whispered as he reared onto his hind legs.

The villagers jumped back, wide-eyed at the gigantic white stag. He stomped his front hoof a few times to prove a point before Aurora dismounted and rubbed his neck. She loomed over the smaller statured men. The villagers took a defensive stance, the men pointing their spears almost vertically to even have a shot at defending themselves. They were unsure of how to react to this tall stranger with hair the color of fire.

Aurora smiled at their leader and bowed her head. He lifted his head, smiling but carefully scanning her with his eyes. Aurora did not move. She waited until she had passed his visual test. Once it seemed he was satisfied, he gestured for the rest to lower their weapons. Aurora gave him a long, slow blink as she stepped forward. The leader put his hand out and dropped to one knee, his palm up and open as a sign of respect to Aurora. She bowed her head and placed her palm on his in return, her hand eclipsing his in size. The two leaders stared at each other. She looked toward Theadova, and he nodded toward the man.

"We mean you no harm," she said as best she could in their native tongue. Her hair danced about her.

The leader of the clan studied Aurora's hair. He licked his finger and stuck it into the air. He held very still. He spoke to the rest of his clan in a primitive language consisting of monosyllabic sounds.

Aurora ascertained he had observed there was no breeze except around her. She shifted a bit, uncomfortable at his quick perception of her.

Primitive they might be. Stupid they are not.

The hunters of the clan examined Theadova, encircling the large, white stag.

Their attention stressed Aurora. "Stop. Do not come any closer." Her voice held power in its tone. The men glanced back at her, pointing at the antlers adorning their headdresses. "He is not to be touched, nor are his kin." A warning as her power crackled through her words.

She looked at the mammoth tusks at the end of their spears. The mammoths' numbers had decreased in the area and now she knew why. These humans needed to be taught respect toward nature and how to live in harmony with it. They required food and nourishment but wiping out an entire species was not the way. They were hunters and gatherers. This was all beyond their comprehension, of that she was sure. They called for a guiding hand. Her eyes zeroed in on their leader.

He stepped toward Theadova, who stood still but kept his eyes on Aurora. "Sinn," the leader said as he pointed at Theadova. The men all bowed at the white stag, chanting "Sinn" repeatedly.

The women laid flowers at Theadova's front hooves, keeping a respectful distance from the oversized stag. He was the height of a glistening pear tree, approximately nine feet tall from the tip of his antlers to his hooves. It was no wonder the humans were enamored with the stag. He did not bear any resemblance to the deer they were accustomed to seeing in their forest. Theadova had a regal neck that was unusually long for a deer. This was a trait of the Aubane faction. He had a short, silver trail of fur cascading down the back of his neck that disappeared into a sea of flawless, pure-white fur. His front legs were long and graceful with powerful hind legs. Their muscles undulated even with the slightest twitch of movement. His hooves, much like his antlers, were scattered with glimmers of golden dust. The only part of Theadova that was dark were his eyes. At this point, those dark pools were focused on his queen.

"My queen?" Theadova asked, confusion and fear gripping him.

The villagers delivered offerings of berries as they laid their spears at his hooves, continuing their bowing and chants.

"They believe you are some type of god, Theadova," Aurora explained. *Sinn*. She rolled the name in her head, making quick translation of the name in the human's native tongue. *God of the hunt!*

"What shall I do?"

Aurora took the moment in stride. "Humans. He is Sinn, your god. He is a humble god, but do not hunt his offspring, or you shall be punished." Her voice vibrated with energy in their native tongue.

The villagers looked at her and at back at him.

Theadova caught on and prolonged the sentiment. "I will bless you all, but do not touch any of my kin, or you will incite my anger." Theadova looked at Aurora, shaking his antlers.

Neither of them knew what they were doing. But as the villagers showered Theadova with accolades, Aurora noticed a change in his demeanor.

The white stag stood a little taller. His coat gave off a glow. His purple eyes flashed to reveal a green highlight. "My queen, I feel a weird sensation of force rising up, like I can run a thousand miles and not tire."

"Theadova? Are you well?" Aurora moved toward him.

The emotions of the situation twisted and changed. Their fascination disintegrated like a snowflake melting on a hot coal. The villagers understood this was a god, but now they wanted a blessing. They wanted to touch a god. The circle collapsed on Theadova as quickly as it assembled. Theadova was overtaken. He didn't want to hurt the humans. His reflex was to kick but he fought the urge. So many hands came at him, looking for a touch.

Aurora stopped it with a small air pulse, like a tropical breeze. The wind knocked the villagers out of the way, freeing Theadova from the mob.

The faces of the ones who remained contorted as their eyes and mouths froze wide.

The leader dropped to his knees, chanting, "Azuta." The entire village followed his lead.

From what she could extrapolate from their language, it meant Mother of the Wind.

Theadova made his way to her as the villagers once again circled the two Fae, chanting "Azuta."

"What should we do?" Theadova whispered to his queen. "Get out of here."

However, the crowd had grown exponentially, and the circle closed in on them, their cries for blessing more desperate. The leader tried to gain control of the situation, but the mob became frenzied.

Aurora felt a shudder of power pass through her, and her eyes glowed much like Theadova's had. The harried horde only paused at her emerald eyes. They saw this as an indication of her power and it drew them in even more. Aurora commanded them to stop, but nothing helped.

Theadova looked at his queen, horror on his face. If he kicked, he risked killing the fragile humans. Aurora could send a current, but anything stronger than what she'd just done might break them like dolls. She was still figuring out how to control her wind pulses as a weapon. They were inches away from drowning in the horde.

A familiar tingle crept up Aurora's spine and spread across her back. In a gust, she catapulted above the pack. The stunned humans raised their eyes skyward in unanimity as their crimson-haired Wind Goddess streaked upward. Aurora felt a vibration of power. She knew, somehow, deep down she could throw a true force wind gale. Where a second ago there was self-doubt, now there was only confidence.

Aurora inhaled and placed her palms together. She harkened back to the days when she protected the element of Air. She called upon it and an orb of translucent blue energy formed. She felt the breeze it contained and let it fly toward the group. It was just enough to distract them but not harm the humans. Aurora had sprouted the same type of energy wings she had that day with Serena, giving Theadova the chance to escape.

As Aurora shot up, the white stag's dark eyes traced upward, keeping his queen in his sights. The sun's rays broke through the treetops, lighting up her hair and... wings? Yes, she had wings!

The stag smiled, briefly stunned, but he found his legs and fortunately, he took the opportunity to run from the masses. Theadova's hooves did not dig into the ground as he ran, but instead, he bounded and leaped upward, propelling to help follow his queen.

Aurora sailed in the air to protect Theadova, losing sight of him as she fought to maintain her concentration. Perhaps it was the moment of contemplation, her concern for Theadova's whereabouts, even the exhaustion or the shock, but her wings dissolved instantaneously. She plummeted to the ground.

The stag watched her descent. With a gallop he leaped to meet her halfway. The ever-reliable Theadova caught his queen. With renewed speed from all the excitement, he carried her back to the palace as if he ran on the back of a comet's tail.

EIGHTEEN:
WHERE THERE IS LIGHT THERE IS DARK

The humans were too stunned by their new goddess' sudden departure to move, they stared upward. Many of the men had removed their head pieces, dropping their weapons on the ground. The elder of the village stiffened, sensing something wrong. Not a leaf or a blade of grass moved in the wind.

The forest was still when a large figure appeared from the rear of the village. He had been there all along, watching and waiting. Covered in black earth, he moved silently through the crowd. He wore a headpiece with several jagged points like a crown of rock, and its darkness was a striking contrast to his flowing white hair. His honey-colored eyes scanned the humans who sensed his ominous demeanor. Women held their young close. His right arm was bare, except for an ebony mineral gauntlet burned into his skin. The same charred stone pattern continued on his right shoulder. He walked with a stealth that held power.

One unlucky human's curiosity got the better of him, and the man reached out to touch the figure.

He didn't look at the poor soul or break his stride. He simply grabbed the man's hand before it reached him. The sounds of bones crunching and the agonizing scream brought a brief smile to the figure's face. He stopped in the center of the crowd and gestured for them to kneel. They did as instructed, fear on their faces.

A voice called out, "Mot." God of Death.

Jarvok looked down at the humans as he spoke in their native tongue. "Fear me, humans, but worship me or my wrath shall be swift but painful."

The humans chanted his name, "Mot!"

The energy pulsed through Jarvok with each chant of the name they bestowed upon him. His head lolled back, his eyes closing for a second in pleasure as he drank in their worship. He lifted his head and funneled the force into his Elestial blade, unsheathing it. The blade burst into white flames, growing larger and burning brighter as the humans chanted his name louder and louder. Jarvok scrutinized the blade, felt the power from it. The energy flowed throughout his body.

"Yes, this will do nicely," he said as the glow from his new blade reflected off his luminescent skin.

Every crackle of thunder and howl of a wolf needs a god. The pretty flowers and sunshine are not the only elements that should receive attention from these primitive humans. While the Court of Light uses love to garner respect from their human subjects, fear will prove just as effective.

NINETEEN:
A Wing and a Prayer

Theadova ran faster than he ever had, carrying his queen back to the palace. What should have taken him at least half a day's journey took him what felt like minutes. His hooves barely touched the forest ground. He rebounded and leaped over the terrain with ease and grace. As the palace gates came into view, he yelled for them to open. The guards recognized him and obliged.

Desdemona met Theadova in the courtyard. "What happened?" she cried as she took Aurora's limp body from the large, white stag's back.

"The humans...surrounded us... She had wings," Theadova panted. His chest heaved and his glittering antlers bobbed with each breath.

"Theadova, calm down. I need you to tell me everything." Desdemona's voice and eyes held a steely reserve he lacked in the moment.

Theadova swallowed, trying to control his breathing but was speechless to her request.

"Follow me. I must get her to a healer."

The white stag nodded. He sighed in relief at the presence of Desdemona's cool, composed aura. She was swift in her steps as the two made their way toward the West Tower.

The bishops joined Desdemona and Theadova moments later in the West Tower. Queen Aurora lay on the meeting table, her arms folded over her stomach. "I have called for Lady Ambia," Bishop Ingor said, his eyes scanning the queen's body for signs of injury.

Bishop Ward picked up her arm, examining it, but his efforts were futile. Bishop Ingor watched the other bishop but his temper got the best of him. "Stop wasting time, Ward, on things that are not our specialty. Leave it for the healer."

The younger bishop ceased his curiosity and fell into line with the others, placing his hands at his sides. Ingor eyed him as he took his place.

"Theadova, please tell all of us what transpired today." Desdemona's question was more of a command than a request.

Transfixed, the five Fae listened.

"The queen's aura has changed," a gravelly yet melodic voice broke the spell of Theadova's words. All eyes turned to the tall figure with horns adorning her head, outlined in the doorway.

The figure entered into the room. Long white hair streaked with powder-blue and candy-pink strands fell to her back. The two glistening, golden antelope horns curved slightly toward each other as they stretched upward swirling, capturing the light as if sculpted of pure gold and ivory. Her light-blue robe glided across the floor and her gold bracelets jingled with each step she took. A musky, pungent scent of spicy tarragon, lemon, and fresh-cut grass wafted into the room with her.

Lady Ambia of the Calendula Faction met each Fae's eyes. The entire clan was dedicated to the art of healing, but Lady Ambia was the best of them. She bowed her head to everyone in the room, giving all a view of her crowning glory. Her spiraled horns bore her faction's name. An explosion of colors, orange, yellow, and red-hued marigolds, sat nestled between her horns.

She slowly lifted her head and glided over to the queen, scanning her body from head to toe.

"What do you mean: changed?" Bishop Caer inquired.

Lady Ambia said nothing as she hovered her right hand over Aurora's body from her feet to the top of her head. She turned to Theadova, her eyes crinkling at the corners. She stepped toward him and used the same hand gesture. "Your aura is different as well, White Stag."

"Well?" Bishop Geddes's impatience grew as his jaw clenched at the lack of an immediate response.

However, Lady Ambia, never one to be rushed, glowered at the bishop. "I must be sure before I give a diagnosis. I heard a bit about what happened, but I require all of you to leave, except Theadova. I will read his and Queen Aurora's energy." Lady Ambia was telling, not asking.

Desdemona took the lead. "All right. You heard the healer—out!" She pointed toward the door.

This time it was the bishops' turn to glare, but they left. Desdemona nodded toward Lady Ambia as she closed the doors behind them.

"What do you need, my lady?" Theadova asked, trying to be as cooperative as possible.

Lady Ambia stepped closer to examine him. His eyes had dark circles under them. The gold sheen on his antlers had dulled and his legs were shaky. Theadova stared back at her, noticing how her horns gleamed in the light. He swallowed hard, suddenly uncomfortable. He glanced past the healer to his queen lying lifeless on the table.

His eyes dropped to the floor and sighed. "I...failed her," he murmured.

"The aura reflects every creature's energetic, emotional, and physical connection to its plane of existence. The colors represent emotions, ailments, and in the case of an attack, vulnerabilities," Ambia explained.

Theadova's eyes softened as he struggled to maintain his composure. "I am aware of the aura and the relationship to the chakras, Lady Ambia." His voice trembled.

The Healer's blue robe rustled as she walked and her bracelets chimed when she folded her arms. "The aura is linked to each being's core, drawing its information from the chakras, our seven distinct energetic pools of emotion. Each one is plugged into our emotional conscience, spinning at a key vibration and tone. Physical symptoms can develop when these vortexes of energy spin faster or slower. Tell me about the humans and their reaction when they saw you both." Lady Ambia ignored his self-admonishment.

Theadova took a deep breath and retold his story for the third time in less than thirty minutes.

Lady Ambia listened intently. "What did they call her?"

"Azuta," Theadova replied with no inflection, no emotion. He was exhausted. The events of the day had taken their toll, or perhaps it was his guilt.

"And you? What did they call you, my mighty stag?" Her fingertips stroked his antlers, helping to calm him.

Theadova closed his eyes and exhaled. Tears rolled down his cheeks. He shook his head and muttered, "I am so sorry, so sorry." As he repeated the name the humans had chanted in their frenzied state. "Sinn. Sinn. Does either name mean something to you?"

She ignored his question, but he knew she was not asking the question to be nosy or pedantic. He hoped she had a purpose.

"I have one last question for you, Theadova. And for this, you must think hard. What else did you notice about the humans?"

She looked directly into Theadova's bottomless eyes now as if she could see his memories. Lady Ambia's blue-bell-hued eyes penetrated like ice.

Theadova closed his, trying to recall that moment.

He heard her faintly ask, "What were they wearing? Tell me, White Stag."

He exhaled slowly, relaxing to watch the moment come into focus in his mind. He smelled the dampness of the forest, the rich musk of the moss, and the ever-green trees around him. He felt the rocky terrain under his hooves. He could feel the sunshine breaking through the tree canopy onto the fur on his back. He saw Aurora in all her winged glory, but he needed to pull his gaze away from her to see the humans.

"They had antlers on their heads, like mine... Oh, by all that is blessed, they were antlers from stags they hunted. They wore antlers from the faction of our young. They had red paint smeared on their faces. The men who wore the antlers, they held spears. The same ones I have seen hunt my young kin with, and they had symbols carved on the handles." Theadova's eyes flashed open, his breath fast and hard.

Lady Ambia stroked his neck.

Jolted from the memory, he shuddered, looking around.

"You are safe," she said in a hushed voice. "I know what happened now." She began to pace, the corners of her eyes crinkling for a fleeting moment, her mouth growing tight.

Theadova could hear the whoosh of blood from his beating heart. His chest was still heaving. The vivid memory had not relinquished its grip just yet. He licked his lips and attempted to swallow past the dryness making it hard for him to speak. "Can you please share your knowledge, Lady Ambia?"

She faced him, tilting her head with a slight upturn of her lips. It was not a smile, for it did not reach her eyes. It was more of an empathetic grin. "They likened you to a god. You were the embodiment of their god of the hunt. When you appeared, it was a divine blessing of sorts. They wear the antlers of your young kin as homage to you as their deity. To touch you would be a blessing for a good hunt and the safe return for their hunters."

Utterly befuddled, Theadova looked around as if searching for a way to make sense of it. "I don't understand. Aurora said something similar to me. I remember that now. But why hunt my young? Why am I a god to them?" Lady Ambia gave a thoughtful smile. "You really do not know how special and magical you are, White Stag. You are such a unique creature. A primitive human's mind could not comprehend the wonder within you. Choosing the form of a deer makes you no less than those of us who kept our original form and made some adjustments. You are still angelic in essence. You cannot hide that. Your light shines. The humans sense your power.

As for your young, they too are angelic, but with each passing generation their energy mingles with nature and changes. It is still fantastic and wonderful, but it is different. The humans perhaps cannot sense your young's magic. They are still immature. What they do not understand, they either worship or kill. The young are easy prey. You, my mighty stag, are not." She patted him on the side to allow him a moment for the information to sink in.

Theadova had always considered the Aubane faction lesser to the others, due to their decision to merge with their animal wards so long ago, but perhaps, she was correct.

"Thank you, Lady Ambia. I must protect my young from them, but what about my queen?" He wanted to take the focus off himself. He hadn't fooled her but he was grateful Lady Ambia played along. "They called Aurora Azuta after she generated the wind gust. It must be a term for a wind goddess. They dropped to their knees and looked to touch her. This is much like the Powers' position of humility. I believe they were looking for a blessing from Aurora as well."

Lady Ambia approached the sleeping queen and held her right hand just above Aurora's body. Theadova watched as faint, translucent colors came into focus just underneath Lady Ambia's palm. The colors hovered about three inches from Aurora's body. They looked like stained glass suspended in the air, frozen in time for a fraction of a second. Lady Ambia waved her hand and the colors followed her movement. She closed her eyes and her lips moved in a silent dialogue.

Theadova realized Lady Ambia was communicating with Aurora's aura. She stopped and swayed for a minute. "That was amazing, but I am still confused," he said.

Lady Ambia steadied herself on the table and glanced at him. "What part?" She tried to muster a smile.

"The beginning, middle, and what just happened with her aura." Theadova shook his head. His front hoof tapping gave away his bit of anxiety over his lack of understanding.

The healer sighed. Her antlers bobbed and her bracelets jingled as she nodded. Her eyes were warm and soft. "The humans thought the two of you were gods. The worship they showered you with saturated your aura, giving you an energy surge. Queen Aurora had more of a surge than you because of her direct elemental connection. She manifested wings. You ran faster than ever before. You've burned through your reserve already. However, the queen is in a magical stasis while her aura acclimates to the energy change." Her voice was very matter of fact.

Theadova tried to process the explanation. "But why didn't that happen to me?" He gestured to Queen Aurora with his head, antlers catching the light of the candles, glinting as if they were winking at Ambia.

"Because you ran. It is a natural state for you. The energy used did not need a new conduit or tool. The queen has not flown for centuries. These wings she manifested were not her angelic wings. Her body sprouted fresh wings. This is a new state and energy level for her."

Theadova nodded, his antlers emphasizing his acknowledgment. He gave a long exhale for the first time since he had entered the West Tower. Aurora had not sustained any permanent damage. However, just as he began to relax, he stiffened at a new realization.

"So, now what? The humans will come looking for us. My young are not safe. What do we tell the others?" His eyes were large, his mouth was tight, and his front right hoof scraped at the floor.

Lady Ambia listened to his ramblings without judgment. "You are a compassionate leader, concerned about your kin, and from what I can tell, you are becoming a trusted member of the queen of the Fae's advisors. These concerns are what come with being a leader, my White Stag." She stroked his neck, her eyes glassy. "The queen will have much to deal with when she awakens. For now, your faction is safe here in the palace. Queen Aurora will see to your faction's continued safety. Do not borrow trouble, White Stag. You are no longer alone. None of us are anymore. She saw to that. I will brief Desdemona and advise her that Reva the Oracle of the Fae should be notified of what has happened."

Lady Ambia kissed Theadova between his antlers and walked him to the door.

He paused and looked up at the healer. "The queen will be all right? Won't she?" His eyes wandered back to his queen and his friend.

TWENTY:
Everyone Needs a Mermaid

L ady Ambia briefed the group of Fae eagerly waiting for her. Desdemona and the four bishops gathered in the hallway outside the private meeting room. Her first order was to have Desdemona send for the Oracle Reva. Bishop Geddes protested and wanted his update immediately, pounding his fist into his palm, looking like a petulant child.

"I want answers now, Healer!" Bishop Geddes demanded. "I am a Bishop! You answer to *me*!"

"I am a Healer. I am *Lady* Ambia. I answer to Queen Aurora," she stated calmly, but there was a cold fire in those bluebell-colored eyes, her horns glittering in the light.

One job of the Oracle was to keep the history of the Fae, and this was a new chapter. Therefore, Lady Ambia held steadfast to her plan and waited until everyone she requested was present to brief them on the queen's condition, despite Bishop Geddes's disparaging commentary.

Next, they were required to come to an understanding about how to handle the factions until the queen woke up.

Lady Ambia had already given her prognosis. She excused herself from the conversation. "Politics are not for healers. My mission is to close wounds, not open them. I will leave strategy up to you." She bowed and took her leave.

The bishops did not give the healer's exit a proper goodbye, or perhaps they did not care to as they returned to debating their plan. They wanted Theadova to stay out of sight and keep quiet about what had happened. Desdemona did not agree, but the bishops reminded her that, in essence, she was "hired muscle in charge of the guards, not diplomacy."

The bishops felt having Desdemona make a general statement about the queen's health would be best to keep the rumors to a minimum. They would call for the heads of the Royal Houses for a briefing instead of an open meeting as Aurora had originally planned. The bishops proposed making the heads wardens to keep all the Fae at the palace for their own safety. Besides keeping the Fae at the palace, the rest went against Aurora's plan. It was deceptive and manipulative. Desdemona was uncomfortable with the direction of this strategic meeting of the minds, but she was unsure of what to do, so she stayed quiet, observing and listening.

A few hours later, Desdemona walked down the long corridor to call the meeting for the bishops. Her obsidian boots made no sound on the quartz floor. The Spelaions had done a magnificent job finishing the meeting hall and the adjacent hallways. Their crystal work really is mind-blowing.

She stopped at the clover-shaped window. They had outlined it in black tourmaline as per Aurora's instructions. The stark contrast of the rough black crystal against the smooth, pink-tinged quartz walls made her smile. It was a perfect representation of Aurora. "Lovely and girly on the outside, but strong with a streak of edge on the inside."

Their queen would pull through. She just had to. They had come so far. Desdemona briefly gripped the window-sill, letting her head fall forward. Her braid swayed in time with her breathing. Praying was a practice in futility because no one was listening to her. Desdemona lifted her head and straightened her shoulders. All that was required was faith in her kin and the universe. She returned to her mission to call the meeting to order. Her resolve took over, and once again she was Desdemona, the most feared Fae warrior.

Running her hand over her Harbinger scarabs, Desdemona glided down the hallway. However, she could not push back the thought this meeting did not feel right. Twelve hours have passed since the queen's return. If Theadova had not gained a burst of speed, everyone would still be planning their arrival for tomorrow.

Unfortunately, the bishops were the queen's advisors and temporary rulers as a collective in times of crisis. Aurora had not set up the terms of succession yet. The monarchy was still in its infancy stage, and Reva gave her input on succession discussions. It was unclear if Aurora could have an heir, given her background and not having a ward to bond with. All of that aside, Desdemona wanted to wait and see when Aurora would awaken, but Theadova made quite the dramatic entrance so by now gossip was running rampant, which was why the meeting shouldn't be limited to just the heads of the Royal Houses.

Desdemona "forgot" the exact wording the bishops wanted her to use regarding the queen's health. She was not about to lie for them. Instead of just informing them of Aurora's condition she happened to invite the heads of the secondary houses to the bishops' meeting with the Royal Houses. Whoops. They could do their own dirty work. She followed her queen's original plan—in her eyes, the better plan for her kin. The bishops would reprimand her later for her oversight. They were in charge of inviting the four royal heads of the houses. Apparently, she was too lowly to invite them.

Desdemona's job was not to question but to act on behalf of the Fae as the collective, not as the voice of a ruling monarch. Aurora had said her oath was to stay loyal to the kin, not just the royal power. Desdemona had the authority to protect the monarchy only when it was for the good of the Fae. If a monarch ever put their needs above their own kin, it was Desdemona's job to stop them by any means necessary. As a former Power, Aurora felt Desdemona was the only Fae who could handle the responsibility.

Desdemona walked into the Great Hall deep in thought, mulling over her conundrum. As of now, she did not have reason to stand against the bishops. Technically, the bishops were not putting her kin in danger. She disagreed with the way they were handling this, but that was her own opinion. There was no imminent threat.

The loud chattering brought her back to reality and her task. She took to the platform and the sea of Fae immediately silenced at the strong Fae form standing before them.

Desdemona was not the tallest of the Fae, standing at five feet and eleven inches, but her shoulders were wide and honed to muscular perfection. Her Fae skin glowed under the Great Hall's Cathedral ceiling with its intricately carved geometric design. The crystal lotus flowers captured the light and bounced it back to the platform. She wore her long, raven hair in a formal braid. It shone like liquid ebony with rich, cherrywood highlights when the light hit it. The blood red tips of her bangs swept across her left eye, hiding half of her delicate face. The hair covered the scar where her Angelite disc had been when she wore another life. Her eyes were the color of thunder clouds on a summer's day, accented by a single black diamond under each eye. Her lips matched the dark diamonds, and it fit her. The diamonds represented the last tear she would ever shed for having to kill anyone who dared try to bring harm to her kin.

Her heart was as cold as ice when it came to defending her kin, and she was unbreakable under the pressure of her oath. A diamond was fitting.

The midnight theme continued in her vest with its double buttons and a longer hem design in the back. The vest had a hood that when pulled forward allowed her to cover most of her face. Desdemona liked her enemies to see her smile when she fought. The pleasure of besting them in battle brought her peace. Most of all, she relished them seeing her just before she took their light. Each forearm was dressed in black-and-blue-etched gauntlets with hooks curving at the elbows for striking and impaling. A leather pauldron on her right shoulder with the seven-pointed star cutouts appeared delicate upon first glance, but the silver and gold spikes made it a deadly weapon. She wore black pants with thigh-high boots where she was currently hiding her weaponry, though she was working on a set of new swords and this was the most recent testing area. Because she was the captain of the Royal Guard, Desdemona had a shoulder cloak for ceremonial occasions but rarely wore it.

Desdemona didn't need to be tall or have a scary black cape to be imposing. She just needed to stand there. Her aura did the rest.

She scanned the crowd. Once satisfied she had their attention, her husky voice brought the meeting to order. *Yeah, they're going to notice the sea of Fae instead of just a small gathering. Troll's balls. Me, my big ideas, and my even bigger mouth.*

"Please rise. I present the bishops on behalf of Queen Aurora. Treat them with the same respect as you would Her Grace."

Desdemona stepped back, allowing the bishops to take the platform.

The crowd rose. The bishops were so busy arguing among themselves over who would speak first, they missed their introduction. Desdemona repeated herself but still... *nothing.* She rolled her eyes and leaned over toward them, clearing her throat in their direction. The crowd shifted uneasily until they stopped bickering and the four bishops entered from the opposite side of the platform, Bishop Geddes shoving the others out of his way to be first.

However, it was Bishop Ingor who stepped forward as Geddes froze, gazing out over the platform, noticing the crowd was much larger than expected. Geddes gave a sideways glance to Desdemona, while Ingor's concern for his fellow bishop initially distracted him from what the real issue was. The other two bishops were immediately aware of the overflowing state of the Great Hall and glowered at Desdemona. Bishop Caer and Ward, not wanting to draw any more attention to the gaffe, stepped to the side of the stage and put their hands over their hearts in the customary sign of respect.

The crowd followed.

"Be seated," Bishop Ingor began. "We will not delay in divulging information. Que—"

Staring out upon the sea of faces, he realized she had indeed invited all the Fae. His right hand balled into a fist and sweat formed on his forehead. He understood Geddes's reaction. "As I was saying, Queen Aurora met with the humans as planned—"

"She was attacked!" a voice from the crowd yelled.

Bishop Ward, hands raised, stood trying to silence the crowd. Murmurs became louder.

"Is she all right?" another voice called out, which was quickly followed up by more inquiries about the queen's health.

"The queen was not attacked," Bishop Geddes responded dismissively. Desdemona raised an eyebrow at the blatant lie.

Bishop Ingor patted at the air with open palms in an attempt to quell the growing chaos. "The queen is tired from her journey and feels until she can make a public statement, it is best for all Fae to stay within the walls of the palace." He exhaled, satisfied at how he handled the situation. The group of Fae continued to talk among themselves, ignoring the bishops.

"Did the humans understand the queen?" a female voice called out.

"Will they leave the Aubane faction alone?" said another male voice from the back.

This time Bishop Geddes took the lead, standing and walking to the edge of the platform. "The humans are primitive creatures. They must be handled delicately. Queen Aurora will continue to reach out and establish a dialogue with them. Until we have established a set of rules, once again, the queen asks all Fae to remain in the palace for our safety. She does not have time to sit and hold every Fae's hand. Do not be such larvae."

Desdemona's left eye began to twitch with Geddes's insult.

The crowd erupted into a frenzy of gasps and questions. Demands to speak with the queen from the crowd became more prevalent.

"Where is our queen?" voices called out from different areas of the room.

"Did she really sprout wings?" another yelled.

"Why must we stay inside the palace? Are we all in danger?" a deeper voice yelled.

The crowd agreed, wanting an answer to that question in particular.

Bishop Caer tried to answer the onslaught of questions. "The queen is tired, as we said. She is busy. No! She did not sprout wings," he spat back at the tumultuous crowd.

Bishop Geddes glowered at Desdemona, his nostrils flaring as his right hand balled into a tight fist. A golden light suffused from his palm until his entire hand burned bright.

"I will deal with you, Captain, and your blatant disregard of my instructions. This is your fault. I will teach you your place and what it means to respect your superiors." He watched her from his lowered brow as he muttered through a clenched jaw.

Bishop Ward glanced at him as the scent of clay and wet stone rose from the bishop. "Not here, Geddes," Ward spat.

"She is a dog who needs to learn her place. I hold her leash. She must be choked a bit." He did not look at the other bishop as he spoke. His pewter eyes flecked with moss green burned with hatred. Desdemona watched the bishops but her job was to keep every Fae safe, not worry about the bishops' bruised egos.

Ward stepped in front of Geddes, placing his hand on the bishop's shoulder and gesturing toward the crowd. "Not. Now."

The sound of the throng of Fae and their cries for answers gave Geddes reason to pause, the light extinguishing from his hand. "I will have my time with the mongrel."

Ward nodded as the two directed their attention back toward the assembly. Just as the crowd seemed as though they might storm the platform, the air became heavy with the scent of the sea and the floor beneath the hall rumbled like a tidal wave was about to crash into the castle. Everyone stopped and looked for the source.

The large doors opened in a thunderous boom.

Desdemona drew her Harbinger swords, ready for what lay before her, as four other Fae, identical to her, dropped from the ceiling. These were the mysterious Illuminasqua she had been training. The four Illuminasqua, with their hoods pulled up, exchanged quick hand gestures. Desdemona nodded as they fanned out, ready to protect their kin.

However, there was no threat. A guard pushing a wooden barrel on wheels stood at the door and in the round wooden container was a Fae with hair like the sunrise on the most perfect summer morning.

Lady Serena lay in the barrel, her rainbow fin languidly draped over the top for all to gaze upon its beauty. She made this common barrel look like a throne. She held herself with such beauty and power everyone forgot what they were fighting about for a brief second.

Desdemona glanced at the Illuminasqua, noting there was no threat, and the four Fae disappeared as if they were never there. She gave a wry smile of pride. My troop's training is coming along nicely.

"Silence, all of you!" Serena's normally whimsical voice was hard and cold, holding the edge of the deepest parts of the ocean to it. The guard wheeled in the mermaid. The crowd parted, bowing their heads as she made her way through the Fae gathering.

Bishop Geddes found his voice first. "Lady Serena. What is the meaning of this interruption?" He didn't even try to hide his annoyance. Serena's eyes turned from their aqua-blue to red as they focused on him. "Shut up, little man. I am head of the Merfolk faction. I was the first of any Virtue to change, yet I did not receive an invite to this meeting. I am the queen's oldest and most trusted friend. So sit down while I try to salvage this."

Bishop Geddes sat, his mouth going slack. Desdemona smiled at Serena's moxie.

Serena regained her whimsical composure, blinking her eyes back to their sea-blue color and painting on her genial smile before she turned back to the crowd of her peers. Her voice was once again melodic.

"My fellow Fae, I have seen Queen Aurora. I can assure you she is well. She is resting from her encounter with the humans. The rumors are true. She did manifest energy wings when she met with the humans."

The bishops exchanged uncomfortable sideways glances as the room began mumbling. "However, it was not the first time she has manifested wings. It had happened once before with me. It happened briefly when she first became queen."

The room was a complete circus. Questions were yelled from each corner at Serena. Even the bishops joined in, demanding an explanation.

The mermaid remained steadfast in her resolve. She simply made a graceful gesture for silence. "My kin, let me finish."

The room obeyed.

The bishops wanted to continue to protest, but the room's compliance won out.

"It was on the beach months after she began construction on the palace. We were discussing the idea of being a queen. She had an emotional outburst of sorts and the wings materialized for a few brief seconds. Nothing like what happened with the humans. After speaking with Lady Ambia and Reva, I believe Queen Aurora is coming into her own as Fae and as our queen. I am confident Queen Aurora will address all of us on how we will proceed together for what is best for the Court of Light. Until then we need not question her wishes. We all stay put and avoid contact with the humans. Queen Aurora said our well-being is her first priority, and she proved it by putting herself at risk for us. Let us be respectful to her while she rests. Do I have your cooperation, my kin?" She raised both her hands in an all-encompassing gesture.

The crowd broke out into applause.

Serena glanced back at the sullen bishops. "Anything to add, bishops?" she chastised.

They shook their heads avoiding her eyes.

"Good, it is agreed upon. We will follow the queen's plan to stay within the palace and when she recovers from her new appendages, she will address her kin. Merry meet."

"Merry meet," the crowd responded with exuberance.

"Desdemona, will you close the meeting, please? I need to get into some real water now."

The crowd laughed at the mermaid's charm. Serena smiled and the guard moved her barrel aside, allowing the captain to dismiss the crowd while they continued to applaud the mermaid.

As the crowd dissipated, Serena turned to Desdemona. "I need to speak with the idiots times four if you don't mind." There was no remorse for her gruff insult.

The bishops opened their mouths to protest, but Desdemona slowly shook her head, warning them not to challenge her.

Serena winked at the guard and they moved toward Aurora's private meeting chamber. Theadova waited in the wings, listening to the meeting. He had told Serena what had happened, prompting her grand entrance. He now trotted alongside the finned creature, escorting her to the chamber. The bishops shuffled behind them. Desdemona brought up the rear. The seven Fae entered the meeting chambers, and Serena cocked her head, giving the guard the signal to leave. He gave his sign of respect to her and exited posthaste.

As soon as the doors closed, Bishop Geddes launched in with his verbal attack. "How dare you insult us! You are just a lady. Furthermore—"

Serena rolled her eyes and splashed her fin into her barrel, sending water all over the bishop. "Did you shrink your dick or just your brain when we changed?" she spat at him. It took all of Desdemona's self-control not to laugh aloud. Theadova choked on his water at the crude commentary.

Bishop Geddes, drenched in seawater, wiped his face. "I beg your pardon!" His eyes wide.

"Oh, cool it, Geddes. I need you to be quiet. But seriously, do any of you have a brain?"

The other bishops were responding with righteous indignation when Serena looked at Theadova and smirked. "Guess they just don't learn."

She raised her tail fin higher this time and sent a wave of water in the other three bishops' direction, dousing them. "Shut up! You lied to the heads of the factions." Her voice was back to its icy tone. "You lied about everything. Her wings and her condition. You told them she was too busy for her kin. Aurora would skin you are alive if she heard you say that. Get your heads out of your asses. Aurora treats her kin with respect. Follow her example. You acted hastily. Call for me next time, or better yet, whatever your first impulse is, ignore it and do the opposite!"

She faced Desdemona. "Des, call for me when Rory awakens, please. I have to return to the ocean." Serena whistled and the door opened. Her guard wheeled her out as she looked at the bishops. She folded her fins so her middle fin on her tail stuck up at the bishops. "Later, trolls."

The bishops stared and as soon the doors closed, they became emboldened with talk of punishing Serena and her "insolence," but Theadova spoke up. "She was correct," he said in a solemn voice. "Queen Aurora always treats her kin with respect. We would be wise to remember that." Theadova had more than a touch of disappointment in his voice.

"Remember what?" a voice said from the doorway.

Everyone looked up as a slender figure came into the chambers.

Aurora stood strong and smiled with an inquisitive arch of her right eyebrow and tilt of her head.

"You have much to catch me up on."

TWENTY-ONE:
You've Got Some Explaining To Do

E ach bishop avoided eye contact with their queen. Geddes stroked his goatee as the rest dropped their heads in some form of contrition.

Theadova looked at them and back to his queen.

"What is it you have to tell me?" Aurora asked again. Her voice held a tinge of annoyance at having to question them a second time.

Bishop Ingor glanced at his comrades and stepped forward. "Your Grace, we are so relieved to see you well. How are you feeling?" He motioned for the other bishops to bring a chair for Aurora, but she waved her hands in refusal.

"I have spent hours, if not days, lying down. The last thing I want to do is sit." She glanced around the room. Her eyes widened and her mouth curled into a smile as she spotted Theadova.

Aurora hurried to the white stag, threw her arms around his large neck, and buried her cheek in his snow-colored fur. The soft bristles tickled her neck as she hugged him and breathed in his scent. He smelled like sunshine and fir trees, the soul of the forest.

"Are you well? Lady Ambia said that you brought me to safety. Because of you, I was able to rest and recuperate in the palace. Thank you, my friend." Her voice was barely audible with her face pressed against his neck. Theadova turned his neck to cradle her back, closing his eyes in appreciation of her kind words and sentiment. "No, Your Grace, it was you who saved me. Your energy wings and wind pulse kept the humans at bay. I just carried us home."

Aurora put her forehead to his. She stroked his back. "We both did it, fair?"

Always the diplomat. Theadova simply nodded in agreement slowly as not to break their intimate moment.

The queen gave him a coy smile and continued to stroke the back of his neck while she spoke to the rest of the room. "I need to be filled in. What has happened since my return? Did you inform the lords and ladies of what transpired between me and the humans? Were all the Fae made aware of the situation as well?"

The room's energy shifted from joyful to uncomfortable. Bishop Geddes stroked his cheek, avoiding eye contact. The bishops had some explaining to do to their queen.

When the bishops did not respond, Desdemona spoke up to goad them into a confession. "If I hurry, maybe I can catch Lady Serena before she hits the ocean. I think we will need her." She pivoted, her black boots skidding on the floor.

"Why do I need Lady Serena?" Aurora's eyes narrowed on the room. "Desdemona, answer me. Why do I need Lady Serena?"

Desdemona was not responsible for delivering the information. She lifted her chin and her cold stare zeroed in on the bishops.

Aurora followed her captain's gaze, gave a subtle nod, and sucked in her cheeks. "My bishops, they should be able to explain this to me. Perhaps now would be a good time for them to start."

Desdemona stood at attention and gave the bishops a look to let them know she was not about to cover for anyone, but she was not going to confess their sins for them, either. It became a standoff between the bishops and Desdemona.

"I believe Bishop Ingor should address the methods in which they handled your absence, and you can decide for yourself if you would like to speak with Lady Serena and hear her point of view, Your Grace." Desdemona gestured toward Theadova and opened the doors for them to exit and let their queen handle her bishops.

"Thank you, Desdemona," Aurora said as they left her with the bishops to sort out their issues.

Aurora watched the door close and gave the four Fae a scathing look. "Bishop Ingor? As my first advisor, I will give you the opportunity to tell me what happened while I was out of commission."

The older Fae separated himself from the other three, or perhaps it would be better to say the other three bishops took a few steps back to leave Bishop Ingor on his own to face the queen. The color drained from his face. The contrast of auburn hair held back in the traditional ponytail all the bishops wore only highlighted his suddenly sickly pallor. "Your Grace, if I may begin by saying we did what we felt was best for all the Fae. We were not aware of all of the particulars surrounding your interaction with the humans until after we had the meeting and um...We may not have been completely forthcoming with all the information." He tried to sound both contrite and resilient in his handling of the situation.

Aurora shook her head. She was not satisfied with his answer. "That tells me nothing. Why was Serena involved?" Her tone was pointed, and her gaze did not flinch.

"Lady Serena was initially left out of the meeting in an unintentional oversight. When she arrived, she was understandably upset and felt a bit slighted, which we explained was not our intent at all." He gestured back at the other three bishops who all nodded in agreement. "Lady Serena did not agree with how we handled the meeting and how we doled out the information. In retrospect, she may have had a point, and upon further self-reflection, we agreed with her logic and followed her lead." The other bishops nodded their emphatic support of their peer trying to protect all of them.

Aurora paced the room, mulling this over. "You were left in a difficult position, and everyone advised against me meeting the humans alone."

Bishop Ward took advantage of her interpretation of the problem. "Yes, Your Grace. We all warned you, and you did not give us time to form a contingency plan in case something happened—you departed so suddenly."

Bishop Geddes added his two cents, "You were so determined to fix the situation. We understand why you left so quickly, Your Grace." He hoped to smoothe things over while adding just a tinge of more guilt.

It was Queen Aurora's turn to look embarrassed. Her cheeks flushed pink and her lips disappeared into a thin line. "You are correct, I was irresponsible. As queen without an heir, I need to think about these things. I should never have gone without Desdemona, and you are also correct... we must have a plan for succession." Aurora's own embarrassment at her mistake made her much more amenable to the bishops' faux pas, and she decided to be more reasonable than judgmental.

The bishops were both relieved and disturbed by this. "Your Grace, if I may be so bold, do you plan to commit to a life partner and produce an heir?" Bishop Ingor inquired carefully.

Their queen walked the room, placing one foot in front of the other in a narrow gait, as if walking a thin line. She was slow and deliberate as her steps mimicked her contemplation, "It is a fair question you present, Bishop Ingor. I do not plan on giving myself to a life mate or attempting to produce an heir. We are unsure if I even could, considering our angelic lineage and the fact I did not morph. I think it is best if the line of succession is left to the bishops. One house should not be given all the power. If you, as the bishops, can choose the next ruling Monarch of the Fae, it will open the possibilities for any of the heads of the Fae Houses to become ruler." Determination flashed in her eyes.

"Is that your final decision, Your Grace—the bishops choose the ruling monarch if there is no heir?" Bishop Ingor asked, making sure he fully understood her request.

"Yes, please see Reva draws up the contract and enters it into Fae law. If the ruling Monarch leaves no heir, the bishops will select the next king or queen from the heads of the Four Royal Fae Houses. However, bishops, this is a heavy responsibility." Her voice was a cocktail of frostiness, criticalness, and hopefulness.

TWENTY-TWO:
You Had Me At-We Shouldn't Be Doing This...

T he salty air was pungent as the sea churned, the white foam denoting the ocean's irritated mood. Aurora scanned the waves for a glimmer of Serena's rainbow fin. A reflection of yellow and green caught Aurora's eye, a graceful arc of colors breaking the surface. Serena's lithe body disappeared for a brief moment, and in a whoosh of water, she reemerged like a sea goddess, flipping her flax-en-streaked tresses up and over her head and revealing her oversized aqua-blue eyes, high cheekbones, feminine jaw, and smiling bronze lips.

Serena pulled herself up onto the sand. Aurora bent down to hug her friend. Rolling up her long dress, she took a seat in the damp sand. The mermaid watched, flapping her tail rhythmically and splashing cool water over her own head as Aurora stuck her legs in the surf.

"I am so happy to see you!" Serena said. "Are you feeling better? I would have come to the palace to see you—"

"I know, I know. But from what I heard, you certainly did more than enough while I was...indisposed." Aurora's royal manners placed a polite twist on her recent episode.

Serena rolled her eyes. "Yeah, well, those bishops of yours aren't the sharpest crystals in the bunch, Rory."

Aurora bristled a bit, squinting at the commentary. "Everyone is on a learning curve with this whole ruling-a-kingdom thing. They made a mistake. We are all trying. They meant well."

Serena picked up a shell and tossed it into the water. "You didn't drag my fine-looking tail out of the water to debate the effectiveness of the idiots-times-four. So, what's up?"

It was Aurora's turn to roll her eyes. "Okay, first, can you please stop referring to my advisors as idiots? And you are correct. I did not drag your fine tail, as you so eloquently put it, out of the ocean for idle chitchat. I have an idea I want to run by you." Aurora's eyes focused on an unseen presence. Her face lost its light as her mouth twisted, the tone of their conversation turning more serious.

"I will lay off the bishops," Serena conceded. "What's this plan of yours?" She rolled onto her stomach, flapping her tail up and down.

Wringing her fingers and biting the inside of her cheek, Aurora gathered up her resolve to tell her friend the plan.

"Oh, my. I have not seen you like this since we first got to this planet. Now I am intrigued." Serena poked her friend in the arm.

Aurora gave her a lopsided grin. "I know. This is kind of big, Serena, and I am not sure if I should even do it. In fact, I am positive I shouldn't do it at all. However, it might be the only way to protect the kingdom from the humans and keep us all safe." Aurora's voice became introspective as she stared out upon the horizon; there was a hitch to her words.

"Oh, I am in!" Serena slapped her tail in the wet sand with a thwack for emphasis.

Aurora whipped her head around. "What? You haven't even heard my plan."

Serena shrugged as she drew in the sand with her finger. "I know, but you had me at 'shouldn't be doing this.' That is my kind of plan."

Aurora cocked her head. Her eyes widened and her brow furrowed. "Huh?"

Serena sat upright, dusting off the sand from her hands. "Look, Rory, you are the most caring person I know. If you say this could keep us all safe, I trust you. Whatever you need, I will help you." Her voice was calm and sincere.

Aurora gave her friend a smile and squeezed her hand. "I appreciate it. Here goes... I have been doing research since I woke up. Looking at our old Virtue texts—"

Serena immediately perked up. "You kept the old texts?" She did not try to hide her disbelief. Aurora pulled her knees to her chest. Serena turned her head away from her friend, fixing her hair and swearing under her breath at the lack of tact.

"I'm sorry, Rory. I am sure it was hard for you to go back and look over those texts. Please go on." Serena gave her a half smile, encouraging her to continue.

Aurora, rocking back and forth while holding her forearms around her knees, cleared her throat. "As I was saying. I went over the old texts and discovered something about a new level of angel He had planned to create once humans populated the planet called Guardian Angels. These

Guardian Angels were supposed to protect the humans and guide them. I am not sure how, but it isn't important. What I did find is they would have existed in an ether-like dimension, one that mirrored this world. These Guardians could slip in and out of this dimension undetected by the humans and walk alongside them. Kind of like a veiled dimension." Aurora raised her brows at her friend. "Do you see where I am going with this?"

Serena scrunched her face up and started flapping her tail in the sand again, indicating she was thinking hard. "Um... Well... So..."

Aurora looked hopefully at her friend as she leaned forward, waiting for her answer.

"No. Sorry." Serena gave a long, low sigh as she slumped back onto her elbows.

Aurora exhaled out of frustration. "Serena. Follow my logic. You know how He operates. This was His plan. The groundwork has been laid. I bet the framework for the dimension already exists. I think we can tap into it and create a Veil for us. Utilizing elemental magic and our innate connection to the Earth." Aurora's hands shook, her eyes were wide.

Serena backed up a bit, scanning her friend up and down and taking a long pause. "Whoa, Aurora. You are talking about acting like Father? Creating a dimension? It is crazy. I have never heard you speak like this." Her voice dropped as she whispered the last sentence. Serena's eyes darted toward the blue sky and back to her friend.

"But you said you would help me." Aurora's voice was harsh, but her eyes showed more hurt than anything else as they glistened with the beginning of tears.

Serena slumped, her shoulders rolling forward as she released a long exhale, blowing her hair out of her eyes. "Oh, I—of course I am going to help you. I was taken aback. Look, it's a great idea. You are right. Let's give it a shot. What must we do?"

Aurora's eyes lit up and she rushed to hug Serena.

The mermaid looked up toward the heavens as her friend embraced her. She didn't know if this was a wonderful idea or if this would be their undoing, but damn it to Lucifer. If she was going down in flames, she would go down fighting with her best friend by her side.

TWENTY-THREE:
Who Said Creating a New Dimension Was Easy?

Aurora pulled away from their embrace. "Okay, so there are a few things we must talk about. It will affect your faction directly."

Serena pursed her lips and squinted her eyes. She raised her finger to her cheek. "And...they would be what?"

Aurora gestured toward the water with her palm up. "I can't Veil the entire ocean. The Merfolk faction will have to move offshore. I will make a gateway into the palace deep in the ocean no human will find. Your kin will have the key. Your faction can access it at any time. It will lead into a lagoon. From the lagoon, there will be channels that will direct you into the palace and the Great Hall for meetings. This way, you will not have to create doorways like the other factions will."

Serena took a few minutes to ponder everything Aurora had explained. "But we will have direct access to the palace?" she reiterated.

"Of course. I can even create a second gateway in a different part of the ocean if you would like."

Serena nodded. "I had already given the orders for my faction to move offshore to avoid accidental human contact. It is not a major change for us. Do you know how much of this planet is covered by ocean water?"

Aurora thought about the question. "No, I don't believe I do."

Serena flipped her fins faster. "Almost seventy-five percent of this planet is covered by water. My faction can stay hidden in the ocean, as you wish. There are plenty of secluded beaches for them to come ashore where humans will not find them. However, only two gateways will not be enough. If I present this option to my kin, it will make them feel as if they are being kept away from the palace. I need a minimum of four, one for each direction." Serena's voice was flat, and her logic was pragmatic.

Aurora could not help but smile to herself at her friend's mature attitude and strong sense of leadership. She knew, one day, Serena would make a fine queen. It was part of why she had told the bishops the next monarch should come from a head of the Fae Houses. She hoped it might be Serena. "You will have four gateways, Lady Serena." With a bow of her head, their negotiations were complete.

"Thank you, Your Grace," Serena said in acknowledgment. "So, how does one create a new dimension?"

"I am still researching it, but I think the next piece is blood," Aurora said grimly.

"Blood? Like a sacrifice?" Wrinkling her nose, Serena's face paled.

"No, nothing so gruesome." Aurora waved her hand. "I want to use a drop of blood from each Fae faction as a type of key to unlock the gate. Our blood will be how we pass in and out of the dimension. Our connection to the elements, to nature, will be the lock and our blood the key. One will recognize the other."

Serena's eyes flicked side to side as she mulled the idea over. "A lock and key mechanism. Using our elemental energy power as the lock and our blood the key. Hmm…I have to say, you are pretty smart."

Serena gazed at her childhood friend, and a sly smile crept across Aurora's face. "I haven't done anything yet. It is a working theory. Save the praise for after I pull this off. Then you can tell me how wonderful I am all day long." Aurora winked. "By the way, you know you could manifest legs and walk to the palace, saving the Spelaions from having to dig more trenches."

Serena, looking scandalized, brought her hand to her chest. "What? And ruin this fine piece of tail? No, I won't hear of such blasphemy! Do you see how jealous those Fae are of me and my faction now? Can you imagine if I sported an even more perfect figure than this? If I strolled into the Great Hall on a stunning set of stems? Please! Those prudes would not know what to do. I like my fins. Besides, I don't think I could manifest legs anymore. It's been so long. How would it look to my kin if I changed back to legs, and they couldn't?" Serena's voice was harsh, yet wistful.

"Oh. Point taken. I hadn't thought about it in those terms. You are a good leader, Serena."

"Well, this good leader must return to her faction, and you have a new dimension to create." Serena smiled and hugged her friend. "I am glad you are better. Oh, and congratulations on new—well, old wings, since I saw them first!" Serena jumped into the water and disappeared into the waves.

Aurora waited and watched until she could no longer see any remnants of Serena's rainbow tail under the water. Her gaze wandered to the lazy puffs of white cotton drifting across an otherwise perfectly brilliant, blue sky as the seagulls called overhead. Her mood changed from hope to apprehension.

Was her friend correct? Was she playing like their Creator by trying to produce a new dimension? Should she listen to her first instinct? Perhaps she shouldn't be doing this. But she wanted to protect her kin. Wasn't that what a queen was supposed to do? Doing the correct thing was not always easy. Aurora headed toward the palace, walking through the dunes and waving the top of her hands over the tall grass, feeling it tickle her palms. She decided to take a longer stroll, gathering some wildflowers along the way. There was a stop to make. She followed a small, rocky path that led to another isolated beach. The path was winding and uneven. Aurora picked up her long dress to keep from tripping. She stumbled, coming too close to face-planting more than once.

She was being silly. Glancing right to left, Aurora closed her eyes and concentrated on the wind, the call of the breeze. Listening for it, she thought about the wings on her back and the chants from the humans. Sweat formed on her brow. When she began to think it was useless, she felt a surge from her back. She opened her eyes slowly. On the sand her shadow had changed. Her breathing accelerated. She turned, examining her new silhouette. Her shadow had wings. They were oval-shaped. There were four of them—two larger ones on top and two smaller ones at the bottom. She mentally commanded them to flap as she used to with her old wings. They responded slowly as first. Her smile grew along with the intensity of the speed of her wings.

Her wings thrumming, she lifted off the ground. She had wings and was in full control of them. She had manifested them. Willed them into existence! Aurora was ecstatic, lifting higher off the ground, following the path from ten feet above. There was no need to worry about the uneven ground now.

Hovering for a moment, she closed her eyes and listened. *Ah, there it is.*

The sweet, delicious sound of the wind, her lost language.

"Oh, my friend, how I have missed you." Tears rolled down her cheeks as she smiled. "I will never leave you again." She was giddy, swooping and spinning, flying faster, skimming the ground. Aurora was so enraptured by her wings she had almost forgotten why she was even at this part of the beach.

Aurora reached her destination, and the somber reason for her visit hit her. She felt ashamed for her joy in this place. This area of the beach was always quiet. There were no gulls. Even the crash of the waves was muted here. She touched down silently and closed her eyes, gently folding the wings into place. With a cold tingle on her back, they disintegrated. She shivered in reflex, feeling a fleeting sense of worry she may not get them back. However, her worry would have to wait.

Aurora, squarely on the ground, took a few steps on the blue-stained sand. No matter how many rainstorms this beach endured, the sand never changed color. The blood of the murdered Powers permanently marked this place. Their blood acted as a stamp of sadness. No animals came here and nothing grew around the area. The sun's rays were diminished. She walked carefully to the first armor marker and bowed her head to pay her respects. It was a woman's armor. The breast plate was the only giveaway. She thanked her for her sacrifice and laid the wildflowers she had collected at the foot of the memorial.

Aurora moved on to inspect the markers. While she was there to pay homage, she also wanted to see if Ward was correct. She had noticed the markings but never paid attention to see if new names had appeared on the armor. She walked among the armor until she came to the final marker and gasped. "Avesta" was inscribed on the armor.

The Black Kyanite armor was rough and fresh from its recent alteration, not smooth from weathering like the others. A single Power is of no consequence. Perhaps one day he might even join us—maybe help Desdemona in protecting the Court of Light. She would welcome him with open arms.

Aurora stood, hands folded in front of her chin, trying to take in the magnitude of the site. She visited here at least twice a month, and each time she came it was still overwhelming. Since discovering the memorial, she had tried to bring each set of armor flowers. It had taken her years to accomplish her goal. Aurora looked out among the memorial markers. This must be included in her plan. She had to preserve it and protect it. The humans could not find this. Tears welled up and slowly trickled down her cheek. She didn't know why she cried for these Powers. She hadn't known them.

However, they had a connection. When they fought, she had done nothing. Perhaps that was a mistake, and she would not fail them in Oblivion.

TWENTY-FOUR:
DIMENSIONAL ANALYSIS

Aurora did not have as much resistance to her plan as she had expected. As per Serena's advice, she called a meeting, explaining the idea of the Veil and how it would conceal the Fae from the humans. Queen Aurora wrote up parameters for human interaction with the Fae. For now, only the heads of the Fae Houses would be allowed to interact with the humans. This helped to establish the first of the primitive elemental and agricultural god and goddess cults. Pairing up the Fae as synergistic gods and goddesses fulfilled Aurora's safety concerns and helped the humans spread their worship to all the factions.

Aurora felt confident in the rules she had set forth and how receptive the clans and their leaders were. Everyone understood that with the adulation of the humans, there was much to gain. Lady Ambia explained how the queen's aura had changed and the gaining of her energy wings had come about with the humans' worship. However, it did not come for free. The Fae had to truly be gods and goddesses to the primordial humans, guiding them and at times giving them discipline when needed. If the Fae handled this with courtesy and respect, the rewards could be more than they'd ever imagined. To complete their ethereal façade, the Fae could not have their home easily discovered. Therefore, the Veil was not just a clever self-defense mechanism, it was a necessity.

Aurora stood in the palace's highest tower, ready to make her theory a reality. Dressed in a plain linen cloak, she wore nothing underneath it.

When it was time, she would need a connection to all the elements and clothing impeded it. Aurora readied herself for the most important energy work she would ever attempt. She had spent the day meditating, aligning her chakras. She would need to tap into them to help guide the energies. Aurora took the blood vials from Desdemona. It had taken her over three weeks to collect the blood from every Fae faction in the Court of Light. She poured them into a gold bowl with Desdemona adding her own blood straight from the source. The bowl was set aside.

Aurora looked over the two physical models of the Court of Light standing before her. One model represented how her kingdom looked presently, vast and wide. She had constructed it from clear quartz; her job was to make it invisible with this spell. Clear quartz acted as a generator, amplifying magical intention. The other was a more condensed version with a few key changes.

The Power Angel Memorial was added much closer to the palace. It was to the east of the main gate toward the lagoon. Blue-stained sand from the memorial was placed in its new location. The second model also had a new second lagoon for Serena's Merfolk faction. It would be a "welcoming gateway" for them. Malascola's kin would carve water channels so the Merfolk could swim directly to the palace. The lagoon would also be a safe haven for the Merfolk who wished to frolic closer to the shore and lay in the surf as they liked to do without worrying about human interaction. This second model was constructed from Rutilated Quartz and Black Tourmaline crystal. The milky-white quartz had rods of Black Tourmaline crystal growing inside it. The combination of the two crystals was highly effective for protection, precisely what one would need when creating a barrier.

The final distinction was the border of mirrors surrounding the new kingdom model. The mirrors faced out toward the human world, acting as an actual reflection to any humans who got too close to the Veil's border. It was also an extra precaution in case any humans gifted with sight saw through her spell. This spell had taken weeks to perfect, and she still had her doubts. Figuring out the lock and key design was the easier part. Constructing the correct words and tapping into the energies of the elements would be the test.

It was time to set the "lock." Aurora took the bowl and pricked her finger with a special crystal Galena blade, adding her own blood. She carefully poured a thin, dark-blue line around the border of what was to become her new kingdom. The blood flowed thick and slowly.

She nodded to Desdemona, who opened the door. One by one, the bishops filed into the room. Following her instructions, they each took their respective places, representing their element. Bishop Ingor walked to the south-facing wall representing Fire. Bishop Geddes, representing Earth, stood at the north wall. Bishop Ward represented

Air at the east-facing wall, and Bishop Caer stood to the west representing Water.

Once the bishops were in position, Desdemona exited to stand guard and make sure under no circumstances they were to be disturbed. With the door closed, Aurora faced her bishops. They stood tall and ready. "Bishops, you understand I do not know if this will work or what will happen, but as we discussed, this is our best course of action. I thank you for your trust. I need you to focus. Do not waver. Once I begin the incantation, there is no going back. Am I clear?" She made eye contact with each Fae. Each bishop answered without hesitation, starting with Bishop Ingor.

"Yes, Your Grace." The others followed suit.

"Thank you. Let us begin. Each of you must conjure a representation of your element and hold it." Aurora turned to ready herself.

Bishop Geddes said, "Hold it, Your Grace?" His voice went up in tone but was not disrespectful.

"Yes. Bishop Geddes, concentrate and hold the manifestation of the element. I must have a physical representation of the elemental energies present to tap into and magnify. I am going to try to act as a conduit and direct the power." Aurora spoke with confidence. She could not afford to question herself.

As a Virtue, she had been versed in energies. Energy play or "magick" was about intention. Intention was energy. Energy vibrated, it moved. Creating the Veil was matching her vibration or intention to the energies that surrounded them and bending it. Aurora needed to align herself with

Earth's natural energies and match the speed at which it vibrated, then draw it into her and direct its flow. Magick was like a raging river. She could guide it, she could harness it, she could even stop the flow at times or slow it down a bit. But no one ever truly controlled magick. If one was foolish enough to think one could, eventually, like a river, it would carve a chasm right through that person. The Virtues had the discipline to work magick, and it was why they had been the only ones instructed in the discipline.

Not waiting for any other bishop to question her, Aurora took the gold bowl with what was left of the blue liquid and dropped her cloak. The time for modesty was over. Dipping her fingers into the bowl, she found it was cool to the touch. Stirring the thick blood clockwise, she watched the deep blue fluid swirl about until her fingers were coated enough to begin. She lifted her index and middle finger from the bowl, waiting until they stopped dripping, not wanting to waste any of the precious liquid.

Aurora slowly and deliberately painted the concealment spell symbols on her body. The blue blood seeped into her skin. With each stroke, she repeated certain words, keeping her mind focused and clear.

Each bishop held his elemental manifestation. Geddes had a balance of rocks. The formation before him was otherworldly. The boulders supported one another at odd angles. Out in nature on their own, they would have never reached the height he had stacked them, but with his control, they were steady and sure.

Bishop Ingor held an arch of fire between the palms of his hands. The bright hues of orange and red reflected in his auburn hair. His red irises with their yellow pupils gave his face a warm glow against his iridescent skin.

Caer commanded the water from the barrel to encase him in a bubble. His hair floated above his head as he closed his eyes and held the liquid manifestation.

Lastly, Bishop Ward stood steadfast with his palms up and small tornados in each hand. Perspiration formed on his brow as he concentrated to keep his control over the miniature windstorms, his gold ponytail flapping behind him.

Aurora saw the strain on Ward's face, but she could not hurry or be concerned. Magick should never be rushed, and once the concealment spell was written she needed to transfer it to the kingdom and create the Veil. The Veil would appear as a reflection of the world. Unless one was of Fae blood, one could not enter it. The Veil would vibrate at a frequency calibrated to the Fae by their blood. This was the key to the lock. Aurora closed her eyes to match her energies.

She glowed with power. From the base of her spine, globes of color appeared. A rainbow ascended her body as each chakra ignited. Aurora acknowledged its arrival with a chant. As the throat chakra blazed, her voice reverberated in the room. "I speak only truth. This guides my intentions."

The last color of her chakra burst out, emanating from between her eyebrows, encompassing the room in violet light. The blue symbols on her body illuminated, and a wind whipped her hair around, indicating her own innate energy gathered.

The bishops watched as a vortex of energy swept Aurora up into it. Ribbons of red, orange, yellow, green, and blue swirled around her body, the crackling of power lighting the room up as she elevated higher. She was fourteen feet off the ground. The symbols on her body gave off their own brightness. She opened her eyes, releasing a blindingly bright emerald incandescent light. She was at the pinnacle of her power.

Aurora's voice resonated like she called from the edges of the cosmos, speaking in the light of a newborn star. Power and wisdom vibrated her vocal cords. She raised her arms over her head and chanted:

"East carries Air, let winds soar.
South unchains Fire, let the flames roar.
West unleashes the currents, let Waters flow.
North nurtures Earth, let the seeds grow.
Let all the elements be present and blessed.
So mote it be.
Orb of power, orb of light.
Ever peaceful, burning bright.
Orb of light, orb of power.
I conjure thee this sacred hour."

As she spoke each element, the bishops' representations of power grew. Geddes's rocks sprouted ivy leaves. Ingor's flames roared. Caer's water bubble became a waterspout. Ward's tornados grew.

She repeated the chant three times until a pure, white light radiated from her chest. With her hands, Aurora took the light from her chest. She strained and grimaced against the light, trying to compress it into a smaller orb. It pulsated and crackled with energy. Her breathing was ragged as she elevated the orb, and as she pulled her hands apart it grew into a larger energetic sphere.

She lifted her hands above her head and spoke:

"In between time and space, from a dream do not awake.
Only Fae shall see it clear, for all the rest we disappear.

Blood of my blood, hear my call:
All Fae are welcome. Come one, come all.
With the blood of the Fae, I consecrate on this day.
They are now the keys to finding their own way.
Through the Veil only Fae shall pass.
The oaken door shall light their path.
When they look, sight unseen,
where they go, we will not be.
Elemental powers, surround my land.
Invisibility be granted. We shan't be found.
The Fae circle I now cast.
Take effect, large and fast.
Here, my kin, we may reside from human eyes.
In the Veil is where we hide.
Weave this with love and light.
Let us be beyond their sight."

She threw the power globe into the new kingdom model, repeating the chant as the sphere crashed into it. The elemental representations retreated from the bishops one by one. Geddes's rocks, Caer's water, Ward's tornados, and Ingor's fire all hovered above the model until they folded in upon themselves and each became a glowing orb of pulsating color—red for Fire, green for Earth, blue for Water, and yellow for Air.

Aurora settled to the ground and poured the last bit of blood over the model, miraculously still intact after the orb had collided into it. The four elements responded to the blood. A light shot from the center of the model palace and the four spheres joined together, forming a seven-pointed crystalline star. The star shimmered and shined, reflecting the four colors of the elements.

Aurora held her hands out to the bishops and they walked forward, mouths open, eyes wide at what they witnessed. Joining their hands together, their queen repeated the last section of the spell:

"The Fae circle I now cast.

Take effect, large and fast.

Here, my kin, we may reside from human eyes.

In the Veil is where we hide.

Weave this with love and light.

Let us be beyond their sight."

The star altered its colors and exploded, but no one dared let go of one another, their knuckles turning white. They held steadfast, repeating the spell. The star dissolved into glitter, landing on the new kingdom arrangement. The old map and model disappeared.

Bishop Geddes released his hand first and tried to touch the new model. When his fingers crossed the new boundary, his hand briefly shimmered, then disappeared before reappearing on the Fae side of the line. They all looked up at Aurora, awestruck.

"By the universe, you did it, Your Grace." Bishop Geddes's eyes held surprise and disbelief. Mouth open, he covered it with his palm after he spoke. Aurora dropped her hands to her sides and stumbled back. Ingor grabbed her cloak and wrapped her in it, supporting her, but she shrugged him off. "We need to see if it worked," she said, her eyes weary from exhaustion.

"How will we return to the palace?" Bishop Ward asked.

Aurora's eyes fluttered. "Only a bishop can conjure a door to come home when the elemental magick is in its natural state. You can open a door, Bishop Ward, when there is a breeze playing with leaves, or Bishop Caer, where there is a well spring. All other Fae must open a door where two elements meet at an elemental crossroad. A seashore, Water and Earth. A volcano is Fire and Earth. A geyser, Water, Earth, and Air. All Fae will leave here through the oaken door outside the palace gates. Go now. Test this. Make sure we have succeeded." Her hand shook as she handed pieces of parchment to Bishop Ingor before Aurora passed out, her head lolling to the side.

Bishop Ingor took the parchment and shoved it toward the other bishops. He moved the queen's hair from her face. "You heard her. Someone has to go and test the Veil. Who is it going to be?"

Bishops Geddes, Ward, and Caer stepped outside the palace front gates as the queen had instructed. It had been midday when the ritual began, but now they looked at the pitch-black sky, complete with sparkling stars. They stumbled around, a bit dumbfounded. Not much should have changed, yet things were surprisingly different. Even in the dark, the world had a new shimmer and shine—otherworldly.

Bishop Caer bent over and gently grazed the tops of the blades of grass as he walked. The coolness of the evening dew felt different. How, he was not sure, but it felt cleaner, crisper. The stalks of taller grass pulled and caught at his cape as he hastened his pace. The fresh release of green moss and earth flooded his senses. Everything was more intense somehow.

The three bishops went to the large oak tree outside the palace. It was so much larger than it had ever been before. The tree called to them. Each one felt the energy pulsating from it deep within their chakras.

Bishop Ward stepped closer and ran his hands over the bark. Together, they watched the trunk twinkle in the night air. A gold handle with carvings and symbols slowly revealed itself. It glowed more as it became more tangible. Bishop Ward reached to grasp the handle. The tree flashed as a door came into focus. The door bore Bishop Ward's elemental symbol for Air. He looked back at the other two bishops, who raised their eyebrows, egging him on. Ward swallowed hard, opened the door, and walked through. He disappeared from sight as the door closed behind him. The other two bishops rushed forward and opened the door, but he was gone.

Bishop Ward walked out into a meadow in the evening. Cicadas sang their midsummer song. The warm breeze was nice on his skin, but the colors there were not as bright. It was as if someone had turned the vibrancy down. He looked around, expecting to see the palace, but it was not there. He looked to the right. There was no lagoon.

"Damn it to Lucifer. Where the hell am I?" he said, true realization crossing his face. "She did it. By the universe, she did it."

There was a rustling and Bishop Caer walked toward him with the same look of triumphant wonderment followed by Bishop Geddes.

The three bishops explored the human world, searching for confirmation they indeed had crossed through. With the map in hand, the bishops looked for the small village, ample proof their queen had succeed in her task. Still, Geddes looked around, shuffling his feet, perspiring, rubbing his arm, sneering at every little comment the others made in regard to the queen's triumph.

"Now for the true test," Ward said. "Getting back." He pulled out three pieces of parchment and handed one to each bishop. "Remember, you must find your elemental representation in nature. Good luck. I'll see you back at the palace."

The three Fae split up. Minutes later, they met back in the Great Hall of the Palace.

"She did it! By all that is holy—"

"Caer! Do not invoke His name," Geddes spat out, his eyes shifting right and left. "We do not know if Father allowed this or if this is by another's hand."

"What do you mean, Bishop?" Caer's shoulders hunched from tension. "This is a display of too much power. I am leery. Is she the right hand of the Father or the tool of Lucifer?"

Geddes spoke in a hushed voice. "But she saved us."

Caer's voice rose.

"From what? We were in no immediate danger," Geddes said, annoyed.

"But you both agreed the humans were a threat—"

Geddes grabbed the other bishop by his coat and pinned him against the wall and said, "She said they were a threat. How do we really know they are a threat? So far, all the humans have done is given us worship. We are restricted from interacting with them one on one. That was her stipulation, not ours. Does she have something to hide? How do you know the hired muscle isn't plotting to be worshipped as a goddess too? There is much we do not yet know." Geddes leaned into Caer as Ward stood behind him, arms folded at his chest, wearing a smug look of satisfaction.

Caer's eyes darted between the two bishops, his lips pressed tightly together. "But we are supposed to advise the queen. It sounds like you do not even like her, Bishop Geddes. She has been kind and—"

Geddes's cheeks flushed red as his nostrils flared. "Fool, this is not about whether I like the queen or not. This is about survival. If she makes a mistake, she ruins it for all of us. I will not allow that. It is about playing the game, Caer. Pick a side. Think about it. If Father did not allow this to happen, then who did? And why?" Geddes made quick gestures with his hands, his agitation growing. "I will not fall for her trickery. I will watch her carefully. No one creates a world except Father. If He blessed this event, He will come for us. I will not follow her blindly. My eyes are opening. I suggest you all do the same." Geddes pointed at both bishops before turning on his heel and leaving the Great Hall. Ward followed closely behind him.

Caer mumbled, glancing up to see he was talking to himself. Weighing the other bishops' words, he stood and ran to catch up with them.

TWENTY-FIVE:
IT'S ALL IN HOW YOU SAY IT

Perched on the veranda while Aurora was deep in thought about her ritual, a small-winged dragon sat quietly watching. He stealthily climbed inside a window, seamlessly blending from his amber hue into the palace's translucent crystal walls. A Black Onyx Quartz crystal cluster barely tucked under the side of his front leg. The asymmetrical points of the hard rock stuck into his leathery side, making small indents on the dragon.

Los was not useless as the Draconian faction had thought. No, Los was so much more. Across the lilac trees of the Forehelina Forest and the turquoise ribbon of the Nimbue River, another saw everything the creature observed. Asa, formerly known as the Power Brigade's seer, mentally connected with the dragon, taking copious notes on everything Los observed. In Blood Haven's throne room, Jarvok scrutinized a familiar setup. Two models of his kingdom lay out on the table. His models were not as elegant as Aurora's, no shiny crystals polished to perfection. His were rough and dark, constructed from the same

magma Blood Haven's foundation stood upon. Mirrors arranged around the new layout, as per the instructions viewed by his small spy dragon, set the stage. The only blood needed was his kin and the Draconian faction. Only former Powers and dragons would be granted access to their kingdom.

Jarvok glanced in the directions of the four corners representing each element. When Aurora's spell reached its height of magical intensity, Los would siphon the excess energy in the room with the Black Quartz cluster and bring it back to him to act as the magical generator for his own spell. As a Power, Jarvok had an innate energy flow, but he was not versed in spellcasting the way the Virtues were. The extra dose of power would help him increase his chance of success. Jarvok had all the tools. Aurora would speak the spell, he would make a few small changes, and it would be perfect.

Los waited until the right time. As Aurora lifted the growing power orb above her, the sparks of energy sizzling off, Los knew now was his chance. He slipped farther into the room. With the commotion of the spell and his ability to camouflage into his surroundings, no one noticed him. He held up the Black Quartz cluster over his head, standing on his back legs, gathering the excess energy while it fizzed and popped around him. The little dragon's arms shook as the energy zipped into the cluster, filling it. Los felt the hum of power contained inside. As it neared capacity the energy trail decelerated until it ceased completely. He slowly backed away, taking his place to finish .

observing how the spell ended to make sure Jarvok had all the instructions he needed to complete his incantation.

Los understood the gravity of the situation. He would not fail Jarvok. This was to keep his new pack safe. He was honored Jarvok trusted him with this task, even when his own kind thought him useless. Jarvok had given him a place, a home, and most of all respect and a purpose. Los had seen what Jarvok had done for Dragor, but then again, Dragor was mighty and large. How anyone could have ever denied Dragor would be useful was beyond Los' comprehension.

Los, on the other hand, was small and born sickly. He had no oral defenses but like the impressive Dragor, the two dragons bore the label hopeless by their own kin and were to be sacrificed, if not for Jarvok. Jarvok had found Los on the outskirts of the Draconian caves as he crossed the border of the Impolita Valley.

The Impolita Valley marked the borderline of the Fire-Breathers' territory. All the Draconians lived in separate sections but met at the Spark of Life once a year to pay homage to "that which brought the dragons life." During this meeting, the faction made sacrifices to the mountain as a way of recycling to the Spark. According to lore, the mountain would erupt and the blood flow would give life to newer, stronger dragons. The mountain was covered in ice like the Ice-Breathers but produced fire like the Fire-Breathers and had pockets of exploding acid geysers around it like the Acid-Breathers. The Spark of Life was housed within the sacred mountain, where all three of the Draconians' oral defenses could be seen at work.

If a dragon was born without wings or malformed, they were not worthy of the Spark of Life and should be given back to the mountain. Their essence would be transmitted out into the world to be reborn again. A dragon born sickly was a curse and sent back to appease the mountain and the Sacred Fire.

Los had been such a case. Born small and vomiting, he could hold down no nourishment. His father reported him to their Chief Peandro, and he was to be sent back to the mountain as a sacrifice. Los' mother had not protected him and the small dragon had almost given into his father's wishes. However, Los' stealth camouflage talent developed during this stressful time.

When the chief sent his guard to pick up the cursed dragon, he had disappeared before their eyes. He wandered around invisible to the others, unable to reappear of his own accord. It had been a happy accident or perhaps destiny because while he wandered around on the border of the Valley trying to reappear, he happened upon a tall, imposing figure. A creature standing on two legs with magma for skin as if he had walked out of the Sacred Mountain itself. He had white hair with black tips and scars on his body but no scales.

Los had never seen anything like it. Beside the male was another smaller creature, a female. She had blue hair and scars on her face. She wore similar magma, but as Los leaned forward, he saw the rock on the female was not part of her skin the way the male's was. Her eyes didn't match— one was blue and one was white. As Los had observed the strange creatures for a short breath, the female's eyes focused on him. He froze in place. Can she see me?

The female reached out. The air around Los felt cold. The one simple act caused Los to materialize. The blue-haired creature placed her hand on his head. He was too scared to move or defend himself. Besides, what could he do? He was a defenseless dragon. Pathetic, his father had said. His mind flooded with thoughts and images, and his life flashed behind his eyelids. She pulled back, and Los knew their names. Asa and King Jarvok.

Los felt safe with them.

King Jarvok knelt down. He met the small dragon's gaze. Jarvok's eyes looked like honey, but they were sad. His smile did not reach those golden eyes. Jarvok extended his hand to Los and softly said, "Come, my friend. You have nothing to fear from me. You are not useless, nor a curse. I will give you a home. No one will sacrifice you unless you choose that for yourself."

Los took Jarvok's hand, and so it was written.

The dragon shook his head, his ear feathers rustling, ridding himself of the memories. Los had a quest to complete. He observed Aurora ending the spell. He would need no further instructions. Los snuck out and launched from the window, opening his wings, gliding on the wind, carrying the black quartz cluster on his back, as he returned to Jarvok. He flew until the sun disappeared and the moon rose. Jarvok's fortress was far from the Court of Light's palace.

The Nimbue River was a large and winding body of water separating the two kingdoms. It was crystal blue. Long, purple willowy trees decorated its banks. Los flew over the river, dipping in and out of the trees in an acrobatic dance until he saw the red glow of the fortress marking the beginning of Jarvok's territory.

Jarvok had built his fortress on the exact spot he had crashed back to Earth after his attempted return to the Shining Kingdom, hundreds of years ago, maybe even more; Jarvok had lost track of time, trying to block out that night. He used the crater he had thought would be his grave as the foundation. The land had never healed from the explosion, nor had Jarvok fully, making it the perfect spot to symbolically reclaim his life. Both he and the land bore the scars from the fateful night.

The small dragon flew into the arched observation window of the fortress' throne room.

Jarvok stood waiting. "Ah, my little Los, I knew I could count on you." The dragon presented Jarvok with the Black Quartz crystal cluster proudly. "Thank you, my friend. As always, you fulfilled your duty." Jarvok gave a nod.

Los was practically giddy, bouncing from foot to foot, hearing his praise. After he finished soaking up Jarvok's adulations, he curled up in the corner, tired from his day's work, but ever ready should Jarvok call on him.

"Rest for a few breaths, Los. I will need you to represent the Air element. You will fly for me, flapping your wings to generate a wind," Jarvok commanded.

The sleepy dragon lifted one eyelid, gathering his fortitude.

"Yanka, you will face the west wall, and when I give you the signal, breathe a thick sheet of ice over the entire height of the wall." Jarvok stared at Yanka, Asa's Ice-Breather. She was a young burgundy-colored with royal blue tribal swirls down her back. Yanka would represent Water.

The dragon turned to face the wall as she was told, looking back at Jarvok, ready to go, her ice tusks' scales alternating and curling upwards releasing small wisps of vapor.

"Inu, my Acid-Breather, you will be Earth. Face the north wall where the pile of rocks are. I need you to melt it. Spit acid when I say."

The large yellow dragon with its iridescent wings and deep blue eyes lumbered toward the wall, almost knocking the table over.

"Be careful. It's crowded in here." Jarvok spoke through his teeth with forced restraint. "Los! You are up. Face the east wall. On my word, you will create wind for me. You represent Air."

Los did as he was commanded.

"Dragor, you are my element of Fire. I have two jobs for you. Stand at the south wall and when I say, you are to melt Yanka's ice wall to give me water, and you have to hit the quartz crystal cluster to unleash the energy. I need two breaths of fire from you rather quickly. Can you do it, my friend?" Jarvok asked as he patted the large grayish-black dragon at his side.

Dragor gave him a snort and a look as if to say, *Of course. Give me a real challenge!*

Jarvok smiled. "Message received."

He grabbed his bowl of blood as Aurora had done. Making a few key adjustments, Jarvok painted the incantation symbols of concealment on himself and on the dragons. He did not want to risk the dragons not being protected in his spell. Keeping his mind clear and centered as he did it was easy. The more challenging part was finding skin that was not scarred or puckered from his burns. The left side of his body proved to be the best site.

Once complete, Jarvok was ready to conjure his own orb of power. He gave each dragon one last look to make sure they were in place and signaled them to create their element. Yanka roared, and her ice wall went up. Inu's melting process initiated. Los flew, and the wind circulated in the room. Jarvok heard the inhale and the click of Dragor's teeth, the rush of heat at his back let him know Dragor had done his job. It was his turn. Jarvok's powerful voice chanted:

"Orb of power... Orb of might... Ever stronger... Burning bright... Orb of might... Orb of power...I conjure thee this sacred hour."

He repeated the chant six times until the orb formed. It was small, not nearly the size Aurora had created, but it was present. He raised the orb above his head like she had and heaved it at his model. The sphere crashed into his kingdom and created a dome over it.

It flickered. He only had a few precious seconds to complete the invocation. He grabbed the black onyx cluster and held it over his head. "Dragor, be ready!"

The dragon took a breath. Inu was out of acid, but her royal acid had done its job. The rocks were still melting as the slick, rust-colored acid bubbled and smoked. Yanka breathed more ice into the melting water, hoping the boiling water would keep the water flowing. Poor Los was ready to pass out from flying, but he kept his wings moving.

Jarvok bellowed the last part of the spell. All his will and might poured into his words:

"Fire, transform my kingdom. Air, move my kingdom. Water, reshape my kingdom. Earth, heal my kingdom. Spirit, hide my kingdom from those who I do not wish to see. Only the blood of my blood shall reside in here. So mote it be. Death will fall on those who try to cross my kingdom's path. They will find their gruesome end but swift and fast. Only the blood of the dark will cause the reaper to miss his mark. So mote it be."

He flicked his eyes toward his Fire-Breather.

"Now, Dragor!"

Dragor's jaw plating compressed, releasing the gasses into his mouth. The click of his back teeth sounded and a steady, concentrated stream of purple fire blazed into the Black Quartz crystal cluster. The cluster heated and exploded as shards scattered and rained down, releasing Aurora's energy into the air. The glowing dome shimmered and encased the model of the kingdom. Branches of electricity pulsated through the dome as it disintegrated around the model. A blue wave of energy washed over the model. Then green energy erupted like an earthquake, shaking the model. A yellow breeze of energy followed. Lastly, red energy sizzled through the model. Each piece in the model lit up with the colors before the next wave of power came through.

"Everyone, stop," Jarvok announced, and the room fell silent. "Los, find Zion."

Zion had been outside the throne room and heard Jarvok calling for him. Los sighed and wiped his forehead in a mock gesture of relief. He didn't want to fly anywhere else.

"Success, my liege?" Zion asked.

"Take Raycor and fly outside the fortress territories. I did not create multiple doorways like she did. Our border is much smaller. The front gate is a one-way door. Fly your dragon over the main gate with your Elestial blade drawn and pointed to pierce the Veil. When you wish to return, cut yourself with your Elestial blade. With blood covering the tip of your sword, draw this symbol on parchment and throw it in the air directly in front of you." Jarvok took a piece of parchment and demonstrated what to draw. It was a long vertical line ending in an arc, and a horizontal line three-quarters of the way up with two shorter lines attached diagonally on the right and left of the horizontal line. He finished with small circles located under the horizontal lines on each side of the vertical line and at the base of the arc. "This will act as the key for you to cross back into the Veil."

Zion scanned the parchment with rapt attention, nodding in admiration of his leader's shrewdness. "Clever, my liege. You are combining glyphs, using the language of the moon. Literally translated, this means 'blood of the dark.' The Court of Light will not revert to the old language, and by now, I am sure Desdemona doesn't remember it. Nicely done."

"I am glad you approve, Lieutenant. Now go and see if my ingenuity paid off." Jarvok pointed to the door.

Zion gave a graceful bow from his waist and swiftly exited the throne room. Stepping outside the confines of the fortress, Zion was stunned. He had been standing guard for hours, yet it seemed like only minutes. Jarvok had started the spell in the dead of the night, but now it was early morning. The sky was sun-streaked with ribbons of gold, blue, and pink. The rays chased away the navy-blue tentacles of the night. The remaining stars blinked out one by one like torches extinguished by the spirit of the universe. The colors around him popped. They were more vibrant, more alive. He rubbed his eyes before he placed his Black Kyanite helmet on and called for Raycor.

A cry erupted from behind the mountain, and the white, acid-breathing dragon shot skyward. She stretched her wings, bathing herself in the morning sun's rays. The mixture of the dawn's light highlighted her lithe body. She was white with a tinge of light blue iridescence on the underside of her wings, sweeping black horns, and a small black spot on the tip of her tail indicating her age. She was young, four hundred fifty years old, and eventually the black spot would grow. By the time she was about seventeen hundred years old, she would be completely black. All dragons, no matter their oral defenses, became black between nine hundred and two thousand years old. Dragor was the exception to the rule, but then again, nothing was normal about him.

Raycor spotted Zion and dove, rolling as she sped toward him. Her eyes had amber pupils with ice blue irises. Those haunting eyes narrowed on him. Zion stood his ground. At the last minute, she pulled up her long tail, nearly grazing him in her quick upward turn. Zion laughed. "I win!" Their game of chicken had become a tradition before quests.

The dragon circled back around and snorted as she landed. She gave a graceful bow of her neck, acquiescing to Zion.

The tall Fae dramatically bowed in return. "We are tied. Four to four. Next one decides it, girl!" He hopped on her, sitting between her back spikes, and the dragon ran, jumped off the launch tower, caught a current, and glided into the morning sky.

"We have an important mission. King Jarvok may have created the Veil to protect all of us. We have been asked to test it. We must fly over the front fortress gate."

Zion drew his Elestial blade. It glowed white. He did as his king instructed, pointing the blade outward and launching himself over the main gate. As he and Raycor passed over the gate, his Elestial blade hummed with power, and the air around him shimmered and shifted. As they gained altitude, the clouds parted. He felt heat all around him, then nothing. He turned.

Behind him, the fortress was gone. He held Raycor for a moment as she hovered in the air.

"By all that is Holy, he did it," Zion mumbled, blinking rapidly. He looked around, expecting to see the fortress somewhere, but saw nothing. "Raycor, he did it!" Zion exclaimed triumphantly. "Fly, Raycor. Let us see where we are!"

Zion flew, exploring where the doorway had released them. He scanned the landscape and found the glistening of River Nimbue over the hills. They were close to their fortress. His triumph curdled quickly into confusion. "Raycor, we are just over the hill from Blood Haven. Fly toward where the River Nimbue opens from the falls. We should be able to see the fortress."

The dragon banked right and with a few short strokes of her wings, Zion saw the Niamia Waterfalls. He knew just over the falls one could see the outline of Blood Haven, yet the tall, imposing fortress was not there. Zion and Raycor flew black toward Blood Haven, but the fortress never appeared in their sights.

Not wanting to waste any more time, Zion took a gamble. Using his Elestial blade he pricked at his skin, drawing blood, he did not draw the symbol. He pointed his Elestial blade toward the horizon in another attempt to get into the human dimension. Zion concentrated on his intentions to leave the Veil, launching himself forward. His blade glowed green and the air sliced open, tearing a hole in the sky. The world shifted as the sky's wound gaped, but this time it was cold and jarring, unlike the first time.

Disorientation took hold of Raycor and Zion as they came through the portal. Spinning, the large, acid-breathing dragon unfurled her wings to their full extension to quickly regain her bearings. Zion, focusing on the horizon, found the muted colors of the human world a welcoming sight. Jarvok had made a miscalculation. His king had in fact created two Veils. He had hidden them in a deeper layer of Aurora's Veil, essentially creating two layers. Zion remained unsure of how Jarvok accomplished this.

"Well, it looks like our king was clever—perhaps a bit too clever. He hid us deeper into the Veil than we planned. I hope his method for getting back will work."

The dragon glanced over her shoulder, conveying concern. The two companions gazed down, Raycor swooping to afford Zion a better view. Humans engaged in some kind of pilgrimage. The tropical heat finally hit, helped them shake off the energy exchange from the Veil jump.

"Quickly, Raycor, take cover." He was not prepared for an appearance, and he was uncertain of their location. They landed far off in the distance.

Zion dismounted to assess the situation. "No sense in disturbing the humans, but I would like to know where we are."

Raycor took the initiative, flying away toward the ocean.

"What are you doing, Raycor?" he yelled, watching her disappear.

Zion waited for her return, tapping his middle finger at the place on his helmet where his Angelite disc would have been. It was a bad habit he had gotten into all those long years ago. Commander Michael had hated when he tapped on his disc. He remembered having to clean boots for a week once when he had pissed him off for not stopping when asked.

The dragon reappeared with a carcass her mouth. She had not killed it. The animal had been dead for at least a few days based on its rancid scent. Raycor landed and dropped the remains for Zion to examine.

The Acid-Breather had been careful to hold the animal in its front teeth and not allow her acid bite to disturb the remains. It was pear-shaped and about the size of his forearm with black markings on its head and white on its stomach. The beak indicated it was a bird. The bird's belly was bloated. One leg was missing but the other one had a webbed foot. This had been a penguin. Given the temperature, he knew only one area in which penguins were indigenous to warmer climates. With this vital piece of information, he was able to recognize the large group of humans, the Bantu people.

Many of the adults were tall and muscular with dark skin. They decorated themselves with beading. As a society their elders were highly revered. They had been spreading their culture all over the continent, sometimes peacefully, sometimes not so much. Many villages had been assimilated into their tribe but if necessary, they forcefully took what was needed. Their weapons were superior to many of the tribes they came in contact with. They worshiped nature and their ancestors.

This area was part of Azrael and Pria's dominion. Zion was not familiar enough with the Bantu people and their culture or the full scope of their beliefs. It was best not to interact.

It was time to head home. He nodded at Raycor. "Nice work, my friend. Now we have to try the doorway and go home." He mounted the Acid-Breather.

Zion unsheathed his Elestial blade and cut his left forearm, drawing a line of blue liquid. Making sure the tip of his blade had blood on it, he visualized the symbol from the parchment. Raycor found a ledge to take off from, looking back at her rider and waiting for the go-ahead to jump. Zion nodded to his dragon and she took the leap. As the two climbed higher into the heat of the midday sun, Zion created the moon glyph on the parchment.

As he completed the last piece, his blade lit the symbol in a soft glow. Zion took it as a sign to toss the paper. The parchment hung in the air for a second, sizzling as if branding the oxygen around it. The edges of the paper dissolved as the symbol enlarged, becoming a bright blue sparkle of lights. Raycor flew directly into the symbol. It swallowed her and Zion, collapsing in on itself once the mighty dragon passed through.

The quiet of the Veil met Zion, and he looked at the fortress and the tall molten rock towers below. The symbol had taken them directly back to the fortress. He vaulted off Raycor in his usual fashion, landing in the sparring courts and interrupting a few Weepers who were practicing. Zion paid them no mind and raced up to let Jarvok know of his journey.

Zion strode into the throne room where the Council of the High Guard waited for him as well. Their unyielding gazes fell upon him. Yagora looked unimpressed, but she always did. Pria appeared more inquisitive, while Ezekiel, Johan, and Azrael were stone-faced. Asa stood beside Jarvok, unreadable, although he caught the subtle note of her shoulders relaxing, maybe a sign of relief at Zion's initial presence.

"My liege," he said, bowing to his king first and showing respect to the members of the High Guard second.

Jarvok remained standing while the council members all nodded. "Lieutenant, what say you?" Jarvok's eyes narrowed.

"My liege, you have created a Veil within a Veil," Zion blurted out.

The Council of the High Guard looked ready to celebrate but suddenly stopped, confused by the news.

"Explain, Zion." Jarvok's voice was curt.

"It seems the doorway over the gate takes you into the Veil Aurora created. Using the same mechanism of our blood and the Elestial blade to pierce the sky, the second doorway takes you into the human world. Upon return, the glyph takes you back to your Veil, essentially skipping the Veil in between." Zion remained silent, letting his words seep in.

"I am confused." Yagora grimaced, most likely because she had to admit she was perplexed. However, as Zion scanned the table, many of the council members had a slack expression gracing their faces. Jarvok pulled at the hairs on the back of his neck, his nostrils flaring. Either he was upset they were confused, or he did not know how to explain it to them. If Zion did not intervene this would not go well.

"The best way I can describe this Veil is that it is essentially two doorways. One takes us to the first layer just beyond our border. The second takes us to the human world. It is a bubble within a bubble. When you exit the first one, the doorway opens up to the River Nimbue.

Using your blade, you can pierce the Veil to enter the humans' world from there. That doorway is stronger. It needs more energy. The first door is like a curtain and the second is like a drawbridge spanning a moat."

Out of ideas on how else to describe the Veil, he glanced at his king, who gave him a slight curl of his lips. Asa tried to hide her growing smile at him. The council all muttered to one another, indicating they were satisfied with Zion's lesson.

Clearing his throat, Azrael broke the tension with his inquiry. "Where in the human world did you end up?"

Zion looked at Jarvok, brows pulling in, asking permission to share the information. "It is a pertinent question, Lieutenant Zion," Jarvok prodded, granting him permission to answer Azrael.

Zion turned to address the council. He stood tall, hands behind his back, chest out, and shoulders squared. "I was in your and Pria's territory, Azrael. I witnessed the Bantu during their migration, but I did not engage." Azrael tilted his head as he exchanged a look with Pria. Leaning forward, placing her elbows on the table, Pria settled her chin on her folded fingers.

Her aqua lashes could not conceal the suspicion or disapproval flashing in her deep-set eyes. "So you were in the eastern sector of my territories?"

"Yes, where the flightless, black-and-white waterbirds reside."

"But you did not engage with our humans correct, Lieutenant Zion?" Pria's eyes narrowed, and she tilted her head slightly, awaiting his response.

"No, Pria. I did not. They are not my subjects. My cults are big enough, thank you. I am not looking for any more human subjects. I do not poach."

Pria gave Zion a condescending smirk in response. Her reputation for trying to poach other's smaller cults had made her paranoid.

Zion normally loved to play into it, but now was not the time as he observed Jarvok.

Unconcerned with the growing tension between Zion and Pria. Jarvok paced, rubbing his chin. "But you were able to return with no issues or complications? The glyph worked?" Jarvok asked.

"Yes, my liege, the glyph worked perfectly."

Asa perked up. "My liege? If I may shed some light on this?" Her voice shook.

Jarvok extended his hand for her to continue. Asa stepped forward. The Council of the High Guard looked on, a few more interested than others in what she might say.

"I believe the answer is in the incantation wording. Your intention was that we be hidden from those who can see. There is a chance Aurora's Oracle could see us, due to the nature of our individual Oracles and their metaphysical ties. Thus, the spell hid us in another layer of the Veil."

Jarvok raised his palm to cup his chin, his long index finger tapping at the tip of his nose, eyes fixed on the ceiling. He moved his hand away from his mouth and made a fist, pacing once again. "I see your point regarding the wording of the spell. Very astute, Lieutenant Asa. Do you have any suggestions on how we can control our exit points from the second layer of the Veil?"

Standing tall, hands behind her back, Asa tilted her chin upward. "If we used moon glyphs in the cardinal directions when we exit the Veil, one could direct where one wanted to go."

Lifting his heels and the balls of his feet a few times, Jarvok balanced with his hands behind his back. "Use the elemental symbols and their corresponding directions to guide us? Interesting. We will try that. Is there anything else you would like to add, my third-in-command?" A fleeting gleam crossed his eyes as he looked upon Asa.

"I believe the dragons should have a vial of their rider's blood on their necks along with the symbol to reenter the Veil in case they are ever separated. We need to ensure the dragons can return to the Veil from the human side. They seem to have no issues roaming this side of the Veil. However, they will need blood to come home from the human side. If the symbol is drawn on the underside of the vial cap with the Elestial blade, the dragon would have to mix the blood and the symbol to activate the doorway." Asa swallowed, hoping she had not overstepped her boundaries. A pinched expression crossed Pria's face after listening to Asa.

"But should the vial fall into the Court of Light they will have a way in," Pria argued, as Jarvok gave a momentary look, weighing Pria's logic.

Pria seized the opportunity. She shot up and inched her way closer to her king, continuing to plead her case.

The High Council Guard observed in silence. Their lack of eye contact with Asa gave the impression they were supporting Pria. Zion glanced at Asa, as if to throw his endorsement to her. "What if we brand the dragons with the symbol? If it is small enough, the Court of Light won't see it, and we will not risk the dragons losing the key." Pria crossed her arms at her chest and gave Asa a crooked smile.

"But it will hurt the dragons and they still need our blood," Asa retorted. Pria rolled her eyes and huffed.

"The vial holds the blood. The top has the symbol on the inside. We can give the dragons only enough to use it once. They will shake the vial to activate the spell and throw the vial in the air. This will open the doorway. The incantation burns up the blood. There is nothing left over." Asa folded her arms, mimicking Pria's smug pose. "It will be for dire circumstances, anyway."

Pria's fists tightened, her knuckles turning white. She flared her nostrils and sneered. Asa dropped into a defensive stance as Pria stalked two paces toward her.

"Enough!" Jarvok extended his arms, keeping both Powers separated. "Pria, stand down!"

Her eyes fixed on the blue-haired opponent before her, her breath ragged.

"Pria, I said, stand down."

She blinked and glanced at Jarvok. "Yes, my liege." She gave Asa one last look before taking her seat.

Jarvok watched her before he returned his attention to his third lieutenant. "Asa, I leave it up to you and Zion to make sure each dragon has a vial. Once it is done, I want the entire council taken out into the human world to make sure they know how to get in and out of the Veil."

Asa and Zion bowed.

"Pria and Azrael, see to it your Bantu people are still worshiping nature. We cannot afford to lose any power bases. I have plans for us and I need all of you to be ready. Dismissed."

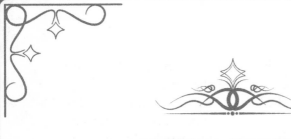

TWENTY-SIX:
WORSHIP EQUALS POWER

J arvok watched from the throne room as Zion took the Weepers through spear patterns and self-defense. Jarvok tried to keep the Weepers on a strict routine and training schedule. He had found this worked best for their emotional and mental stability. Adjusting to the Abandonment had not been as easy for the Weepers as it had for others. They required the regimented lifestyle, the hive mentality that the Power Brigade provided.

Jarvok remained hopeful these Powers would acclimate to their new lives and fall into rank. He set up training exercises to keep the soldiers busy and put Zion and Asa in charge. All this had helped, but they compulsively picked at their Angelite disc scars, causing them to reopen and bleed. The blood ran down their forehead and past their eyes, giving the illusion of "crying," thus the nickname the Weepers. He was rethinking the name as he watched from above. Perhaps they needed a distraction, or he wasn't utilizing their talents properly.

Jarvok called for his smaller dragon. Los was ninety-five years old, a young dragon. His ability to camouflage, much like a chameleon, was growing stronger, and he could control it longer as he aged. While many dragons didn't develop their oral defenses until they were one hundred years old, they passed certain developmental milestones at eighty-five, ninety, and ninety-five to indicate they were developing properly. Fire-Breathers were the exception, developing much earlier than any other dragon. If Los planned to develop any oral defense, like acid or ice, Jarvok believed he would have demonstrated some indication.

Los had his growth spurt in the spring and was roughly the size of a juvenile red wolf. He wouldn't grow much bigger. Therefore, he often stayed close to Jarvok and Dragor. Acting as Jarvok's gofer, Los was loyal and dependable. He delivered messages throughout the stronghold, and with his camouflage abilities, he was invaluable for reconnaissance.

The amber dragon flew up to the observation window. Hovering with an occasional wing flap, he patiently dangled in the air, awaiting Jarvok's request.

"Los, bring Zion to me."

Los chirped, then flew toward the combat courtyard.

The cool breeze moved Zion's dark ponytail, and he took it as a signal to don his helmet. Jarvok's second-in-command stood, armed with a wooden Bo staff. Fifteen Weepers encircled him. They all had sharpened spears pointed at him.

Zion surveyed the circle and smirked. He lived for the fight, relishing a challenge. "Come and get it, guys."

The Weepers collapsed on him. Zion jumped over the first few. Landing without as much as a thump or a cloud of dust, he quickly backflipped, kicking a charging Weeper in the chin on his way over. The crunch of his foot connecting with the Weeper's jaw fueled his excitement. He gained his footing and used his staff to sweep the legs of two more Weepers who converged on him. Three more Weepers stabbed at Zion. He dodged and parried their spears, using their momentum to throw them off balance. He thrust a front kick into one of them, which knocked the other two down, clearing his path. He side-kicked another. Holding the end of the staff, he jumped and spun his staff around, hitting the remaining Weepers. In two minutes, fifteen Weepers lay on the ground, nursing their wounds.

He tilted his chin and spun his staff behind his back in a flashy move before slapping it on the ground. The crack of the wood acting as a victory cry, Zion removed his helmet and handed his weapon to a nearby arsenal keeper. They nodded in appreciation as Zion stepped over the groaning Weepers at his feet.

Los waited outside the training circle for Zion to finish. The small dragon flew to keep pace with the tall Power as he marched along, toweling off after his training victory.

"Yes, Los?" Zion's eyes focused on the other training sets as they walked past, tightening his lips at the sloppiness of the exercises. "It's a thrust and then a parry," he yelled as he mimicked the movement. "Sorry for the interruption, Los."

Los motioned toward the observation window of the throne room. Zion stopped to look at his direction. "Oh, King Jarvok wants to meet with me? Of course, Los, I'll be right up. Thank you." The dragon snorted and flew back toward the tower.

Zion knocked and entered the throne room. To call it a throne room was incorrect. It was more of a strategy room. A map of the Court of Light and its fortress, along with the newly erected human villages, sat in the center of a large table. Adjacent to the table was an impressive weapons wall boasting each type of weapon Jarvok was proficient at wielding. There was a large chair carved from the molten rock of the crater Jarvok had made when he crashed back to Earth the night he attempted to return to the gates of the Shining Kingdom. It was grey with a rough texture. The cooled magma still had drip marks down the side. It was unfinished, inelegant, and not at all graceful but symbolic, forged in fire and strong as hell. It was the perfect throne for Jarvok.

His king stood at the observation window, his partially bare right arm with its fused Black Kyanite gauntlet burned into his wrist behind his back. Zion knew the stance all too well. His king's contemplation posture. Jarvok was developing a plan.

"My liege," Zion announced himself.

Jarvok gave a quick glance over his shoulder. "I have a mission for you." His voice was flat. It usually was when a quest was involved.

He closed the heavy, black tourmaline double doors behind him. Striding over quickly to his king, Zion stood shoulder-to-shoulder with Jarvok, eagerly awaiting his commands.

"I had asked Los to gather information on the human worshipers, regarding their rituals with the Court of Light. They are planning a rain ceremony for their crops. They want a blessing from their storm god or rain-bringer. They call him Aded, better known as Arceria of the Dinay Mera clan. He is a low-level lord and has basic elemental Water play."

Jarvok left the window and walked around the map, stopping and moving a few pieces around. He picked up a small, clear, quartz-shaped crown figurine. Jarvok rolled it between his fingers as he stared at the map. "I want you to send a few Weepers to kill Aded. Let the humans see us kill one of their so-called gods."

"I don't follow, my liege." Zion met Jarvok's eyes and a cold chill ran up Zion's back as if an Ice-Breather was standing behind him.

His king closed his fingers around the quartz crown. It was a silent break, and a second later, the dust spilled from his palm as he slowly opened his hand. Zion swallowed as Jarvok closed the distance between them.

"It's simple. I'm looking to provoke Aurora. I no longer wish to share or act as though we do not exist. I tire of the games the Court of Light is playing."

"Games? My liege?" Zion's hand was at the back of his neck, no longer able to contain his confusion.

"While we may not have made as many appearances to the humans as the Court of Light, Aurora cannot possibly believe the stories of monsters and dark gods the humans tell are all made up to act as the balance to their loving light gods. If she does, then she is even more naive than I thought, and that's even more reason to act now. I will make her an offer. Aurora can surrender her kingdom and stop allowing the humans to worship the Court of Light. If she does, I will let them live in their little palace under her, or she can meet me on the battlefield and face certain Oblivion. Either way I win. The less Court of Light for humans to worship, more power for us. I will not share our power base any longer. Take a platoon of Weepers and go. Chaos be with you."

Zion paused, his mouth abruptly closed as he tilted his head, trying to make his reflex response of "Yes, my liege" fit his king's unusual exiting commentary. His sapphire-blue eyes lifted to the magma ceiling. The irregular cones and points suspended above held no answer to his riddle. The word "chaos" ran through his brain, like Los hopped up on sugar plum wine. It flickered and bounced.

He straightened his spine and faced his king. He conceded his king knew best. "Yes, my liege. I shall be a creature of chaos raining destruction upon Arceria."

Los stopped scratching his ears upon hearing Zion's retort and wrinkled his nose. He folded his wings around himself and hunkered down. Jarvok observed the small dragon's reaction, a grin ghosting for a brief second before his honey eyes melted into a pool of frustration. "No, Zion, I did not ask you to be a creature of chaos."

Zion's posture slumped. "I do not understand."

Jarvok leaned over the maps, staring at the figures and territories. He glanced up at Zion then returned his gaze to the map. "No I suppose you do not."

Zion joined him, scrutinizing what lay before them. Jarvok returned his attention to his second-in-command.

"To be a creature of chaos is to be used by the energy of disorder, to be a tool of it. You are allowing confusion to lead you. I want more for us. We will take control of the pandemonium. Those who control chaos control their destiny. Do not let it lead you like a pet on a leash."

He turned and walked to the window, hands behind his back. "Now go, and Chaos be with you, Zion." Zion smirked. His blue eyes glowed with comprehension as his shoulders pulled back. "No, my liege. Chaos be with us." He turned and ran with a renewed vigor for his mission.

Jarvok briefly curled his lip as he gazed out the window at Zion's enthusiasm, but his stoic expression returned. He waited for the bang of the heavy doors to exhale. His shoulders slumped as the weight of his rule took him under. He leaned his hands on the window, the magma crumbling and sliding from his palms as the pressure caused small fissures to appear in the sill. His head hung low, his hair falling to his face as he raised his honey eyes, looking out over the training yard. They would need to train every day and even do night formations. No rest.

The scent of cedar and sage wafted up from the bonfires below. He knew his plan to attack was sound but his timeline was of concern. If Aurora continued to gather and unify her human worshippers, she could have the magick to overtake his kin and force them into serving the Virtues as their army. The thought of his kin living a life of servitude caused Jarvok to force the acid back down his throat. No, he would not risk anyone gaining the upper hand over him. He had hidden his kin in his Veil, established them as gods to the humans, and formed an alliance with the Draconians. He would not force the Draconians to fight alongside him against Aurora but if they chose to stand with him he would accept their help.

He had been strategic in observing her, watching and waiting. She was a naive, idealistic, egotistical ruler with no battle experience. An almost certain victory. By making an example out of Aded, the humans would fear his kin and as Jarvok had learned, it was better to be feared than loved. One just needed to ask his Creator.

TWENTY-SEVEN:
Even A God Bleeds

The large, monolithic stone formations seemed imposing to Zion as he passed over them. Almost imposing. Each large blue stone stood approximately thirty feet tall. The humans thought their circular design afforded them some sort of sacred protection.

How trivial. These humans do not understand energies or magick.

Making a circle with large blue stones and deeming it sacred did not make it so. Had the Court of Light given them this false bravado? If they had, it was about to crumble.

The center of the circle housed a wooden altar surrounded by smaller pieces of timber arranged in a half circle. The humans had neat piles of tools. Each stack was organized by function: digging, cutting, and weapons respectively, over a mile away from this site which meant it was still undergoing modifications. A six-foot trench bordered the entire circle.

The trench's function was unknown to Zion. This was a new addition to the structure since his last visit. He traced the trench with his eyes. It began at the right of the two gigantic welcoming stones one passed through to enter the circle. Zion had walked through it as their serpentine god. They had sacrificed many animals in his name, and the rocks still bore the red stain of his offerings' blood.

Zion could still feel the rush of the first night he appeared to these humans. He had arrived in a blue blaze of fire, using his Elestial blade to harness the power of plasma in lightning to strike down a wooden mock-up of the structure he now gazed upon. It was to the west of where this one stood.

His white dragon, Raycor, had been a striking sight against the night sky. She had broken the peaceful tranquility of the summer's darkness with her battle cry as she unfolded her large iridescent wings, so bright they matched the full moon. For a brief moment, her sheer size blocked out the celestial ruler of the night's bright beams. She hovered, letting the humans take in her magnificence. He loved his dragon. She had a flair for the dramatic nearly as much as he did. He gave a wry smile at the particular memory.

On his command, she dove as if she were going to crash into the sea of humans, then pulling up at the last moment, she opened her large jaws. Her black forked tongue lifted and her telescopic fistula aimed to unleash her poison. A stream of rust-colored, noxious liquid known as Aqua Regia acid spewed from her mouth. It was a sight these humans had never seen, a true acid-breathing dragon. Her potent concoction melted the large stones waiting for placement. With this display of awesome power, the humans had fallen to their knees declaring Zion, Dracontia—"serpent god who eats the sun."

He dismounted Raycor, stroking her neck for a job well done. Speaking in the human's native tongue, he informed them he was indeed their God, Dracontia. Zion had felt the power rush as he had many times before with each new coven of humans he collected. He unsheathed his Elestial blade. It had grown three-fold. He raised it skyward, and lightning charged into the Auric weapon. Zion smiled. Yes, they had feared him and more power was his, just as his king had promised.

Zion had given his demands for tribute and warned if he was not happy, he would be a vengeful god. The humans had shuddered as he mounted Raycor and launched skyward. Zion returned every three months or when they summoned him for help. He did take care of his followers. If there was a plague or bad luck of some kind, he returned to help impart judgment and punishment, which usually consisted of death.

Staring at the circle of stones, a stroke of genius hit Zion. Instead of killing the accused as he normally did, he would enact a new form of punishment. He would incinerate the offender and spread their remains outside the circle, confining their spirit to forever walk outside the circle. Never to walk inside the hallowed ground for all of eternity. Their job would be to protect it from anyone who might want to enter it for nefarious reasons. Once they had served their time, maybe they might be allowed into the afterlife.

That's how you make a circle sacred, not by digging a trench. Yes, it is perfect!

He would introduce his plan after today. Policy changes had to wait, for now he was there to remind them who their god truly was.

He gave the Weeper Platoon the order to land and immediately found a surveillance position in a cover of woods far enough away for them to keep watch but not be detected.

Miles away from Zion's observation camp, the humans arrived. The humans chose a site that had representations of the elements—the river, the mounds of earth, and the firepits. The winds were known to whip through the area. One after another, they pulled their rafts up from the river to begin the long pilgrimage to the consecrated site, unaware of what awaited them. They marched in a long, single-file procession.

Large stones lined their path toward their revered gathering place. Each stone represented a sun Dracontia had eaten. Each day his priests had a group of worshippers whose sole job was to find the largest rocks to place for the passing day. They inscribed the number of times Dracontia had "eaten the sun" on the rock and worked to place the stone as a tribute for their god. Some days he would send a small dragon to help them when they had made him especially proud with an offering of great size.

Today was not about Dracontia. They were there to pay homage to their rain god, Aded. They needed him to give rain for bountiful crops for the harvest season. The young virgin they intended to offer him was dressed as Aded liked her in a long, flowing, cream-colored dress and a cloak covering her body and face. Pastel-hued wildflowers adorned her wavy raven hair, peeking out from her cloak. She was Aded's if he approved of her. She would be his and his alone from this day on. She would offer her womanhood to him. If he was satisfied, he would grant them a good harvest, and she would become a soothsayer in his coven. Aded only spoke to the tribe through females. He decided on them, and it was an exalted position within the tribe.

The young girl remained silent, praying she would be enough as four men carried her on a chair decorated with fragrant flowers.

From a copse of trees, Zion watched along with his Weepers. An elder woman dressed in a long, grey tunic and carrying a gnarled walking staff taller than her shuffled to the two large welcoming stones. She dropped to her knees and pulled herbs from a suede pouch on her hip. She mumbled to herself and raised her hands skyward before using the staff to pull herself up and hobble into the circle.

"She is the head priestess of his coven," Zion said, looking back at the Weepers. Their bodies were coiled and ready to strike. He felt their anticipation.

"Can we kill her?" one of them asked.

Zion briefly mulled over the question. He knew there would be a few human casualties, but since Arceria—Aded—had a female-led coven, he wasn't sure what kind of impact female casualties would have on humans. With Powers, gender was a moot point. Male or female, power knew no gender. In the end, Oblivion was Oblivion regardless of gender.

Everyone bled and everyone died.

"After we kill Aded, see who fights back. If they fight, kill them. If not, leave them alone." It was a diplomatic answer. If a woman drew a sword against them, she deserved a warrior's death.

The humans filed into the circle, their loud chanting filling the large area. They carried the young woman to the center, and the crowd parted as the head priestess came to inspect who might be the newest addition to their ranks. The men set the chair down in the center of the timber horseshoe shape. The people settled down. The time for socializing was finished. It was now all about the pageantry. The priestess used her staff to sprinkle some kind of water to bless the young girl. Dragging her feet around the girl, using her walking staff for balance, she chanted and asked Aded to find their offering acceptable.

"Do you come here of your own free will?" the priestess directly addressed the girl.

"I do." There was no hesitation in her voice.

"Do you swear to serve our rain god Aded until the next life? Forsaking all others, should he deem you worthy?" The priestess inspected the girl as if looking for any signs of doubt.

"I will." Her voice was steady, calm.

"If he does not find you worthy, or you have laid with another man and are not of true virtue, will you allow yourself to be sacrificed as tribute?" The priestess eyed her suspiciously.

"I will." The girl's unfaltering, corn-flower-blue eyes met the priestess's gaze.

The priestess turned to the crowd. "The offering has passed the first test. I will summon Aded."

The mass of people erupted jubilantly.

Four women appeared, dressed in colored tunics of the cardinal directions. Each woman took their place in the stone circle to indicate one of the four directions.

The woman in the green tunic walked toward the north of the altar, carrying a handful of soil. "I represent the Earth." Her voice reverberated against the stones.

The woman in a pale-blue tunic stepped toward the left of the other woman, approximately twenty-five feet apart from each other. She carried a clay pot of water. "I represent Water."

The woman in the red tunic moved to the south of the altar, perfectly spaced, carrying a torch. Taking her place, she lit the torch. "I represent Fire."

The final woman dressed in a soft yellow tunic took the last spot. She held nothing. She spread her arms out wide and turned her face skyward. "I represent Air."

The four women surrounded the offering. The high priestess led the four women into a chant. "Guardians of the elements, we summon thee. Guard our circle and the magic herein."

The crowd responded, "So mote it be."

Zion rolled his eyes. All this pomp and circumstance the Court of Light had taught these humans was so unnecessary. His followers sacrificed something in his name and called him. His kin were so much more efficient than their counterparts.

The priestess swayed and moaned. The other women soon followed her lead. "Aded, our rain god. We beg of you to hear our plea. We call to you in this hour of need. Your offering awaits you. We summon you, so mote it be."

The crowd joined the women in the chant. Before long, the entire stone structure was echoing in the chant.

The chanting droned on for what seemed like an eternity, when suddenly the torch of the woman in red went out in a quick whoosh. The crowd fell silent at the swift development. The ground shook, and the river they had traveled upon swelled. The river was miles away, but the water came up to the welcoming rocks of the stone circle, flooding the trench.

In the distance, a figure emerged from the direction of the river. He was tall with broad shoulders, dressed in a simple white shirt and dark pants. He looked as if he had come from a fishing boat. His damp hair, grey—not from age—was the color of storm clouds and trailed to his shoulders in waves. Even from a distance, his eye color was visible, a striking blue as if the brightest summer sky had been lit with Laborite crystals. His every step echoed with thunder.

Zion chuckled. He had seen this creature on his reconnaissance missions. The form marching toward them was not Aded. No. Aded was short, and one of the few, blue-skinned members of the Dinay Mera faction of Fae. "Interesting, the Court of Light changes their appearance when they meet their human worshipers." Zion always presented in all his true glory to his worshippers. Jarvok will find this information most useful. Zion was even more intrigued with the show.

Aded stopped at the welcoming stones. "I am Aded, God of Rain. I have heard your plea for help." The entire crowd dropped to their knees bowing. The priestess made her way to the front of the pack. "Thank you, Aded. We are your humble servants. Please enter our sacred circle." Stepping aside, she bowed her head.

Aded glared at her. "Never forget...I do not need your permission, Priestess Ursula."

The priestess looked up from under her brows at him, his reprimand slapping her. "Forgive me, Aded. I meant no disrespect."

He extended his hand, helping her to her feet. "It is forgotten. Show me my offering." He gave her hand a slight squeeze to reassure her and kissed each cheek. Zion noticed how Aded said the human's mistake may have been forgotten, yes, but not forgiven. He filed the information in the back of his head. In a few minutes, it would not matter. Their rain god would be nothing more than a puddle.

TWENTY-EIGHT:
WHEN THE RIVER TURNS RED

CIRCA 1350 B.C.

Aded entered the blessed stone circle. The silent crowd watched the tall figure take his time. Aded surveyed the eyes staring back at him. Aded stopped, and his focus briefly lingered in Zion's direction.

Zion grew still.

Does he sense me? Even with the cloaking spell Jarvok and Asa wove? Aded only paused and continued toward his offering.

Zion exhaled in relief.

Aded circled the young girl. He did not approach her, keeping a respectable distance at first. His stride was slow and calculated. He looked like a great white shark toying with his prey before its first tasting bite. Aded moved in and slipped her cloak from her head to reveal her raven hair and cornflower-blue eyes to the fading light. He grinned in approval. She did not meet his eyes, her lips trembling.

He gently took his fingers and tipped her chin to meet his gaze. "Be not afraid. I am pleased with you." His voice was a primal growl. It transcended across male species when they sought to possess a beautiful woman.

The young girl smiled, the faintest glimmer of relief crossing her face.

"What is your name?"

"Disa, my god." Her voice a small whisper compared to before.

He leaned in, kissing her on each cheek and on her forehead. It was soft and chaste. Disa inhaled the damp, clean smell of fresh rain as it enveloped her. Zion gave the signal to his Weepers. Aded was distracted. Now was the time to strike. They moved stealthily through the trees, easily leaping over the trench.

Aded stiffened as if feeling the crackle of power in the air. Zion was too close. The cloaking spell was no longer effective. Zion launched into the center of the circle, splintering the wooden altar beneath his feet. Aded jumped away from the Power. The crowd gasped at their night god Dracontia's unexpected arrival.

"What is the meaning of this?" Aded yelled at Zion in their language, not bothering to involve the humans who were now dumbfounded by the two gods and their strange exchange.

"Aded?" Zion's sarcasm seeking to goad the other. "You look so different, but I guess even a god must dress up every now and then. Little do your worshippers know you are the size of a berry shrub and blue." Zion smirked at the insult of Aded's true form.

"However, don't worry. I will take care of them after you leave," Zion promised. He unsheathed his Elestial blade to emphasize his point.

"I am not going anywhere, Power." Disdain dripped from Aded's words.

"Oh, but you are. There aren't enough humans for all of us to share. You need to meet your Oblivion." Zion pointed his blade at the Court of Light Fae and readied for battle.

The Weepers closed in on the circle.

Disa's mouth contorted into a scream as the god she was given to faced off against another. She had sworn her allegiance to Aded only a few short heartbeats ago. Her cornflower-blue eyes flashed anger as her rage bubbled to the surface. Picking up the sacrificial knife she carried in case she was deemed unworthy by Aded, she lunged at the other god Dracontia.

Seeing the human girl brandishing a weapon, the Weepers took this as an act of war. The soldiers descended upon the circle, killing any human who crossed their path. Blood splattered the blue stones. Men, women, and children were all their prey.

Zion turned as the small human girl attempted to stab him. He struck Disa down, decapitating her with ease. He had extinguished the light and fire behind Disa's eyes. Her empty eyes stared up lifelessly at Aded. The Light Fae cried out as the river swelled and flooded the circle. The water mixed with ribbons of red as the Weepers made victims of the humans. The river became a crimson pool from their blood.

The Weepers fought ankle-deep in red water, undeterred by the floating viscera and the mass hysteria.

Zion and Aded met god to god. Aded picked up Disa's blade, twirling it in his hand but he was no match for Jarvok's second-in-command. He charged Zion, lunging and slashing at the trained warrior. Zion avoided Aded's sloppy fighting before elbowing him in his back, sending him into the blood-stained water. He drove his Black Kyanite armored boot into the Fae's side. The crack of his ribs splintering under Zion's force was audible even in the chaos. The kick flipped Aded onto his back, exposing his chest, giving Zion the perfect kill shot. Aded pleaded with his eyes, too weak to say anything else or perhaps too proud to beg for his life to a lowly Power Brigade Angel.

Zion locked eyes with the horrified high priestess of his followers. He smiled as he drove his glowing white Elestial blade into her rain god's heart. So confident in his kill, he didn't even glance down at his opponent. He relished the faith draining from her wrinkled face and true fear setting in. He gave the blade a final twist and listened for the sickening crunch and the wet pop as his blade reached the other side of the broken body.

He gave the old woman a wink as she shrieked.

Looking at the water, she tried to run away from the cloud of blood insidiously creeping toward her. Their god's blue blood mixed with the red-stained liquid, creating a purple hue. She cried and tripped over a body. Zion sensed her fear as she cursed his god name, which fueled him more.

He glanced at the body as it returned to its true form. Zion pulled the chain from his neck. As he relayed the chant Asa had given him, Aded's body eviscerated.

Satisfied with his kill and no longer sidetracked by his mission, Zion gave the command for his Weepers to retreat. The humans' deafening screams dissipated. He no longer felt the charge of their worshipping fear. During his tussle with Aded, the Weepers had gone on a rampage, killing everyone.

Zion stood in stupefied silence, scanning the stones. The megalithic structures that had been so neatly arranged and precise now crumbled like ancient ruins. He leaned on one of the cool blue stones, taking in the sight laid out before him.

Over five hundred humans slaughtered, all in a matter of minutes. He was horrified to see their bodies strewn over the rock formations and timber placeholders. Everywhere he looked there were bodies or remains. Burgundy-splattered rocks surrounded him and red water lapped at his ankles. He waded through the water, moving the remains to clear his path. Death was everywhere.

How did this happen?

He closed his eyes and the image of the priestess's leathery face flashed in his mind. Moments ago he was reveling in her terror, bathing in her revulsion. Now he wanted to heave. The wailing of his Weepers brought him out of his thoughts. In the distance, his Weepers celebrated their victory, smearing each other in the humans' blood. They weren't tired from battle but energized. They were still tormenting the bodies and enjoying it.

This is not normal. The Weepers have never been normal... But this? It is not how my brethren behave. The humans were no real threat.

He watched them suck the marrow from the bones of the dead. He flinched at the slurping. The vomit rose in his throat as they licked their lips of the humans' blood. Powers were dignified soldiers, not barbarians. Their mission was to kill Aded, not wipe out an entire human village.

He stared at the pile of bodies, even small humans. He bowed his head, holding and shaking it. The Weepers had not discriminated. He had given them the direct order—unless a human picked up a blade, they were not to engage them. Except for the girl, whom he had killed, Zion had not noticed anyone else pick up a blade.

Why had they not listened to him? Had they followed his lead? Perhaps he'd incited them. Had he been so lost in his own thirst for blood he did not see what was happening? Had he become a creature of Chaos and let it control him instead of the other way around? Was this what Jarvok was talking about? Was he too busy enjoying the kill? Was he too damaged? Perhaps he was beyond repair, and this was his future. He looked at the Weepers wearing the entrails of a human as hair.

No. No. He pulled himself back from the edge.

He had been commanded to kill Arceria, and he had. He was not like the Weepers and they were not completely lost either. They were not demons. If he truly believed they were, he might as well march himself and the Weepers up to Lucifer's gates and bang on them until they let them all in because there would be no redemption for any of them.

Zion removed his helmet and ran his hand through his hair. He was efficient if nothing else. He had assisted Jarvok in starting a war with the Court of Light and decimated one of their power bases. The Weeper army might be losing their minds or perhaps they were already lost, and Zion was the only one who knew it. "I think I have a serious problem."

TWENTY-NINE:
DON'T KILL THE MESSENGER

I t took Zion longer than planned to pull the Weepers from the human remains. They were enjoying feasting on the blood and marrow too much. Only when there was nothing left that they could lick, eat, or suck dry could he gain their attention. Once their gory feast was finished, they fell right back in line like nothing had happened. A slow, insidious injection of ice crept through his veins as he watched how easily they returned to their "normal" selves.

The Weepers followed Zion onto the large Hematite drawbridge to the fortress they called home. One by one in a single-file line, they marched into the confines of the fortress, taking orders without question.

Another group of Weepers was going through battle formations with Asa as they entered. The empathic Power stared at Zion's group and shivered. Zion met her eyes and glanced away quickly. Zion directed his small group to their armory shed to surrender their weapons and fall into formation routines.

Los waited for Zion, along with a captain, to assist him with his armor and escort the lieutenant to Jarvok for a briefing. The small dragon quietly flew beside him as he stripped off his helmet and gauntlets. He handed them to the armory captain for cleaning.

"I take it King Jarvok is waiting for me, Los?" Zion's voice was steady.

The dragon grunted a few times, then sped ahead of him in urgency. His ears flicked as if listening for Zion's footsteps.

"If you only knew what I had to tell him, you would not move so fast, my little friend," he whispered.

Jarvok stood in his usual place at the large, arched window overlooking the combat circles. His hands clasped behind his back, and he stood strong yet graceful. The sun was setting on this side of the world. The orange and red streaks made it look like the sky bled—fitting for the day. Zion entered the throne room.

Jarvok did not take his eyes off the blood-strewn sky. "Well, Zion? Mission accomplished?" His deep husky voice held a touch of agitation, most likely due to his lieutenant's tardiness.

"Yes, my liege. Lord Arceria, known as Aded, is dead."

King Jarvok turned and faced Zion, his eyes raking his lieutenant. "Is that all?" His tone was suspicious.

"No, my liege. We had some issues," Zion said, unsure of how to explain what had just happened.

"Issues? Did another Fae interfere?" He smirked. "Was Lord Arceria too much for my second-in-command?"

Zion's spine stiffened, and his right fist flexed, feeling the itch of his blade. "Of course not. I killed him easily."

Jarvok walked toward Zion. "Then what?" he said, raising his voice. "Why are you hours late if he was so easy?"

"There was a problem with the Weepers!" Zion yelled. "Forgive me, my liege." He bowed his head and dropped to his knees, his Black Kyanite armor banging against the magma floor.

The muscles in Jarvok's jaw twitched and clenched. "A problem with my Weepers? Explain, Zion." His voice was now quiet and firm, delivering a simple demand. Zion stood, facing his leader, a small bead of sweat forming above his lip. His boldness eviscerated under Jarvok's scrutiny. "At first, the mission went as planned. I engaged Aded and challenged him in front of his worshippers as you commanded. I told the Weepers not to draw swords unless a human drew upon them, but when Aded's offering drew a knife on me, they turned on the humans. They acted like savages, my liege. They decimated the entire village while I exterminated their rain god. When it was over, no human was left breathing." Zion paused. He had much more to say, but he needed a moment to figure out how to describe what had happened next.

Jarvok blinked and shook his head. "Zion, they are warriors, and after hundreds of years, they have been allowed to do what they do best. The human drew a blade; they responded. I would have preferred if they had not killed the humans, but I understand how this happened." Jarvok's head fell back as he exhaled.

"No, my liege, there is more. The Weepers didn't just kill the humans. They *relished* the kill. With each death, they became more frenzied, more ravenous. The Weepers ate the humans."

The horror in Zion's eyes even stopped Los from puttering around. The small dragon comprehended the emotion in the tall Power.

Jarvok stared into Zion's crystal eyes. "They what?" His words were slow and deliberate as if he hoped he'd misunderstood his second-in-command.

"The Weepers. Ate. The. Humans."

There was an awkward silence.

Jarvok's eyes widened before he turned and paced the room. "Did you call them back?" A mixture of outrage and fear filled his voice.

"Of course, my liege, but they did not respond to their names. Only when there was nothing left did they return to themselves." Zion put his head down, ashamed and saddened.

"Where are they now?"

Zion looked up, surprised by Jarvok's question. "I sent them to Asa to train. I thought getting them back to combat exercises would be best."

Jarvok rested his hands on the window, watching as if he could figure out from the many bodies below which one of his Weepers had done this atrocity. He finally hung his head. "It was an anomaly. It has been centuries since they faced an enemy. Keep them busy with more training exercises and away from patrols. Only the Weepers who respond to their names should patrol. In the meantime, we must deliver my demands to Aurora and her Court of Light. Worst case, the Weepers will have a much worthier opponent they can obliterate if she is stupid enough not to surrender."

This was the first time Zion had ever heard Jarvok sound less than fully confident in his plans. "Yes, my liege," he said, trying to give his leader the confidence he lacked. "Los!" Jarvok said, now sounding surer. "Prepare a scroll for me. Zion needs to deliver a message to the Court of Light."

THIRTY:
Old Friends

A urora prepared in her chambers. She was due to make an appearance to her Egyptian worshippers. It was shemu, or their harvesting season. They knew her as Ma'at, the goddess of truth, justice, harmony, and natural balance. She guided her Egyptian followers on the path of honesty, righteousness, balance, harmony, and reciprocity. Together, these principles worked in tandem with nature's energies, keeping the universe from returning into chaos.

Aurora appeared to them with large multicolored feathered wings. Others who had known her from when she was a Virtue might have said they resembled the ones she had worn ages ago, yet there was a difference. These were colorful and bright. Her Creator would have never allowed her such beauty, but she no longer needed His permission. She fulfilled her destiny, and now she flew by her own mastery, on her own wings. That brought a smile to her face.

She had all her Fae change their appearance during human worship. To be a god or goddess was to be

otherworldly. Therefore, they should look the part. Some
Fae were small. She was afraid the humans would feel com-
pelled to either challenge the Fae or touch them. Appearing
godly helped keep their worshippers at a distance.

Their manifestations took concentration and power,
but it helped keep the visits brief and maintain the mystery. She stood in front of her mirror, preparing to turn
her milky-white skin into the color of bronzed sand. She
thought about how her worshippers' hair was the color of
the Nile at midnight—

Frantic pounding slammed at her door.

"Your Grace!" her chamber guard announced on the
other side. "Your presence is requested in the Great Hall.
It's an emergency!"

She flicked her wrist, and the wind obeyed her command and opened her door. As Aurora predicted, her guard
was gone and Desdemona was there, ready for her queen.

"What has happened?"

The captain of her Royal Guard's face was grave.
"Come, my queen. You must see for yourself." Desdemona's
voice was dry.

Aurora followed her into the Great Hall. The bishops
all gathered, staring down at the water channel. No one
else was present. The doors were closed. Bishop Ingor was
on his knees, examining something Aurora could not see
in the water.

When the bishops did not acknowledge the queen,
Desdemona announced, "I have brought the queen. Back
away from it."

Startled, they gave a sign of respect and stepped aside
to allow the queen to see what had them all so captivated.

Queen Aurora took a step closer, unsure of what she was looking at. Her eyes focused on the shape in the water channel, about four feet in length. It was a body.

She scrambled to the edge of the channel. "Get it out of the water. Now!"

Bishop Caer made a few movements with his newly acquired elemental water staff, and the liquid followed his directions, gently raising the body and laying it on the floor. They all immediately recognized the corpse. It was the remains of Lord Arceria of the Dinay Mera House.

Desdemona knelt, running her fingers over Arceria's clothes, inspecting the wounds. Her fists tightened up and she bowed her head, letting her long, red-tipped bangs fall in her eyes.

"What is it?" Bishop Ward bellowed.

Desdemona looked up at him, turning her attention toward her queen. "We have a serious issue." The answer spilled from her lips in a frigid tone.

"Get on with it, Fae!" Bishop Geddes insisted.

Before anyone could react to the bishop's impatience, another sound rocked the palace. The deafening screeching came from the front gate.

Everyone covered their ears to muffle the sound, but it was no use. Desdemona grabbed her queen's arm to hurry her to safety, but the sound stopped. Their eyes darted around the room. Caer wrapped his arms around his chest as Ward mumbled and backed away from the water channel.

"What in the world?" Bishop Caer asked.

A pounding came from the Great Hall doors. "Captain, there is an intruder at the front gate requesting an audience with you and the queen. He has a-a...creature." The guard's voice shook, his fear palpable.

Desdemona's gaze shifted to her queen. "No! Don't even think about it, Your Grace. I will go and see what this about. Stay here." Desdemona's eyes flashed red, a rare occurrence. She turned to the bishops. "Surround your queen." Her authority was final.

"What about us?" Bishop Geddes pleaded as he reached for her sleeve. Desdemona rolled her eyes. "I will send guards to watch the door."

She drew her Elestial blade. She had not drawn the auric blade in over five hundred years. Everyone looked in amazement as the glow of the blue energy sword came to life.

Without hesitation, Desdemona charged toward the front gates. She was prepared to take on the intruder and whatever creature dumb enough to follow them. Whoever they were, they would need all the help they could get if they thought they were getting into this palace.

Desdemona made it to the front gate in minutes, but what she found waiting was not at all what she had expected.

Instead of a fierce enemy, Desdemona found the familiar face of a former comrade. They served together under Commander Michael in his Power Angel Brigade Platoon. She sheathed her Elestial blade. Even with his Black Kyanite helmet on, she knew it was him. He was the only one who had hair like a black pearl, though it was longer now.

A coming breeze ruffled his hair to sway that was almost to the middle of his back. When in the Brigade, their hair had to be short. It was a necessity. Long hair made it easy to pull in a fight. He slowly removed his helmet, and there he was. He still looked the same as the day she had exalted and come to Earth.

There was movement behind him. A large, white beast stretched out its wings. By allowing herself the distraction of him and her memories, she almost did not notice the white-winged creature standing behind him.

She shook her head and stepped back, her mouth open. That must be the source of the screeching.

Her old friend gave an ironic smile. "I see you remember me, Desdemona. It's good to know I still have an effect on you." His voice was smooth like velvet.

She remembered with those looks came arrogance too. "What is the meaning of this?" she called from atop the tower gates.

"It has been so long. Is this how you treat a companion? No invitation to come in?" His voice full of false sadness, dipped in sarcasm.

Desdemona subtly tilted her toward her guards, their crystal-tipped arrows pointed and readied. "Keep me covered." Her tone was hushed.

Her tower commander gave a slow blink.

Desdemona took two strides and vaulted off the tower and waterfall so they would not have to lower the bridge. Landing in a coiled crouch, her left fist bracing the ground, she flipped her bangs out of her eyes, remaining where she had landed as she glared at him.

"Impressive. I see you haven't lost your touch." Zion gave her a long, dramatic slow clap.

She gradually stood, her shoulders back and her head held high. Her black hair tied in a braid blew softly in the breeze, her blood red-tipped bangs shifted, revealing their shared Angelite disc scar.

"What do you want?" Her voice was calm, her face schooled.

"Is this how you greet an old friend? Aren't you a bit surprised to see me? By the way, I have a name. It is Zion. Lieutenant Zion." He gave the customary Power Brigade salute, with the right index finger and middle finger to the forehead.

Desdemona did not return the gesture. Zion shrugged and began to circle her. Desdemona's eyes narrowed on his sternum, trying to decipher his next move. She said nothing, listening, in the hope he would give something away.

The large creature behind him shuffled and groaned. Her tail swished side to side for attention. "Oh, forgive me." He patted the creature.

She wasn't sure if he spoke to her or the creature.

"And this lovely, spectacular specimen of raw power is none other than Raycor, my acid-breathing dragon and my most trusted cohort. I find dragons much more loyal than, well...you know." The dragon straightened up, lengthening her neck and basking in Zion's adulations.

Desdemona huffed at his dramatics.

The dragon quickly turned her head toward the female Fae. Her sinuous neck stretched outward, her white denticle scales glittering in the sunlight to look like she was made of crystal and not organic material. She crept toward Desdemona, her nostrils opened to take in her scent, inspecting the Fae and sniffing the air around her as if asking, "And what is so spectacular about you?"

Raycor huffed, her lips rippling to reveal long teeth. Acid dripped from two of the dragon's long side teeth. As the liquid pooled, the ground dissolved, producing holes in the earth. Smoke along with an unpleasant odor rose from the blackened dirt. Desdemona observed the ground decay and grimaced before flicking her eyes back toward the creature causing the damage.

The dragon exhaled directly into Desdemona's face, blowing her red-tipped bangs back. Raycor turned her nose up at the Fae and lumbered back to stand beside her rider, curling her tail around them both in a sign of protection.

Zion arched his eyebrow. "Well, it seems Raycor is unimpressed. She is a good judge of character." Zion stroked the dragon's side and stepped over her long tail with its black age marking. "Back to business. I am here to deliver a message to your queen. Where can I find her?" He lifted his head, looking past her.

"No." Her response was clear and direct, her cheeks flushed. Raycor gave a low rumble from deep in her throat at her denial.

"I have a message from my king to deliver to your queen, and this might convince you otherwise." Zion smirked and threw a small chain at her feet. Desdemona picked up the chain. The Dinay Mera clan's sigil was inscribed on a circular piece of crystal. The rich, royal blue danced with hues of purple and green. Peacock Ore, Arceria's necklace. Her eyes burned.

Her Elestial blade begged and pricked underneath her skin.

"I can sense your blade, Des. Don't do it. I did not come here to fight. I am the messenger. Let me deliver my message, and I will be on my way. My king is being fair. He means no harm. Take a blade to me, and Raycor will turn this entire palace to liquid." His hands were up in an almost surrender.

Desdemona counted to ten in her head, trying to coax her blade back down. "You murdered Arceria. I was not surprised to see you because I recognized the wound was from an Elestial blade. So I knew a Power must have committed the murder. How have you stayed hidden this long? I do not know. How have you traveled through the Veil? I do not know.

However, why you think I would let you see my queen after you murdered a Fae in cold blood, I do not know or care because it will not happen while I draw breath." Desdemona had revealed more than she wanted, her emotions getting the best of her. Focusing her gaze, her eyes flashed red as she readied her stance. She unsheathed her Elestial blade.

The right corner of Zion's mouth turned up into more of a snarl than a smile as his blade unsheathed. "Now we fight, my beautiful Des. It has been a long time coming."

Raycor snarled and crouched, ready to spring into action if Zion called upon her.

Before the two could clash, a windstorm drove them apart and a figure appeared in the midst of chaos.

Queen Aurora dropped in between the two Fae. "Sheath your blades." The Fae were pinned by two separate cyclones.

Raycor froze where she stood, howling. The dragon looked to Zion for instruction. He struggled to nod and calm his companion.

Aurora closed her eyes and concentrated on absorbing her energy wings into her back. "I will release you if I have your word you will not draw your blade against myself or my captain. Desdemona will give you her word she will not draw hers as well. Your creature must stand down too." Aurora's tone reverberated in the air, with a timbre of the roughest ocean's waves.

The squall slowed enough for Zion to respond, "You have my word." His voice struggled against the wind as it whipped around him.

She turned toward Desdemona. "Yes, Your Grace."

With a fluid movement of her arms, the winds ceased and both warriors fell to their knees abruptly, their bodies exhausted from the beating they endured from the whirlwind.

Zion stood slowly, regaining his composure. "I am Lieutenant Zion, second-in-command to King Jarvok of the Court of Dark, Queen Aurora." He bowed his head out of respect.

Aurora's eyebrow raised. "Court of Dark?"

Zion smiled. "Yes, Your Grace. The. Court. Of Dark."

Desdemona stood at Aurora's side prepared to strike. Aurora subtly touched Desdemona's hand to hold her at bay. Realizing Zion would not elaborate on their name, Aurora skipped it and pursued other information.

"Why have you come here, Lieutenant Zion?"

Zion did not respond to the queen. He extended his hand to reveal a scroll. "My king has an offer for Your Grace."

Desdemona stepped forward and took the scroll from him, handing it cautiously to Aurora. "My queen, he is the reason Arceria is dead. I recognized the wound made by an Elestial blade."

Aurora took the scroll from Desdemona. "Is this true, Lieutenant Zion? Did you kill Lord Arceria?" she inquired as she read the scroll.

"I did as my king commanded. As you can see, he is fair in his demands. Stay in your palace, denounce the humans, and live, or meet him in battle and join Arceria in Oblivion. The choice is yours, Queen Aurora. He will give you his word no harm will come to you and your kin if you choose to live within his parameters."

"Explain his parameters."

"My queen?" Desdemona stepped forward. Aurora shot a look to silence her, and she fell behind her queen.

Zion quirked his lips, enjoying the leash Aurora had on his former friend-in-arms.

"It is simple. The humans will no longer worship any member of the Court of Light. You will denounce all activities with the humans. Leaving all worshipping rituals for King Jarvok and the Court of Dark. If you comply, you can stay here safely in your part of the Veil. King Jarvok will offer his protection in case any humans come across your kind. No Dark Fae will harm any members of the Court of Light. We will all happily coexist. You, as the figurehead of the Court of Light for the rest of your days. Even the dragons will offer their protection to the Court of Light. We have fire, ice, and acid dragons." Raycor snarled in recognition.

Queen Aurora glanced up at the dragon and cocked her head sideways as she held the scroll, looking it over. "And if I refuse his most generous offer?"

Zion threw his hands up as if it was a foregone conclusion. "Destruction of the Court of Light, plain and simple. You would be declaring war against the Court of Dark consisting of all former Power Brigade Angels. We have been here as long as you have been, training, learning. You can't possibly win, Your Grace." Zion's charm and wit evaporated. His sapphire-blue eyes were detached with the frost only a soul that has seen war knows.

"Well, you leave me no choice." Aurora's voice held a hint of defeat.

"I am so glad you are a reasonable Fae." He turned and mounted Raycor.

"I am, Lieutenant Zion. Please give King Jarvok my best and tell him next time he declares war on my kingdom, he should have the balls to meet me in person. I shall enjoy having his head mounted on my wall after I rip it off on the battlefield. Now leave before I take your balls and stuff them in your mouth with my response written on them. You know, for dramatic effect."

Raycor swallowed. She seemed stunned at the queen's graphic description.

Hell, even a dragon knew a cold threat when she heard one.

Zion dropped his head and bit the inside of his cheek to keep from laughing. He had to admire Aurora's nerve. He cleared his throat. "Well, I shall deliver your message. I may class it up a bit, but as you wish, Your Grace. I look forward to our next meeting. Unfortunately, it will not be under such pleasant circumstances." He placed his helmet on and gave Desdemona the brigade salute before his dragon jumped to a large rock near the waterfall's edge, then dove into the mist, disappearing.

The tower guards all leaned forward to observe the white, acid-breathing beast reappear as she caught an up-current. Her underbelly streaked past them as they bent backward to watch her arch up and sail overhead. Her translucent wings were outstretched and beating as she disappeared over the horizon.

The two Fae watched as their courier of bad news ascended upwards.

"So we are at war?" Desdemona's voice was hollow.

"It appears so." Aurora brought her hand to her lips.

"With the Court of Dark? A faction made of nothing but former Powers. And they have dragons—ones who breathe fire, ice, and acid, I think he said," Desdemona surmised.

"Yup." Aurora nodded, watching the large, white beast disappear.

"And we have?" Desdemona asked.

"The only Power to ever exalt and one really pissed-off queen who created the Veil."

Desdemona smirked. "They have no idea who they are messing with, do they?"

"No." Aurora shook her head.

Both Fae slowly looked at each other.

The queen winked at her captain.

A throaty laugh escaped from Desdemona. "No, they really don't."

THIRTY-ONE:
FIRST THERE WAS DARKNESS

Z ion returned to deliver Aurora's colorful message. He was surprised at the steel that lay beneath the silk of the queen's skin. He chuckled at the recollection of how strong and tall she stood in her defiance. Not that it would do her much good. Jarvok would overtake them in mere days, months if they put up a good fight, but it would be over.

His thoughts drifted to Desdemona. Time had been good to her. He would never admit it to anyone, but the exaltation suited her, and she had earned it. Desdemona had done something no other angel had ever done or Archangel had contemplated attempting without help— she survived a head-on confrontation with Lucifer. He had been there when she was brought to the healers. Oblivion had been inevitable as far as they were concerned. He had touched her Angelite disc to pay his last respects. He saw the blue cast of her lips, the grey light that surrounded her aura. He had watched as her light faded, but she miraculously recovered.

Desdemona was one of the few female Powers he had encountered with whom he had not had coitus, much less aura blended with. Not for lack of trying. She had refused his advances, which made him want her more. What started out as a game of conquest turned into something much more for Zion. There wasn't a Power around who didn't either fear or lust after Desdemona. He was sure Desdemona preferred to be feared than loved. However, it was never meant to be. When she'd healed, she exalted and Commander Gabriel sent her to Earth as a Virtue. He was never able to tell her for all his flirting and arrogant quips that he loved her. As a Virtue, protocol would not allow him to ever speak to her without a chaperone.

But here she was, back in his life but once again on opposite sides. She was just as stubborn as he was arrogant. Besides, King Jarvok had a deep-seated hatred for Desdemona. It would be best to keep these feelings to himself and leave the past where it was.

Raycor circled Blood Haven. Zion patted her head. "Go rest, my friend. I'll take it from here." He jumped off her back and rolled, landing in the exercise courtyard. He smiled and waved up at the dragon to signal he was fine. She gracefully banked left, extending her oversized white wings, and headed to her underground cave to rest, he assumed.

Zion glanced about for Los. As if the mere thought of him conjured the dragon from thin air, he appeared a few feet in front of Zion, flapping his wings. "Los, I was just thinking about you." Zion winked at the amber-hued dragon. "I take it our king is waiting for me?"

Los grunted and twitched his ears as he headed toward the tower stairs.

Zion entered the throne room to find the Council of the High Guard in full attendance. Everyone, except King Jarvok and Lieutenant Asa, sat around the large map outlining the Court of Light and the human territories. Zion greeted his king first with a bow as everyone rose in respect of Jarvok's second-in-command. Zion nodded, but he was not sure Jarvok would want all of them to hear Aurora's response.

"My liege, I have delivered your message as instructed." His voice was low.

"And…" Jarvok's tone was noncommittal.

Zion gave a sideways glance toward the warriors seated, hoping Jarvok would read his eyes. "My liege, in private," he whispered.

The Council of the High Guard consisted of the original search party that had found Jarvok in the crater after the Shining Kingdom had rejected him. The others, Pria, Yagora, Jonah, and Ezekiel stayed topside. Asa had made it halfway down the crater to help him pull Jarvok the rest of the way. They had scoured the Earth to find other Powers, bring them together, help them deal with the Abandonment, and heal their broken bodies and minds. Teaching them what it meant to have choices.

Their first lesson was in self-realization and identities. Jarvok insisted the Powers take back their names, which in his eyes had been stolen from them when they entered the Brigade. If a Power did not remember his or her name, Jarvok helped them to select a new one. Initially giving newfound Powers back their identities took priority over everything to Jarvok.

He organized the Powers, sticking with what they already knew, a militaristic-based system. He wanted to keep a sense of familiarity. They had all been through too much. A complete change would have been too jarring. The Brigade was the only life many of them remembered. He built upon it, attempting to keep the structure and discipline without the demeaning aspects of their former life.

The one aspect Jarvok could not control was his title. The seven Powers made Jarvok their king unanimously. He would have been happy with the designation of general, but Zion pointed out this left him vulnerable for possible challenges. He persuaded Jarvok to accept king. For king was a title another could not challenge by brute force.

Jarvok puffed out his cheeks with a forceful exhale. "I trust your judgment, Zion, but anything you have to say can be said in front of the High Council."

Zion repeated Aurora's refusal of Jarvok's proposal, word for word. The High Council broke out into mumbles.

Jarvok smirked and turned to face the window. "Silence." His tone was firm, but he did not raise his voice. He stood tall, his back to the room. He gave a low, husky, and bemused chuckle. He pivoted on his heels slowly, letting his fingers glide through the flames of the candles, undeterred by their heat. "Well, well. It seems our Fae queen has a mouth on her, doesn't it?" His honey-gold eyes locked onto the High Council, his fingers continuing to play with the flames. The table joined him with a low giggle. He walked away from the candelabra, waving his hand in a nonchalant manner. "It makes no difference. I shall relish cutting her tongue out even more."

The table broke out in an uproar of laughter. Jarvok placed his hands behind his back, pacing around the table, each foot carefully in front of the other in a meditative dance.

"We will prepare for war with the Court of Light. It will be quick, but we will abide by our ethics of engagement. Small Fae children are off limits. Only if a Fae draws their blade upon us are they our enemy. Pria and Azrael will be in charge of finding out any information on the worshipping rituals for the eastern human territories. Yagora will take the northern human territories and work with Jonah. Ezekiel and Asa, take the western territories. I will send Los to the Court of Light. He has easily penetrated the palace before. He is responsible for most of the information we have on them. Even if they tighten up their magical defenses, Aurora can't block the fauna of Earth. Los is the only one who can penetrate their security system. She will plan for ice, acid, and fire dragons, but since he is none of the above, she can't plan for him."

"My liege, why not just send Dragor, Raycor, Construct, and Fornia to destroy her palace before she places a new barrier against the dragons?" Pria asked.

"Because, Pria, it is not an honorable fight. Too many Fae would be lost as collateral damage, including young Fae. We do not kill the young!" He leaned on the table, staring at her to drive his point home.

She dropped her head. "Of course, my liege. Forgive me."

He waved his hand dismissively. "We will meet them during human worship rituals and on the battlefield, but first, we gather information."

The table all agreed, and they stood to leave.

Jarvok began to pace again and speak. "The next order of business is our name. I had Zion tell Aurora we are the Court of Dark."

The table erupted into chatter, sitting back down hesitantly.

"My liege? Why did you choose to use their vernacular?" Jonah asked, tugging at his left ear incessantly.

"As much as I hate to admit it, my comrades, Aurora is correct. None of us are angels of any kind. Yes, there are angelic ties, but currently we are not angels and have not been for a long time. We no longer identify as Powers. It is time to move past it. You all have names. I will see that homage is paid to what has been learned from being Powers—discipline, strength, endurance, and combative skills—but we leave behind the submissive nature the title shackled us with. The lies, the servitude—they are finished, just like the label 'Power.'"

The High Council members leaned forward, listening to him, enraptured by his words.

"My friends, they can be the light, but our Father said first there was darkness, then there was light. Don't you see? Darkness before light. We will be the darkness. We will use the shadows to hide. They will not see us coming. Let us take all the power and never will we be submissive again. Even the humans know darkness is the true power. The night eats the day. The dark eats the light. We are not evil. Darkness does not equate to evil. It is power. It envelops all, consuming it. No one fears the light because it holds no secrets. The darkness grasps all its secrets. It is the unknown. We will use this to ensure our survival. Let them be the Court of Light; let them be seen. Under the cover of darkness, we will watch, wait, and take what is rightfully ours. We are the Court of Dark." He pounded his fist on the table, toppling all the small models with the force of his blow.

The table exploded into thunderous applause. Azrael stood, his shoulders pulled back, and slammed the table with his fist. "I am Azrael, member of the High Guard Council of the Court of Dark."

Each member stood, repeating the same mantra until all had pledged, ending with Jarvok.

"I am Jarvok, King of the Court of Dark. Beware all who dare cross the Dark Fae."

THIRTY-TWO:
EMPATHY FOR THE DEVIL

"**D**amn it to Lucifer!" Zion grumbled as he picked up the broken baton. "That was my favorite practice staff." He swung it over his head, trying to see if there was a way to salvage the rowan wood weapon, but the sheer velocity of his swing caused the wood to split more.

"Ugh!" He put the weapon out of its misery by breaking it over his knee.

Asa was unsympathetic to his plight, ignoring his outburst. She leaned up against a snow pollen tree, her fingers tracing her mask's curves, her gaze distant.

"Well, thanks for the compassion," Zion said, tossing the broken sticks at her feet.

"What? Sorry." She shook her head and rubbed at her eyes.

"Could you pay just a little attention to me? You know how needy I can be." Zion pouted, sticking out his bottom lip, and proceeded to flash Asa a dazzling smile. When it did not elicit an acerbic remark, his brow furrowed. "Earth to Asa. Come in, Asa."

"I was actually thinking about what you said."

"Oh, really? What did I say?" Zion's face scrunched up.

"Damn it to Lucifer,'" Asa replied, sliding down the tree to sit, running her hand over the blades of grass.

"Huh?" Zion crouched down to meet her mismatched eyes. One was uncanny milky white and the other a serene ocean blue.

"I was thinking about Lucifer."

"What about the big, bad king of Hell?" Zion smirked. Asa licked her lips and took a breath. "Have you even seen or caught a whiff of a demon since we were abandoned?"

Zion sat down on the grass, extending his long legs, crossing his ankles and placing his weight on his elbows. He reclined, his bangs falling into his eyes. "No. I haven't seen a demon since our last battle, before He..." Zion rolled to the side, picking up his hand and pointing upward, "closed the gates to the Shining Kingdom. Lucifer closed his first because we kicked his ass, and our loving Father locked our butts out. Come on, Asa. We witnessed Commander Michael personally say he was ordered to check on the gates of Hell. Little did we know it meant 'see ya, suckers. I am heading home without you.' We didn't figure it out until after we found Jarvok."

Asa rubbed her temples. "I know, I know. I remember Commander Michael receiving the orders from Commander Uriel to check the locks. None of us knew Lucifer had retreated. But didn't you ever wonder why Lucifer just gave up? One day we were battling for the Shining Kingdom, and then, poof, Lucifer runs back to Hell and takes all his demons with him." Asa stood and shook her head.

"We don't know if Lucifer took his demons back to Hell. We assume he did. Maybe he incinerated them. Less evidence. But it's all conjecture."

Asa was disagreeing before Zion finished his answer. "Lucifer would not destroy his own army. It took him ages to acquire it."

"So what's your point? Lucifer knew he was outclassed by the Brigade, and he retreated to lick his wounds." Zion shrugged, pulling at the weeds. "I don't know, Zion." Asa slapped the sides of her legs and bit her bottom lip. "Lucifer returned to Hell and just accepted defeat, no big warning of vengeance? Not one demon body on this Earth?"

"Asa, you are over thinking this. Obviously, Lucifer didn't want the Brigade to capture a demon and question them."

"Nope, that logic doesn't hold water, Zion. Most of us were locked out. How could they have taken them back for interrogation?"

"So what? Why are you concerned about this? Are you worried about Lucifer being a risk to us? Can we just kick the Court of Light's ass into Oblivion before you bring these delusions of paranoia up to King Jarvok? Please, my dear Asa?" Zion laid back in the grass, arms spread out.

Asa kicked her friend's foot. "I never said I was concerned about Lucifer being a threat. I've been thinking about this for a while, and I wonder if he was really as bad as they say. That's all." She mumbled the last part.

Zion shot up to a sitting position. "Seriously? You are questioning if the King of Hell, the Father of Lies, is just misunderstood? You really do love a challenge, don't cha?"

Asa stomped her foot and folded her arms across her chest. "I am serious!"

He rolled his eyes and stood up, placing his hands on her shoulders, dipping his head trying to get her attention. Asa tucked her chin. He blew on her nose, forcing her to look at him. She fought her growing grin. "You are as cute as a goblin's babe when you mope."

Asa punched him in the stomach. "And you are a goblin's ass."

Zion coughed and laughed as he held his gut. "All right, all right. Let's hear all about your empathy-for-the-devil theory."

Asa growled. "Are you really going to listen? Or are you patronizing me, Zion? Because I'm not going to waste my breath. I'll kick your ass in the training ring and embarrass you in front of Jarvok." She gave him a mocking smirk.

Zion put his hands up. "Whoa. I asked, didn't I? And you can't kick my ass."

"I can, and I have, Princess Sapphire." She winked.

Zion cheeks flushed pink. "You promised you would never bring that name up ever again! It was one bet. One fight, Asa, and I asked for a rematch." He raised his index finger up to her face in protest.

Asa sauntered a few steps away. She paused and struck a pose, tapping her chin a few times. "Ah, I remember. I believe the conditions of the bet were as follows: I said I would not bring up the name 'Princess Sapphire' in public, but it's just you and me, Princess Sapphire. By the way, you looked so cute in a crown. I can't resist. So are you ready to pay attention and listen to me? Because I have already proven I can best you...Princess."

It was Zion's turn to fight his growing smile. "I concede. I am listening. Please continue, Oh Great One." He gave a theatrical roll of his wrist, sarcasm abundant in his voice.

Asa gave a dramatic bow. "Thank you. As I was saying, how many of us were left here on Earth, injured or dying? Our Father abandoned members of the Power Brigade, who served the Shining Kingdom honorably and won this so-called war. Yet we curse Lucifer in our everyday vernacular. It makes me think who the real villain is: the Father who deserted his soldiers and left them behind to perish, the Father who denies us access to the kingdom we fought to defend, or the wayward devil who took all his forces home to save them from harm and make sure he left no one behind."

THIRTY-THREE:
I Am the Storm

CIRCA 1250 B.C.

Y agora and Ezekiel bore down on their attack. The dragons had turned the desert into a paradox of fire and ice around the pixie faction. Ezekiel brought Construct, his yellow-hued Fire-Breather. The beast melted the sand into smooth glass, creating a clear prison to trap unlucky pixies and Will-O-The-Wisps beneath the layers. Their essence was now part of the desert landscape. Yagora and her Ice-Breather Onichi remolded the land. Onichi's ice tusks transformed the large dunes into ice crystalline mounds that reflected just as brilliantly as Construct's glass menageries.

Lady Devas's voice was hoarse as she roared the command, "Ego procella sum," meaning "I am the storm," her call for the Storm Stand Guard, pixies who had the ability to call the storm of north winds to create small squalls. When they all stood in formation, they could create immense sand or dust storms from joining their power. The smaller winged pixies covered the Storm Stand Guard, using their wings to throw their ice darts as they arranged themselves. Their wings formed icicles with the call of cold north winds to freeze the moisture in their wings to materialize razor-sharp icicles. The flap of their wings propelled them, slicing through their enemies, slowing them down.

The taller members of the Storm Stand assembled into two lines back to front, one line dropping to their right knees in a fluid motion as the others remained rigid at the ready. The pixie at the end began to whip his right arm around his head, palm facing up, shoulders undulating as his left followed.

Like dominos, each pixie followed suit as the one beside him or her completed their movement. Squalls formed, raising the desert floor, the grit and dust carried across the landscape to meet the army of Weepers closing in. As the squall grew, the cloud became dense, blocking out the sun and engulfing the Weepers at their backside.

Lady Devas nodded at her kin as they held their concentration, though she knew this only delayed the inevitable. The Weepers would not stop until they met their targets. A screech from above reminded her she had dragons to contend with. She could only hope by all that was light in the universe Queen Aurora would reach her in time. They just needed to hold out a little longer. They had managed to keep their battle away from the humans. Egypt faced its own problems with the slave uprising and the plagues that had descended.

Lady Devas was in this position because her followers had prayed to Amaunet, Goddess of the North Wind, asking for protection when hail fell from the sky. Once the hail hit the crops it turned to fire, incinerating their barley and flax. When Devas appeared in her Amaunet form, Yagora attacked her. The Egyptians saw this as two of their goddesses battling, a story they would not doubt immortalize on a pyramid wall.

The Court of Light had moved the battle to the banks of the Red Sea, away from humanity. They tried to minimize human casualties whenever possible. The Fae casualties were mounting for the Court of Light.

Devas called out to Lord Oromasis. His Will-O-the-Wisps were needed to give her kin time to regain their strength. The Will-O-the-Wisps were strong and well-armed. The female Wisps were the only ones of the faction who had wings. Their green-and-gold antennas that sprouted from their mid-back were imbued with the ability to conjure sparks. Their large, two-sectioned, green iridescent wings had lavender highlights streaking at the scalloped edges and darker metallic green veins running throughout. The wings were capable of throwing the sparks outward at a target, starting fires. The male Will-O-the-Wisps had the same antennae but no wings. They produced sparks and hot venom. Hot venom was particularly nasty. Once introduced into the body, the venom would flood the bloodstream and melt a victim from the inside out. The Will-O-the-Wisps' weapon of choice was the golden sickle, a curved handheld blade they could charge with their hot venom to deliver their special gift.

The Weepers continued their death march, forward through the haze and grit of the north wind sandstorm. Oromasis gave the command and the Will-O-the-Wisps with their fire wings charged headfirst, the sparks of yellow, gold, and red barely visible in the thick bronze air. The subtle glow of Elestial blades began to illuminate the dust bowls as globes of yellow lights twinkled out one by one, denoting a fallen Wisp. The sandstorm slowly began to die down.

"My Storm Stand Pixies cannot keep this up much longer, Oro."

Another screech drew their eyes upward, making it hard to forget the death the blue skies held. Devas looked to her line as her kin began to fall from exhaustion.

"Protect the line!" Oromasis yelled. Devas ran to her kin, adding her power to help hold the storm steady.

A wave of white-blonde braids somersaulted over Oromasis as Lady Kit, leader of the Fire Drakes, stood with six of her elite guards, their ash batons drawn, each topped with a fire globe. Inside the orange glowing orb housed a Snap Dragon flower. The wine-colored flower had elongated, wavy-trimmed velvet petals with a lengthy plum-colored stamen. These flowers were much like their cousin the Fire Lily. The phosphorescent stamen sparked when it encountered air. However, unlike the Fire Lily, the Snap Dragons' stamens were exaggerated and packed much more of a punch. Their stamens did not spark, they exploded into a splendid fire. When the stamen extinguished, the petals snapped tight—earning their name Snap Dragon—allowing the stamen time to regenerate. The flowers were so large they were known to engulf a baby dragon's foot when they closed. Each guard had a quiver full of the flowers, ready to unleash and command.

"Lady Kit, how do the Fire Drakes fare?"

"Better than you, Lord Oromasis. The Weepers are closing in...fast." She passed her hand over the globe of her rod, scooping a piece of the flame from the flower's stamen.

The scent of vanilla and cedar filled the air as she molded the small flame into a gigantic fireball and hurled it into the air. Oromasis' face reflected the blue of her sulfur fireball as it exploded into one of Construct's glass facades. Shards and debris scattered into the air, slicing through any Weeper's skin not covered in Black Kyanite armor caught in its path.

Oro gave a sly grin. "We are grateful to see you, Lady Kit."

However, their relief was fleeting as the sandstorm wavered once more, and the vibrant blue sky could be seen. More importantly, the dragons could see their targets.

Yagora and Ezekiel worked in tandem, a well-choreographed ballet between the two comrades, swooping and swaying in perfect harmony. Construct lit the sky with his deadly purple gift of hydrogen and methane fire, shielding Onichi while she readied to deliver her icy death. It was her turn to use her large red body to protect Construct as he recouped from the energy expenditure and released a precise high-pressure stream of liquid nitrogen from her cartilage tusks, instantly freezing anything it hit. She employed her wings to splinter whatever she froze or a loud victory cry would shatter her victim, sending shards of ice everywhere. The two dragons would replicate the dance, their damage escalating.

Lord Oromasis and Lady Kit ran for cover, calling for Devas to follow. "Pull back!" called Devas to her kin as the pixie line scattered. They used their elemental control of air to form sand dunes as they retreated, the Fire Drakes providing coverage with their fireballs. "Reform the line!" Devas instructed.

The Storm Stand scrambled and began their configuration again, only a small lull in the haze. The three house leaders huddled together ready to make a stand as the dragons and Weepers closed in.

"If we take out just one dragon, we have a chance," Lady Kit said, her tone steadfast.

"Oh, it is that all? Just one dragon." Oromasis rolled his eyes, shaking his head. "Do you have a plan?"

"I actually do, you goblin's ass." Kit was not about to argue. "A well-timed fireball at the Ice-Breather's tusks will take out their oral defense. This will leave Construct vulnerable after he spews his fire. We all know Fire-Breathers need time to recuperate. It is why they work with the Ice-Breathers. His gas bladders need time to refill. His fire plating will not yet have returned to their full protective state. We will have a chance at him. If we can get behind him, fate may smile on us. The beast will not have his consort to protect him."

"But, Kit, you will have to be within a few feet of Onichi to make the attempt. You will be completely—"

"I know, Devas. Onichi will be amid her ice breath, and I will be in range."

THIRTY-FOUR:
KEVAH

K evah spun to his left, falling out of formation as Lady Devas had commanded. It was time to change lines. His time in the Storm Stand was over for the moment. Kevah lifted his helmet, revealing his short lavender hair with its red hawk stripe down the center. He had been self-conscious about it as a Little One until he met her. She adored his hair. He shook his head and wiped the dust from his lips. His shield had covered his eyes and nose. He spat and coughed up the desert grime. His snow-white, quartz Apsaras armor was practically unrecognizable except for the feather-like folds and embossing, even his faction's sigil was buried under the blood and dirt of battle.

Kevah joined the ground and air assault team to keep watch over the Storm Stand Guard. The team was made up of the pixies who still had their wings. They were tiny. Not every pixie grew to the height of an oak sapling such as he had. All pixies were born with translucent white wings the size of dragonflies. As adolescents they were not much bigger than flying fish. During their adolescence a pixie's wings would either molt and roll into themselves, creating beautiful, winged scars on their back and denoting they would grow taller, or their wings would expand, changing their coloring to all different hues of the rainbow and develop the capability of throwing icy darts. If a pixie grew, they would be called a Storm Caller as their height gave them the talent to call the cold North Winds. Kevah was the only one in his family who matured into a Storm Caller. His mother convinced him it was his duty to join in the war.

"Why did I listen to her?" Kevah mumbled as he ran to meet the rest of his kin.

The Weepers fought through the cold wind. They were relentless. "Ready!" a voice called out.

Kevah could hear his heartbeat thrumming, the seconds replacing the sound of his pumping blood.

"Draw your weapons," the voice instructed in the distance.

He reached for his vortex knives, the two razor-sharp, crescent-shaped daggers with the handles inlaid into the knives, forming sleeves for the knuckles. This allowed the pixie's hands to remain free to perform elemental magick while still wielding the knives. The final and perhaps most deadly piece to these weapons was that the knives were split. They fit together to form a perfect circle. The pixie could join the knives and use the vortex as a boomerang, sending it on an air current to slice several targets in one skillful toss.

Kevah twirled his knives over his head before striking them at his sides in unison with his kin, ready for the Weepers. He did not have to wait long.

The Weepers closed in on the unit, stalking forward, fighting the pixies, the Will-O-the-Wisps, and the Fire Drakes. They roared with primal enthusiasm as their Elestial blades slashed and gutted the Light Fae. The more their enemies fought the more emboldened the Weepers became. It fueled them. The vortex knives sparked against the Black Kyanite armor of the Weepers. No damage was done unless they were lucky enough to catch skin.

The Weepers were there for one reason and one reason only—death. They killed for the thrill. It was sloppy and gruesome, their hatred of their targets fueling them. They wanted the kill to be worthy. An easy slay only infuriated them. They were soldiers and relished a challenge. The addition of the Fire Drakes to the battle lines invigorated them. They slashed and charged their way through the pixies with fervor to get to a Fire Drake, their thirst for blood driving them. They had been commanded with the task of annihilating the Light Fae and they loved their job. Kevah watched in horror as his kin dropped under the blood-drenched indigo luminosity of the Elestial blades. They were outnumbered and outclassed.

He had only one thought: Shawna, the mermaid—the love he'd left behind for this Lightforsaken war.

He knew deep down in his aura he would not see her green-glass-colored eyes again. He should have stayed with her. To hell with what his mother thought. They could have made it work. Shawna was everything to him: curious, kind, and intelligent. His entire aura recognized her. She felt like home. Kevah could hear her in his heart. The last thing she said to him resonated there, her words pumping in his veins, giving him life as they crawled under his skin. She had gazed up, her eyes full of hope and resilience. "I will never abandon you. I have been here too long. Though I may not be able to stand beside you, I will be with you." She reached out to touch him, but Kevah turned away, unable to take even the slightest graze of her hands. His resolve crumbled with every word she spoke. Shawna retracted her arm.

Softly touching her own lips, she glanced down before she spoke again, her voice smooth and reassuring. "I will never allow another to walk over me to hurt you. Know I am going to fight for you against all who say we are not meant to be, though my heart submits to you I will never bow to anyone in battle. Leave me if you must, if your heart tells you it is just, but know I will be here waiting and fighting for you."

Kevah was exhausted from the war, tired of all the death. He wanted to see the light, *her* light. No more fighting for either of them. He turned and ran. He ran toward the water. Somehow, he thought if he could get to the water, any water, he could call to Shawna. He needed to tell her he was wrong. He chose her, not his faction or some nonexistent sense of duty. Kevah had made a mistake. This was not his war. He was born on Earth, not in the Shining Kingdom. He was not a Virtue. He was Fae, free to make his own choices. Kevah had lost enough. He wanted his heart back, and it was in the sea with Shawna.

However, Kevah couldn't find the water. The sandstorm was disorienting. Instead he found one of Construct's glass sculptures, which held a dying pixie and a few Will-O-the-Wisps slowly suffocating under the thick glass. He cupped his hand over his mouth as he realized their fate. He banged on it but it just made his hand hurt. He touched the warm glass with his fingertips, pulling them back to his forehead, and dropped his head. There was nothing he could do. He wasn't a fighter. He did not want this to be his fate. He covered his eyes. His shoulders lurched up and down in time with his sobs until he heard the frenetic breathing. Kevah hiccupped and wiped his nose. He recognized the ragged breath. Rubbing his eyes, he glanced over his shoulder, and there stood a Weeper.

The Weeper had tracked Kevah, the pixie's anxiety and fear attracting him like a pheromone. The Weeper snarled at him, his Elestial blade unsheathed, blue-tinged light highlighting half his face. Watching the blade pulsate and glow, the pixie pulled his vortex knives, ready to fight. However, his arms felt heavy, the knives like the weight of the earth hanging off each hand. The fire Kevah saw smoldering in the Weeper's pale eyes, he knew he did not possess in his own. He dropped his chin to his chest and shook his head. "No. I am finished with this war." He tossed his knives down. Shawna's face materialized in his mind. His tears felt warm as they fell. He wanted to see her, kiss her, but it was not meant to be and he was not a match for this Weeper. Even her love could not fuel him.

Love should not fuel violence.

He would never be free if he had to kill this Weeper to get to her. There would be another waiting for him and another, and there would always be another death on the other side. Death and love—it was an oxymoron. Kevah had a thought—or more of a delusion. Perhaps if he did not fight the Weeper, it would feel something for him and let him go. The pixie went to his knees, arms out to the sides, palms up.

"You could let me go because I will not fight." Tears tracked down his face, his white armor stained blue with blood gleamed in the desert sun as his tears fell and traced down the snow-white crystal armor.

The Weeper's nostrils flared as he watched the Light Fae surrender. He started to pace, picking at his Angelite disc scar, blinking and twitching. Blood dripped down his face from the Weeper's scar, matching Kevah's tear tracks, but the two *wept* for very different reasons. He glanced at the vortex knives on the sand and swallowed. He reached for the knives and growled at the pixie.

"Coward," he muttered, venom coating every letter as he grabbed the pixie by his shoulder. His snow-white crystal armor fissured under the Weeper's grip as he drove his Elestial blade through the left side of his gut.

Kevah lurched forward but knew it was not a death blow, painful but not enough to be fatal. "You did not kill me. You are letting me go." A ghost of hope echoed through his voice like a whisper in a cavern before it was swallowed whole. He moved back as the Weeper released him for a brief moment.

The Weeper scoffed, took two strides before seizing the pixie again by his arm, pulling him close. His breath was hotter than desert dry air on Kevah's ear as he spoke.

"You will feel every inch of this." He leaned back, watching as Kevah lost all faith, terror settling in as he trembled.

The Weeper inhaled and shuddered, savoring the pixie's fear as he began cutting off the pixie's fingers one by one, using his own vortex knife. "You robbed me of a fight, and now you must pay...in pain."

THIRTY-FIVE:
LET THERE BE... WATER?
OR LET MY WEEPERS GO

Lady Devas, Lord Oromasis, and Lady Kit reviewed the plan one last time. Oromasis would draw Onichi's fire as Lady Devas propelled Kit upward using an air current. It would be up to Kit to time the fireball just right. The Fire Drakes would lay cover, and Devas would need to concentrate to throw Kit high enough. They decided Kit would have to start on a dune for enough height. This would leave her exposed, but it was the only way to ensure they would have enough height to reach Onichi and give Kit time to spin her fireball.

The Fire Drakes took their positions and began their assault. The Will-O-the-Wisps stood to their backs, holding off the Weepers. Devas nodded and Kit took to the dune. A shadow circled overhead as Onichi gathered her fortitude, a shadowy figure on her back.

"Now!" Kit cried as she twisted off the dune.

Devas swung her right hand over her head, her left following in a high block to command the air to lift Lady Kit, but before she could finish the movement, Onichi swung around and the figure riding her back fell to the ground in a sickening thud. It rolled in the sand to land at Devas's feet, revealing its identity. She screamed at the torso of her kin. A tortured male pixie lay with lavender hair and a red hawk stripe.

With her focus broken Lady Kit began to fall, but not before Yagora surprised her, crawling up the back of her dragon. She jumped to the front as she vaulted off the head of Onichi, Elestial blade drawn to impale the leader of the Fire Drakes in mid-air. Then she back-flipped in a free fall from Kit, trusting her Ice-Breather would catch her.

Lady Devas realized her focus was disturbed and regained her orientation in time to help Lady Kit land. The Fire Drake leader's body settled upon the desert floor silently as each Fire Drake screamed in unison, their fire globes bursting into infernos as the landscape became a conflagration of blue flames and sorrow.

Oromasis ran to gather her body. She was breathing, but her light was dimming.

Yagora and Ezekiel leaped off their dragons, invigorated with their takedown of the Fire Drake's leader, choosing to engage in hand-to-hand combat. The brilliance of their Elestial blades were a blinding blue stained with Fae blood. They moved with efficiency, speed, and skill. The pixies' air guard threw icicle darts from their wings, avoiding the two warriors with acrobatics, but the Weepers were another story.

The Weepers had backed up the Light Fae to the banks of the Red Sea. There was nowhere left to go. The briny scent of the seawater mixed with sulfur-tinged death filled the air.

Lady Devas and Lord Oromasis prepared to make their final stand. They gave each other sideways glances as they dug their feet into the wet mud. Lord Oromasis slipped, trying to gain traction as Lady Devas grabbed under his left arm to steady him as he protected Kit.

Construct and Onichi landed near Yagora, each dragon letting out a primal roar of victory, their wings flapping as their tails waved. Glaring at the two Fae, she glanced at Lady Kit's wound and smirked. Lord Oromasis threw a futile fire spark at Construct. The dragon caught it in his mouth, swallowed, and licked his lips, giving a low growl that sounded more like a laugh of derision at the two Fae. Yagora glanced back to observe the Fire-Breather's reaction. She turned back to the two Fae for their rebuttal, a cocky smile ghosting her face when her opponents swallowed hard, their eyes darting erratically side to side.

Yagora pointed her blade at them, the glow reflecting off the Court of Light's shiny, dark-grey Hematite crystal armor. Yagora tilted her head at her distorted reflection in Devas's chest plate, her blade looking warped and enlarged. Yagora moved her gaze from the armor to her targets, sizing them up as they crouched, ready to attack.

With a snort, she said, "Surrender."

Devas refused. There were no quick quips or banter. Just a simple, "Never."

Yagora glanced over her shoulder at Ezekiel, and with the subtlest of head gestures the Weepers rushed at the small group. Lady Devas and Lord Oromasis retreated farther into the water, dragging Kit with them. They were knee-deep, ready to fight to the end.

"It has been an honor, Devas." His golden sickle was charged with Hot Venom.

"It's not over yet, Oro. Get Kit to Lady Ambia. Her sacrifice will not be in vain." Lady Devas raised her hands above her head. Spinning, light-blue and yellow orbs grew from her hands. Devas prepared to call all the power of the north winds. It would be her last time. Harnessing all the elemental force into her would allow for one gigantic energy pulse, buying her kin time to escape and destroying her in the process.

Oromasis jumped in front to shield her. His antennae threw sparks as she gathered her fortitude. Lady Kit was cradled in his right arm, his sickle in his left hand.

They suddenly felt the pull of the current. The two glanced down, their boots free from the water as they stood on dry land. The stagnant odor of decaying algae caused their eyes to water. Stunned, Lady Devas glanced around, the glow of her orbs dissipating. There was a tug deep inside her, a place she employed to call her element. Recognizing the power, she cast her eyes upward. Her lengthy rose-gold braid whipped erratically in the tempest with dark clouds marching along the horizon.

Queen Aurora hovered in a tornado made of water. Just barely visible, their queen drew the Red Sea to her, winding the sea around her as she disappeared in the center of the waterspout. Devas released the elemental force, saving it for another day. She dropped her head to her chest and released a long exhale. The swirling energy vortex expanded. Celadon light suffusing through the air grew brighter and larger as the portal opened.

Aurora was giving them a chance to escape.

"Retreat!" Lord Oromasis yelled to the pixies, Will-O-the-Wisps, and Fire Drakes. He handed Lady Kit to her kin, but knew it was too late for their leader. Her light was almost nonexistent.

The pixies flew toward the portal, but Devas noticed the dragons making their way toward Aurora.

"No! Wait. Oromasis, have the Fire Drakes direct their fireballs toward the dragons. Draw their fire. We must keep them away from the queen until everyone is safe."

Yagora wasted no time mounting Onichi as she and Ezekiel headed for the sea tornado to meet Aurora head on. The Weepers followed the pixies and Will-O-the-Wisps into the dry seabed, hungry to continue their fight. Aurora quirked her mouth. "Yes, that's right, follow them." Aurora's eyes flashed green. She planned to drown the Weepers. As the Weepers stepped farther into the wet silt, their heavy Black Kyanite boots stuck in the dense and thick sediment. The pixies and Will-O-the-Wisps flew over without issue, helping their kin who did not fly. The horde of Weepers glanced up at the waterspout, figuring out this was a trap.

"Too late, Weepers." Aurora released the airstream holding the water back, allowing more water to fill the area. The Weepers balked as the sea rose to their knees. Lord Oromasis and Lady Devas headed toward the Veil's portal. Aurora's plan was working. The Weepers did not move. They would rather die than dishonor themselves running from a battle and would only withdraw if given a direct order of retreat. Aurora watched with grim satisfaction until a gathering of humans cut her celebration short.

A man leading a mass of humans appeared at the bank of the Red Sea holding a wooden staff. He looked skyward and had asked for a path in the name of his Lord. He planted the timber staff at the shore and believed his action correlated with the sea retreating. The humans rejoiced. Their God had heard their prayers. They danced, celebrating their freedom, too caught up in their newly formed escape route to notice the last of the retreating Fae far from shore. Aurora turned to the group of uninvited humans, her ego bruised more than anything. *He did this? Stupid humans!* Aurora rolled her eyes.

The Weepers were only knee-deep in the Red Sea. They were far from the shore. If she let the water go completely, she would cause a tidal wave drowning all in its path—humans and Weepers—but all her kin were not through the portal yet. She needed to keep the humans separate and allow her kin time to get through to the Veil.

Yagora and Onichi circled the queen. "What now, little queen? Let them drown? If you hold back the waters, I will give the orders for my Weepers to return to the shore and feast on the humans! A lesson to the slaves for turning on their masters from their Goddess Meretseger." A vicious grin crossed her face as she stuck a forked, serpent-like tongue out at Aurora.

"I will stop the humans from going farther if you create a portal and get your Weepers out. Alternatively, I will drown them all. Humans and Weepers. It is far better to let the humans drown than let them be eaten."

Yagora's eyes widened. "You wouldn't dare!" she growled.

Aurora let the water reach the Weepers' thighs. "Try me." She stared at the Dark Fae.

Yagora glanced at Ezekiel and back to the Weepers a few times before mumbling under her breath. Jarvok would have her head if she lost an entire Weeper unit. It was a gamble she could not take. Yagora released a frustrated groan. Onichi mimicked her sentiment as her ice tusks' scales erratically flicked upward, ribbons of vapor escaping them. Yagora subtly patted her dragon's cheek before finally giving Ezekiel the order to open the portal. "It is done. Recede the waters and hold the humans back as you promised," the Dark Fae commanded.

"Not until you say please." Aurora flashed a bright smile. When Yagora said nothing, she let the waters rise a bit more.

"Troll's balls...please!" Yagora gritted out.

"Of course, since you asked so nicely." With a sweet smile, Aurora pulled the waters away from the Weepers.

Ezekiel gave the order to retreat. The Weepers marched into their portal.

Yagora gave one final disdainful look, curling her lip and snarling.

Aurora winked back. The human man ordered his people to hurry into the dry seabed. She let water flood back toward them, the group praying to their God to protect them. She used a gust of wind to create a wall of water to block their view.

Like cattle, the humans slowly and guardedly waded through knee-deep water as the water wall protected them from the Fae battle coming to its climactic end.

Aurora glanced down at the man leading the humans and noticed an army of her Egyptian followers chanting and riding toward them. Obviously, the man and the people he was leading were the slaves she had heard so much about. The slaves had nowhere to go, blocked by the water she had put up to guard the Weepers' escape. The humans cowered at the wall of liquid as it defied gravity.

Aurora swore under her breath. She was not in the mood for involvement in human politics but as the Egyptian army closed in, she could not turn her back on the slaves. "Now I guess I have to help you guys."

She dropped the wall of water once the last of the Weepers disappeared through their own portal. Using the wind, she parted the waters from each side of the shore, carving a chasm to allow the slaves to begin their trek. The bearded man urged the group to run as they praised their God for His mercy. The thundering hooves of horses and chariots could be heard even over the rushing sea. The Egyptians were fast approaching the slaves. If she did not do something, they would be caught, and she knew the pharaoh would not be kind. With a heavy heart she released the waters behind the slaves, drowning any of those who chased after them. Concealed in her waterspout and storm clouds, Aurora watched as they attempted their trek to the other side.

The slaves walked all night to cross the sea. In the end, with the sun resolutely below the horizon, as darkness was still fighting to resist its inevitable surrender to the dawn's light, the final Israelite stepped foot on the opposite side of the shore. Aurora released the last remnants of water and the Red Sea was as it was before, serene and placid. The Israelites were joyous as they thanked the bearded man and their God above for His generosity and for choosing them as His children.

The humans' words struck a nerve with Aurora. Something happened here.

Have I been a pawn in the Creator's game all over again? These complex emotions came bubbling to the surface like a geyser ready to explode. She bit the inside of her cheek, unclenched her fists, and slowed her breathing. However, there was no indication the Creator paid attention to these humans in particular. Her shoulders were no longer grazing the bottom of her earlobes. She stretched her fingers and wiggled them.

Aurora looked skyward. Only a few faint stars remained as the golden rays of hope began to fill the expanse. She knew the feeling—to gaze upon a new day and be hopeful for what was to come, to believe you were the flame who could burn and fill the sky with possibilities. Aurora waved her index finger skyward. "Why do I get the sneaking suspicion that I just did Your dirty work for You?"

EPILOGUE:
WE HAVE ONE
GIGANTIC PROBLEM...

A s expected, Aurora did not receive an answer from above. Against her better judgment, curiosity getting the better of her, she followed the mass of humans and their newly empowered leader. *Why do they worship this human? He is just a man after all, isn't he?*

She was perplexed by the way the crowd cheered after crossing the sea. How they revered this man who took credit for calling upon their God and parting the waves. She wanted, no, she needed to know how this played out. Her war forgotten for a few precious moments, Aurora hovered above, silently observing the humans. They displayed no remorse for the Egyptians who had drowned behind them. Aurora had felt for the loss of life. She did not agree with the way the Israelites were treated, but human politics were none of her concern. Yet here she was.

She had endeavored as the goddess Ma'at to intercede on the Israelites' behalf many times. She preached equality

and fair treatment. Some of her pharaohs and priestesses had followed her advice, but the newer regimes were ego-tistical. Humanity headed in the direction of self-involve-ment the more they evolved. The increase in knowledge was congruent with how close-minded they became. It was a strange dichotomy.

While lost in her musings, the group set up camp for the night, but not before their leader began a worship ses-sion. Aurora listened to the prayers they sang to their God. Grateful for his rescue of them from enslavement, they considered themselves "the chosen ones."

Aurora chuckled. She knew her Creator all too well. He showed no favoritism. Anyone could look at her own plight for proof. If these poor deluded souls thought they were any different, she could guarantee they would suffer some sort of abandonment by Him, just as she and Jarvok's kin had. At some point their God would take umbrage with them for one thing or another and they too would fall out of His favor.

Aurora watched the group for a few more hours, feeling a kinship with them. She understood their hopeful energy. It was reminiscent of when she had first come to this planet long ago. She had prepared it for these humans, and now she was at war for their adulation to keep her kin alive.

My, my...how times have changed. Perhaps if I protect this group and wait until He turns His back on them, I can be their savior and convert them back to the old religion.

She narrowed her gaze on their leader. There was something about the one human in particular. His energy was different, so steadfast in his beliefs. She felt the under-current of his faith. There was more at work than just a changing of a culture. She was various goddesses to many humans. She would continue to monitor this situation. Right now, she had a war to win. Aurora left the desert people but vowed to return to check in on them. How long could they wander around aimlessly, anyway? When they were hot and thirsty they would be praying to a rain god or goddess in a matter of days, then resume their lives, forgetting all about their alternative religious movement.

For weeks, Aurora returned at different intervals to watch the humans walk through the desert and set up camp for a few days before packing up and moving on. The leader, who Aurora had learned was named Moses, told them God was guiding them. The humans waited for their God to give them a sign. Aurora, hoping to convert them back to the old religion, waited for her opportunity. When they were desperate from thirst or hunger she would appear with whatever they needed. A goddess of mercy to deliver them from their circumstance.

On the day as she was ready to make her move, her worst fear became a reality. Storm clouds rolled over the desert, turning a placid sky into an ominous dark precursor of what was coming. The air was thick with the scent of ozone. A charge of energy and a force overwhelming her, Aurora clutched at her throat. She couldn't breathe. Raw power suffocated her. She could not remember a time when she had been in the presence of such awesome might.

Aurora's eyes widened, her body shook. Her mind had not immediately recognized the familiarity of the air, but her body certainly did.

It was *Him*.

With nowhere to hide, she looked around like a scared child trying to shield herself from the monster in a nightmare. As the grey clouds covered the sky and the humans cowered beneath them, her heart was empty. She had no empathy for them. Self-perseveration was all-consuming. *He* was coming. With each clap of thunder, *He* was closer to her.

Paralyzed by fear, she felt the color drain from her face as a deafening, omnipotent, familiar voice emanated from the clouds. The voice held every sound of nature—from a volcano erupting to ocean waves crashing on the side of rocks during a storm, to a cricket chirping on a summer's night. The voice embraced the awesomeness of the earth in one breath and spoke to the frightened humans.

"I am the Eternal, your God. I led you out of Egypt and liberated you from lives of slavery and oppression. You are not to serve any other gods before *Me*. You are not to make any idol or image of other gods. In fact, you are not to make an image of anything in the heavens above, on the Earth below, or in the waters beneath. You are not to bow down and serve any image, for I, the Eternal your God, am a jealous God. As for those who are not loyal to *Me*, their children will endure the consequences of their sins for three or four generations. But for those who love *Me* and keep *My* directives, their children will experience My loyal love for a thousand generations. You are not to use *My* name for your own idle purposes, for the Eternal will punish anyone who treats *His* name as anything less than sacred."

As fast as the skies turned grey and angry, they became tranquil once more. It was a beautiful, pale-blue morning as if nothing astonishing had happened. The remnants of the supernatural deity were the trembling humans left in *His* wake. Some were wailing while others were unconscious from fright. Many were in shock from what they had just witnessed. Most had dropped to their knees, hanging their heads in prayer.

Aurora concealed herself behind a rock, shaking uncontrollably. She wrapped her arms around herself, hoping to stop the convulsing, but it only made it worse. Crying and sobbing, a small hiccup escaped her lips, and she slapped her hand over mouth. Her gaze darted side to side, stunned the sound came from her. She tried to stand, but her legs gave out from under her. She fell to the desert floor, legs sprawled out as the sand rose up around her in a plume of dust and grit. She did not attempt to move again and wept harder.

"*He* answered them. *He* spoke to them," she repeated through her tears.

She didn't cry from being in *His* Glory or having the power sing to a part of her she thought dead. But it had not been dead, just asleep deep down inside her. *He* could wake it up at any time. It was more, so much more. The song of energy felt like...like home. It called to her. She missed *Him*. Even that wasn't what upset her the most. It was these small creatures, these humans. These primitive, narrow-minded humans really were *His* favorites. *He* had answered them. She was *His* child, and *He* still had not answered her. Even when she'd stood on a mountain and demanded it, *He* ignored her. After millennia, she still didn't know what she had done wrong to fall out of favor. She thought she had made peace with this, but she had not. *He* could still affect her.

Now, judging by *His* words, *He* wanted to be the humans' one true God, taking away her livelihood and her kin's mode of existence. What kind of father did this to His own? But maybe they weren't *His* and these humans were. Was this the answer all along? Were the Virtues just laborers, much like the Powers? Maybe they were not so different.

The logical thought was fleeting. Instead, Aurora channeled all her rage and hurt, heaving it onto King Jarvok and the Court of Dark. They had become the source of all that was wrong in her world. It was an easier answer, so much simpler to make them the reason for her strife than look to her Creator and live with a hole in her heart that could never be fixed. The Court of Dark, they were the last remnants of a previous life and an old wound. Once she excised the wound, the infection would be gone and her kin would be safe. She didn't start this war, but damn it to Lucifer, she would finish it. Aurora made it her mission to destroy Jarvok and the Court of Dark no matter how long it took.

ART BY RUXANDRA TUDORICA@METHYSS DIGITAL ARTIST

T hank you for reading Birth of the Fae: Locked out of Heaven. I hope you enjoyed your time in the Veil and are as anxious as I am to return to the world of the Fae! Queen Aurora and King Jarvok will be back very soon. I would love to hear your thoughts, visit my website at Birthofthefae.com to share. Check the website for updates on all things Fae, read short stories and excerpts from my next book, Birth of the Fae: Thine eyes of Mercy. Be sure to keep up with the Fae on Instagram @Birthofthefae_novel.

Chaos be with you ~ Danielle

4 Horsemen Publications

Romance

Ann Shepphird
The War Council

Emily Bunney
All or Nothing
All the Way
All Night Long: Novella
All She Needs
Having it All
All at Once
All Together
All for Her

Lynn Chantale
The Baker's Touch
Blind Secrets
Broken Lens

Mimi Francis
Private Lives
Private Protection
Run Away Home
The Professor

Fantasy, SciFi, & Paranormal Romance

Beau Lake
The Beast Beside Me
The Beast Within Me
Taming the Beast: Novella
The Beast After Me
Charming the Beast: Novella
The Beast Like Me
An Eye for Emeralds
Swimming in Sapphires
Pining for Pearls

D. Lambert
To Walk into the Sands
Rydan
Celebrant
Northlander
Esparan
King

Traitor
His Last Name

J.M. Paquette
Klauden's Ring
Solyn's Body
The Inbetween
Hannah's Heart
Call Me Forth
Invite Me In
Keep Me Close

Lyra R. Saenz
Prelude
Falsetto in the Woods: Novella
Ragtime Swing
Sonata

Song of the Sea
The Devil's Trill
Bercuese
To Heal a Songbird
Ghost March
Nocturne

T.S. SIMONS
Antipodes
The Liminal Space
Ouroboros
Caim
Sessrúmnir

VALERIE WILLIS
Cedric: The Demonic Knight
Romasanta: Father of
Werewolves
The Oracle: Keeper of the
Gaea's Gate
Artemis: Eye of Gaea
King Incubus: A New Reign

V.C. WILLIS
Prince's Priest
Priest's Assassin

YOUNG ADULT FANTASY

BLAISE RAMSAY
Through The Black Mirror
The City of Nightmares
The Astral Tower
The Lost Book of the Old Blood
Shadow of the Dark Witch
Chamber of the Dead God

Broken Beginnings:
Story of Thane
Shattered Start: Story of Sera
Sins of The Father:
Story of Silas
Honorable Darkness: Story of
Hex and Snip
A Love Lost: Story of Radnar

C.R. RICE
Denial
Anger
Bargaining
Depression
Acceptance

VALERIE WILLIS
Rebirth
Judgment
Death

4HORSEMENPUBLICATIONS.COM